Praise

"A timely saga of environmental catastrophe... Drawing on their backgrounds in archaeology, the Gears vividly re-create Paleolithic America in this enchanting and instructive novel."

— *Publishers Weekly*

"*People of the Nightland* is an important story of global warming, trust, vision, and leader-ship...Like all the other Gear books, *People of the Nightland* will stay with me and keep me thinking for a long time."

— *Armchair Interviews*

"Rich in cultural detail. Both longtime fans and newcomers will be satisfied. Another fine entry in an ambitious, long-running series."

— *Kirkus Reviews*

Nightland: Darkness

Also by W. Michael Gear and Kathleen O'Neal Gear

Nightland: Darkness

The Earliest Americans
Book 9

W. Michael Gear

Kathleen O'Neal Gear

WOLFPACK
PUBLISHING
EST 2013

| 13,000 B.C. | 10,000 B.C. | 6000 B.C. | 5000 B.C. |

Paleo Indian

Early Archaic

People of the Wolf
Alaska & Canadian
Northwest

People of the Fire
Central Rockies &
Great Plains

People of the Sea
Pacific Coast &
Great Basin

People of the Lightning
Florida

Paleo Indian

Archaic

00 B.C.	1500 B.C.	100 A.D.	800 A.D.	1000 A.D.	1300 A.D.

Archaic   *Woodland*   *Mississippian*

People of the Earth
Northern Plains
& Basins

People of the Mist
Chesapeake Bay

People of the River
Mississippi Valley

People of the Masks
Ontario &
Upstate New York

People of the Lakes
East Central Woodlands
& Great Lakes

People of the Owl
Lower Mississippi
Valley

People of the Silence
Southwest Anasazi

Basketmaker   *Pueblo*

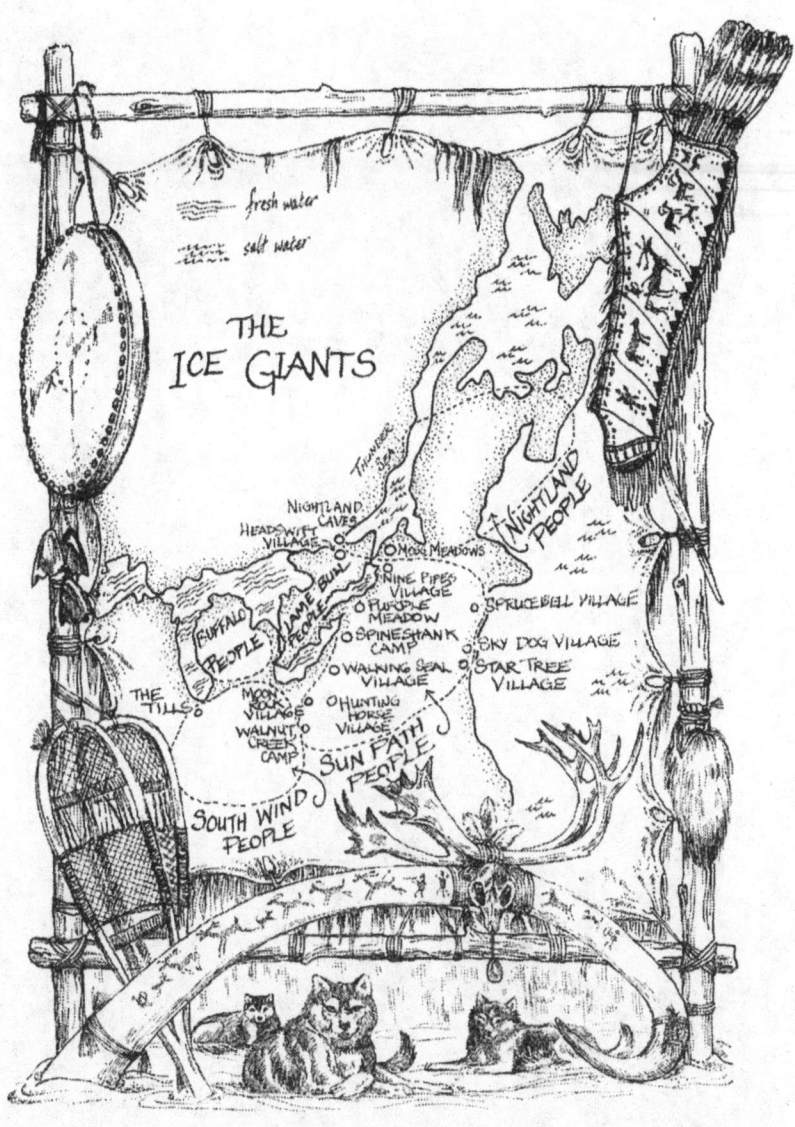

THE
ICE GIANTS

fresh water
salt water

NIGHTLAND
CAVES
HEADSWIFT
VILLAGE   MOOSE MEADOWS
                                            NIGHTLAND
                                            PEOPLE
                    NINE PIPES
                    VILLAGE
LANE BULL   PURPLE   SPRUCEBELL VILLAGE
BUFFALO PEOPLE   MEADOW
PEOPLE   SPINESHANK   SKY DOG VILLAGE
                  CAMP
                 WALKING SEAL   STAR TREE
                 VILLAGE   VILLAGE
THE   MOON
TILLS   VILLAGE   HUNTING
            WALNUT   HORSE
            CREEK   VILLAGE
            CAMP   SUN FAITH
                       PEOPLE
    SOUTH WIND
    PEOPLE

Nightland: Darkness

Chapter One

On his belly, the Nightland war chief known as Kakala sneaked up over the pile of boulders and scrutinized Headswift Village where it nestled in the rocks above him. His longtime deputy, the warrior woman called Keresa slid into place beside him. Dawn's lavender gleam sheathed Keresa's delicately-featured face and reflected in her hard eyes. Her atlatl and war darts were clutched in her right hand and clattered softly as she studied the warren of tunnels and boulders the Lame Bull people called home.

Kakala trusted no one the way he did Keresa. After countless battles and raids, and years of counting on each other, their friendship had strengthened into a bond as tough as dried ligament. Now, neither of them wanted to be here, faced with a battle they had little chance to win. Especially against their old adversary, the Sunpath war chief, Windwolf.

The morning was cold, mist hanging in pockets. A drizzly rain had fallen that night, turning into slushy snow before the clouds fled off to the east. Ice rimed the stone, making footing treacherous.

Not the best time to attack a hostile village.

"What do you see?" she asked.

"Nothing that looks like the kind of trap we laid for Windwolf at Walking Seal Village, that's for sure. Goodeagle is as crazy as a head-struck goose."

The entire hill was a mass of tumbled rocks, gravel, and scrawny spruce trees. Why would anyone wish to live here?

"Those must be the Sunpath People." Keresa pointed to the cluster of hastily thrown-up lodges at the foot of the slope. They looked like little more than broken branches leaned together and covered with ratty hides.

"Yes," Kakala answered. "If we send a handful of our warriors after them, they should run west, away from the village."

"And they'll probably keep running."

"If they're wise, they will." Kakala squinted against a fierce gust of wind. His bearhide cape flapped around him. "I repeat: Tell our warriors they are not to kill *any* Sunpath People."

Her mouth quirked. "What if Sunpath warriors are casting darts at them?" She arched an eyebrow. "Can we wound them?"

"Yes, we can wound them." He chuckled. "We want them spreading the news that Headswift is destroyed, remember? So that Silt hears and turns back."

Keresa heaved a sigh. "Assuming Karigi hasn't already stopped them." She paused. "Are you *sure* that changing your orders to have him come here was a good idea?"

"We came expecting a trap. Where is it?"

She shook her head, looking nervous.

Kakala gestured to the village. "Very few people are out in front of the rockshelters. Why?"

"It's still early. By midday, people will be everywhere."

"Then let's be about this. If three tens of our warriors hit the Lame Bull People fast, we can drive most away. That will make it easier to corner the rest."

She didn't say anything.

He scanned the valley, examining every possible place the fleeing survivors might take refuge.

Keresa's eyes narrowed, and Kakala's jaw muscles jumped at the look she gave him. They'd been arguing for moons now, debating the rights and wrongs of the curious orders they'd been getting. And just now, he could see that same rebellious gleam in her eyes.

"What are we doing, Kakala?"

"I'm trying to stay out of the cage for good. I'm not sure what you're doing."

"The Lame Bull People have never done anything to threaten us. Yet we're here to kill them."

"Some will survive. They always do." But his heart sided with her words.

She shook her head, and her long black braid sawed across her shoulder.

"I don't like this any better than you do, Keresa."

She hesitated for so long it set his teeth on edge. "...I know."

"The sooner this is over, the sooner we can go home."

She gave him a measuring look. "Home? To what?" She slid down the rocks and trotted out to meet the warriors who waited at the base of the boulders.

Kakala scowled at her back. *What i would give to just turn around and leave this place.*

4

Chapter Two

In all the low places, mist had settled, cloaking the village in damp, intense cold. Icicles hung from the spruce boughs. The entire world looked iron gray in the lavender light of dawn.

Windwolf followed Lookingbill as he hobbled toward the back of the ceremonial chamber. The old man had pulled up the hood of his buckskin cape to shield his bald head from the frigid air. His fleshy nose had turned red.

"Dipper is ready. No one likes this, me most of all, but—"

"I don't like it, either," Windwolf said, "but it's the best I can do with the time I've had."

Lookingbill turned, and his wrinkled face pinched. "I had hoped you'd tell me it was infallible, that I needn't worry. Instead, you agree with me?"

"I try not to deceive chiefs."

Lookingbill smiled faintly and continued toward the rear of the chamber where a number of weapons lay piled: Four tens of darts leaned against the wall, their sharp stone points glinting; atlatls were laid out on the floor, ready for warriors in need; and a mound of bone stilettos rested to the left of the atlatls.

Lookingbill pulled a dart, as long as he was tall, from the pile and checked its balance. As he bent to retrieve an atlatl, he said, "When do you—"

"*Chief!*" A young warrior dashed into the rock-shelter and blinked while his eyes adjusted to the darkness.

"I'm here, Lone Eagle. What is it?"

"War Chief Fish Hawk said to tell you that our scouts have reported. The Nightland warriors are coming!"

"Very well. Get to your place."

"Yes, Elder."

The youth ran from the chamber, and Lookingbill expelled a breath. When he turned back to gaze at Windwolf, his eyes tightened. "War Chief, you look like you just stared into Raven Hunter's eyes, and he stared back."

Windwolf did not smile. "Raven Hunter always stares back, Chief. That is my personal nightmare."

Silvertip huddled in the dark angle of two leaning rocks at the mouth of his mother's chamber. He stared down at his deerhide moccasins with mastodonhide soles. His feet looked small in the gloom.

In the rear, his mother sat across from Skimmer and Ashes, the women talking softly.

He reached out, running his fingers along the side

of the Wolf Bundle. Every instinct urged him to stay here, to cower in the darkness and let the fighting pass by.

He wanted to shout: *I didn't mean it.*

But the Dream from which he had just awakened had been explicit. The black wolf had looked at him with glowing yellow eyes, and said, *"It is time for you to die."*

He had stared in terror at the Spirit animal.

"Do not be afraid," Wolf had told him. *"Death is the only passage from this world to the next."*

He had just shaken his head.

"But you must," Wolf had told him. *"You cannot find your future until you lose your past. You must give up this body for the One. Only then will you Dream."*

He did want to Dream. For the moment, however, fear lay locked in his guts. His muscles were shaking, and all of his courage could barely keep him from throwing up.

Goodeagle used all of his skill to worm his way up the slope. He kept low, sometimes crawling between the rocks. There, to his surprise, he found a small shrine. Laid out on a piece of weathered hide, he discovered a collection of shiny pebbles, a long fluted point of sacred white chert, and several twists of mammoth hair. The leather on which they lay had once been painted in the image of a wolf.

A worthless offering, for an imaginary Spirit.

He had a sudden urge to rip it up and throw it down the rocks behind him, but some impulse stayed his hand. Instead, he crawled wide around it, and wriggled up under the crest.

His gaze drifted over the jumble of rocks. The Thunder Sea came into view off to the northeast, glimmering, filled with icebergs. The white swell of the Ice Giants rose like a snowy range of mountains above the salt water.

Looking closer, he caught a glimpse of Kakala's warriors sneaking around the perimeter of the village.

No one seemed to notice them. Far down at the base of the slope, the Sunpath villagers went about their tasks, gathering wood, feeding the dogs, playing with their children.

It seemed odd, though, that there were so few Lame Bull People out. And, looking more closely at the Sunpath, he thought something was wrong. Their postures, the way they acted, was almost wooden.

Goodeagle untied his water bag from his belt and took a long swallow. Though food had been offered, he hadn't eaten in four days, and much of his pain had receded into a blessed haze. It was, perhaps, strange that going without food left a man's soul clear and calm. All the way here, he'd run at the rear of the war party with his two guards. While they'd eaten their daily rations, he'd watched and listened to the warriors boast about what honors they would win when they arrived at Headswift Village.

Honors? What honors were left to win when all the world was busy destroying itself?

At night, he had crawled into his hides, ill, but too numb to feel, or relive any of the nightmares that tormented him like evil Spirits with fiery darts. In too many, Bramble stared up at him, hatred marring the face he had once loved. He would see her choke on the blood welling from inside her. When she called out his name, it was in a crimson spray that coated his skin.

He didn't have to do the silent calculations of how many Sunpath lives had been lost, or would be lost in the moon ahead.

Windwolf, this is all your fault.

The ache in his gut started to rise again. He swallowed and forced it down. Why were so few people out front? He shook his head. Could they be the bait? The thought affected him like a dart in his belly.

For several stunning moments, his thoughts riveted on strategy sessions held over campfires—just him, Windwolf, and Bramble. What fine times those had been. He could recall...

There are so few Lame Bull People out in front of the rockshelters.

He, Bramble, and Windwolf, they'd been stretched out on the dry grass near the Thunder Sea, watching the Nightland People pack up their camps, speculating on what it would take to get inside the Nightland Caves. Insane strategy—things to be tried only when they were already dead men, trapped, and no other path lay open to them. An ice-scented wind had blown off the Thunder Sea, rustling the grasses.

After the Nightland People had gone, he and Windwolf had explored every ice tunnel, trying to learn how the passageways connected.

Windwolf's deep voice rose in his thoughts: "*No, two tens would be too many. If you're going to take the caves, it'll have to be a small war party. Six men, with specific duties, and a crowd. That's all you will need.*

9

The war party will have no more than ten tens of heartbeats..."

"Oh, no!" Goodeagle spun around and ran down the trail with his heart in his throat.

"You...fools! You stupid...stupid fools! Windwolf is going to...to kill all of you!"

Chapter Three

Cloud People filled the brightening sky. The queer leaden light lent an unearthly brilliance to the cold world and turned the shawl of frost on the rockshelters into a glittering mantle.

Keresa trotted up and knelt beside Kakala, expecting a reprimand for being late. "It took longer than I expected, but our warriors are ready. As you instructed, I ordered the three tens of warriors going with us to capture any Elders they saw."

"Good. Did you dispatch a runner to inform the nearby villages that they will have refugees coming in?"

"I sent young Aniya. She's one of the best runners we have."

Kakala squinted up at the village. He looked as nervous as a big cat on a hunt. Sweat matted his black hair to his forehead. "Why aren't there more people outside?"

"I've been wondering that same thing. Something's wrong."

"Do you think they got word we were coming?"

She studied the few people who were outside, mostly women and children, one old man. They acted perfectly normal. The squealing children were playing a game of hoop-and-stick, running and trying to cast their sticks through the hoop to earn a point. The women who stood near the mouth of a small rockshelter were using jasper scrapers to clean the last bits of flesh from a buffalo hide. The old man dozed in the sunlight.

She said, "They look nervously calm."

Nervously calm?

He shrugged it off. "They do. But then, given what the Sunpath People have been through, how could they look calmly calm?" A pause. "Maybe there's a ceremonial in one of the rockshelters—a burial rite, or a marriage."

Keresa whispered, "It's possible. We should at least hear drums and flutes." She stiffened. "I think they know we're here and have run into the rockshelters to hide."

Kakala nocked a dart in his atlatl. "Then...they would have taken the Sunpath People with them. Maybe it's a village Council meeting. That would explain why there's no music or Singing."

Keresa nodded reluctantly and took the opportunity to nock her own atlatl. "It would also explain why the Sunpath People are outside going about their day. They wouldn't have been invited."

Kakala said through a long exhalation, "That makes sense."

"Does it? I'm not so sure."

He started to rise, but suddenly ducked and stared up at the cloudy sky.

"What's wrong?"

He shook his head. "Nothing...I—I thought I saw a shadow. Something black...moving over me...the shadow of huge wings."

Keresa glanced up at the sky, then pinned him with cold eyes. "It's guilt."

Kakala turned to scowl at her. "Remind me to punish you for being insolent."

"I'll bring it up next time I find you in a cage."

Kakala hesitated for a few more heartbeats. "Do you see that woman in the pretty doehide dress?"

"Yes. What about her?"

"You're going to capture her. I'll get the old man. One of them is bound to be valuable to somebody."

He stood up, lifted his atlatl, and yelled a shrill war cry.

From everywhere warriors reared up from the rocks, leaped out of their hiding places, and flooded toward the village.

Two tens of warriors headed straight for the Sunpath People, screaming war cries. Keresa heard Goodeagle, coming from behind, screaming, "No! In the Guide's name, *no!*"

With amazing speed, the Sunpath People grabbed their children and vanished around the base of the boulders. The soft reverberations of screams and pounding feet carried on the wind.

"Victory!" Kakala cried as he charged up the slope on his thick legs.

She followed, but her gaze kept straying to the cloudy sky, expecting to see something monstrous and black swooping down upon them.

Deep in his rocky warren, Silvertip heard the shout of a warrior. Immediately, screams broke out on the still air. A chorus of war whoops and cries followed.

It is time. But he huddled, frightened and shaking. His tongue had gone thick, stuck to the roof of his mouth.

Clamping his eyes shut, he whispered, "I don't want to die."

"*It is time*," Wolf's voice insisted softly from the air around him.

He didn't remember rising to his feet or tottering out to the entrance. He blinked, half-blinded by the light, picked up a fist-sized rock, and hurried out onto the trail that led down to where warriors were running up through the boulders. His mother screamed somewhere behind him.

"I'm going to die," he kept repeating. Tears were leaking down his round cheeks, and the sobbing made it difficult to run.

Keresa charged straight for the woman in the doehide dress; the screaming children scattered, fleeing into the rockshelters.

The woman, running like a panicked deer, rounded a big boulder. Keresa frowned at the rock formation. She could see no way out. It had to be a dead end. She was smiling as she slowed, expecting to find the woman cowering against a sheer stone wall.

Kakala shouted, "Degan, take ten men and pursue them into their hiding places! I want as many captives as you can catch. Kill anyone who's trouble!"

Goodeagle pounded toward them, shouting, "Go back! It's a trap! Pull back!"

Keresa hesitated. *What's he yammering on about?*

The warriors—grinning like wolves on a blood trail — had already ducked into the mouths of the rock-shelters.

Only heartbeats later, new cries erupted—not the cries of women and children, but rather the cries of surprised warriors.

Keresa spun around.

Nightland warriors came flooding back out. Most had darts sticking in their bodies. Three warriors collapsed on the trail, screaming, while their wounded friends ran around them, trying to get away from the hail of darts that sailed after them. Five more men fell before they reached the safety of the rocks.

Goodeagle had stopped, his expression that of dismay.

Then, all along the rim above, whooping Sunpath warriors appeared and began casting darts down at the Nightland warriors milling below the rocks.

For one startled instant, Keresa froze. *It's a trap!*

"Pull back!" Kakala yelled. And Keresa saw a dart whistle past his ear to splinter on a boulder before him.

"They're behind us!" she cried, turning, seeing a line of advancing Lame Bull warriors. Even as she watched, the men nocked darts, bending their bodies into the deadly release.

"This way!" Keresa called, charging full tilt down a trail that led to the west. She could hear feet pounding behind her. A dart hissed past her shoulder, splintering on a rock to her right.

At least two of the warriors had taken captives, but they were hiding them in the rocks below.

In that instant, a boy of perhaps twelve stepped out of the rocks. Keresa had a momentary glimpse of his face, tear-streaked, his mouth racked with sobs. She watched as he drew back and launched a rock straight at her. She ducked to the side, grabbed up her war club where it bobbed on her belt, and hammered the boy with a side-handed blow. She felt the smacking impact, saw his head jerk sideways under the impact, and charged past.

As she did, a woman emerged from a narrow trail, full into Kakala's path. He barely hesitated as he grabbed the screaming woman, spun her around, and propelled her forward.

Keresa turned, caught sight of a pursuing warrior, and cast a dart in his direction, Kakala demanded, "Who are you?"

"I am Dipper! Daughter of Chief Lookingbill!"

Keresa caught a glimpse as Kakala's face slackened and a gleam entered his eyes. "It must have been your miserable sister I killed a few days ago. You don't wish to be next, do you?"

The tears in Dipper's eyes vanished. She gave Kakala a fierce look, but her voice shook when she said, "My son! You've killed my son!"

Kakala bellowed, "I want a woman named Skimmer, and I want Windwolf. I have heard they are both in your village. Is it true?"

"My boy, *you've killed—*"

Kakala slapped her hard across the mouth. *"Answer me!"*

Her split lips bled. She wiped her mouth on her blue-painted sleeve, and she looked up, eyes burning hate. "I'm *not* telling you anything."

Two darts hissed by to clatter on the rocks.

"Kakala!" Keresa shouted. "We've got to get out of here!"

He looked wildly around, shouting, "Quickly! Into those caves."

Keresa hesitated as the warriors charged past. On impulse, she reached down, grabbing the boy she'd clubbed.

Dipper's son? He could be of value to us. They won't know he's dead.

Chapter Four

Keresa's shout—*"Kakala! Look out!"*—was his only warning. Windwolf dropped from a rock, feet impacting with a thud. Kakala spun, shoving the woman, Dipper, away. As she sprawled on the ground, Kakala tried to pull his dart back, only to lock eyes with Windwolf as the man recovered his balance, braced himself, and swung with a stone-headed ax. At the last instant Kakala threw himself backward, the deadly blow glancing across his temple.

Lightning flashed as his head snapped sideways.

"Dart him! Degan!" Keresa's shout seemed distant, as though heard from the bottom of a pond.

Kakala stumbled, careening forward, before he toppled face-first to the ground. In his wavering vision he glimpsed Dipper pulling her son off to the side. Windwolf was trading blows with Pega, their war clubs swinging.

The hills came alive. The Sunpath People ran from their hiding places carrying branches, throwing rocks, using sharpened sticks as stilettos. At the same time, the

Lame Bull villagers flooded out of their rockshelters with weapons.

As though from a great distance, he heard Keresa shout, "Into those holes, hurry!" Then he felt her strong arm slide beneath his shoulders, and drag him to his feet. "Kakala? Kakala, hold onto me! We have to get out of here!"

His knees buckled beneath him.

Keresa dragged him; then other arms lifted his spinning body. He remembered rubbing against stone, then sagging heavily.

More and more warriors scrambled through the opening behind Keresa, bodies blocking the light. Each time it was as if someone drove a wedge through his numb head. And then he was falling in an endless spiral, the world turning gray.

He barely felt his gut heave, vomit spewing. His body was so distant, airy, floating...

And then the grayness faded to black.

Keresa had watched Windwolf strike Kakala down. Before he could strike again, Pega had charged forward, swinging a club. As Keresa tended to Kakala, she had glimpses of Windwolf and Pega trading blows, the clack of wood loud. Seeing Washani and Klah bear Kakala safely into the rock, she grabbed for her atlatl and one of the scattered darts where she'd dropped them. The boy's mother was tugging frantically at the boy's arm. No time for that now.

Keresa nocked a dart just as Windwolf struck Pega down. Her arm whipped back. From this distance, she couldn't miss. Their eyes met—an instant of mutual understanding.

I am going to kill you now.

His slight smile was as eloquent as if he'd shouted, *No, you're not!*

She threw her weight behind the cast. The dart flashed forward, the shaft flexing. Windwolf twisted to the side, her stone-tipped dart cutting through his war shirt, vanishing harmlessly behind him.

Corre and Degan rushed up, arms back, but even as they launched their darts Windwolf threw himself behind the rocks.

The hissing of a dart brought her back to the moment. Keresa heard its impact: a muffled slap as it drove itself into Corre's chest. He wavered on his feet, took a step back, and sank to the ground, staring in disbelief at the shaft quivering in his breastbone.

"*Keresa!*" Degan shouted. "Into the hole! Now!"

She looked for the dead boy, seeing drag marks.

No, he's no good to us now.

She spun on her heel, a dart slicing through her cloak, and ducked into the rock as a volley of darts shattered on the stone behind her. Inside, back pressed to the wall, she panted, struggling for breath. Kakala lay on the gravel like a lump, blood running down the side of his head.

Goodeagle dove through on all fours, looked around, and lunged to pick up an abandoned war club. "Keresa! It's up to you! What are you going to do?"

Keresa, panting from exertion, hauled Kakala into a sitting position, looked into his vacant, half-lidded eyes, and propped him against the wall. Blood streaked his face and had soaked his war shirt until it clung to his muscular body in wet folds.

"Is it true?" Goodeagle stared wild-eyed. "Did Windwolf escape?"

Keresa could only pant, staring out at the narrow opening. She could hear the screams and pleas of her wounded warriors. Despite clamping her eyes shut, she could see too clearly with the eye of her soul: They were writhing, bleeding, staring in horror at the wooden shafts sticking from their flesh.

One by one, the screams stopped. The Lame Bull were repaying blood with blood.

Goodeagle spun around, frantic eyes rising from Kakala to Keresa. "He's killed your *entire* war party. They're all dead. You fool! You let him kill your people! I tried to tell you—"

Keresa rose, drew back, and slammed a fist into Goodeagle's mouth.

Goodeagle staggered backward, sobbing as he hit the floor.

"Deputy?" Degan called. "There's a hole in the rear of this shelter."

She shook herself, gathering her scattered wits, and worked her way back along the narrow passage. In places she had to drop to her hands and knees. Then the tunnel opened, and she saw the high crevice. Bishka and Degan were staring up, their faces illuminated by diffused daylight.

Tell me it's a way out.

"Degan, you and Klah carry the war chief. Follow me!"

It took all of her strength as she levered her body up the narrow crack, then poked her head up into the light.

Some premonition warned her; a shadow moved on the rock. She loosened her hold as an adz whistled down to shatter on stone. She felt the wind of it, stone splinters pattering on her hair.

Keresa slid, her body bouncing off the rocks, to land in a heap at the bottom. She winced, raising her hands to find raw and bleeding palms.

Feet shuffled behind her. She turned to see her frightened warriors emerge into the chamber. They manhandled the limp Kakala between them. Each was looking to her, desperation in his eyes.

She climbed painfully to her feet, turning her attention to where the tunnel forked. She glanced warily around the right bend. Up ahead, sunlight lit the tunnel.

Raven, let this be it!

Wiser now, she proceeded warily, her warriors creeping along behind her. The tunnel narrowed until barely wide enough to pass her shoulders. Looking up, she could see a wide, funnel-like opening, impossible to climb.

Pray no warrior is up there. He could drive a dart down through the top of my head and clear to my foot.

Once through, she turned, grabbed Kakala's arms, and hauled him forward to allow the warriors behind him to get through.

Kakala's eyes rolled. That much, at least, was an improvement. He reeled in her arms, disoriented. He kept saying, "What...what...what..."

Keresa called back, "There's sunlight up ahead. We're going to try to climb out!"

Warriors followed along after her, eyes wide as they stared at the forbidding stone around her.

She grabbed hold of the rocks, planted her feet, and started to climb. The hole at the top consisted of a gap between three boulders. This time, she peered around carefully, easing her way up, fearing an ambush.

She found it—saw the faces of tens of warriors above her, grinning. She jerked back as a stone-tipped dart snapped against the stone where her head had been. The shattered dart dropped past her.

The clattering sound of falling rock echoed through the tunnel. She slid back to the cavern floor, staring with the rest as Degan hurried back the way they had come.

"Oh, gods, Keresa!" Degan shouted, throwing himself back before a cloud of rock dust. The tunnel had been collapsed to seal them in.

The choking wall of dust continued to billow out as rocks and debris thundered down.

Above her, the Lame Bull warriors were rolling boulders into place, sealing the opening.

She breathed, "Blessed Raven Hunter, we're trapped."

23

Chapter Five

Goodeagle hunched in the rear of a chamber, surrounded by five other warriors. When the tunnel collapsed ahead of them it cut them off from Keresa's party. Goodeagle and the rest had been forced to turn around and go back. From behind the curtain of fallen rock, he heard shouts, but the voices were muted, as though coming from beneath a deep layer of earth and stone. He coughed and squinted at the veil of dust that filled the chamber.

The opening through which they'd entered mocked them. When Mong had eased up to the entrance, a long dart had sailed in, opened a cut along his ribs, and clattered off the wall.

As long as warriors were out there, there would be no escape.

A loud thump gave them a start. Owl-eyed, they stared as yet another large rock hit the ground with a thud.

"What are they doing?" Mong asked.

"Sealing us in," Goodeagle said breathlessly.

Rana, who sat against the wall to his right, asked, "What happened to us?"

"Windwolf just destroyed your war party."

"We're still alive," Washani growled.

Goodeagle laughed; it was a low threatening sound, filled with self-loathing. "Not for long."

"Do you think the others survived? Keresa and the war chief?"

"Pray they're dead, Washani. If they lived, right now they're being sealed up in rock tombs."

The end would be long and difficult. They'd die from thirst first, but not before desperate men began killing their friends to drink their blood for the moisture it contained. Then they'd eat the meat...until only one man remained.

Windwolf found Dipper kneeling by Silvertip's side. She used a piece of damp hide to sponge the bulging lump on the side of the boy's head.

"You had a close call," he told her, kneeling opposite. "When I saw you running toward the fighting, my heart almost stopped."

"It was Silvertip," she said, sniffing. Her round face was tear-streaked, panic in her eyes. "I don't know what possessed him. He knew the orders. He was supposed to stay safe!"

Windwolf carefully turned the boy's head, pressing gently with his fingers. "There's a lot of swelling, but I don't think the skull is crushed."

"Will he live?"

He winced at the pain and worry in her voice.

"Dipper, I honestly don't know. Head wounds, well, they're hard to judge. For now, the best you can do is keep him quiet. Make sure that his body is warm, and use that cold compress on the wound."

She nodded, her hands shaking. "Thank you," she whispered. "But for you, they would have had us both."

"You and Silvertip were very brave."

Another tear slipped down her cheek. "I don't feel brave."

"That is generally the way of it."

A worried voice called, "Windwolf?"

He turned, seeing Ashes, some terrible distress behind her large brown eyes.

"What's wrong, Ashes?"

"It's Mother," she said, on the point of tears. "She's gone."

Skimmer bent under the weight of her pack, keeping to the low ground. She stopped when the sound of the fighting broke out behind her. Windwolf was springing his trap.

"May you win, War Chief." *And keep Ashes safe!*

She blinked back tears as she remembered her daughter's stunned expression.

Ashes' desperate pleading still rang in her ears. *"No! Mother, don't leave me!"*

"I had to, baby. This is the only way to ensure your future."

If she could do this thing, kill Ti-Bish, the spirit and will would fade from the Nightland People. Their warriors would slip away, and her people could return to their lands once again.

It will all be over. And I will have saved us all.

She cast one last wistful glance over her shoulder. Then she turned her head back to the route. As she hurried along, her heart felt as if it were breaking. Ashes' face filled her thoughts. Every instinct told her to run back, to gather her daughter into her arms and never let her go.

But Ashes would be safe in Headswift Village. As safe as she would be anywhere. Windwolf would see to that. The man took his obligations seriously.

Now it's up to me.

When she completed her task, if she lived, she would find her way back to Ashes.

She repeated the words she had told the girl. "I'll be back. I promise you. And then it will all be over. We can bury our dead, and grieve, and build ourselves a new life."

The way led along a drainage that wound through rocks. Stands of spruce and willows provided additional cover. From her calculations, if she continued, she should cross the trail that led back toward the Nightland villages.

You didn't trust me, Windwolf? Well, the decision is no longer yours to make.

As she hurried along, memories of Hookmaker's body, of Blue Wing crying after the traitor Goodeagle had tired of her, and of the women in the pen fueled her anger.

She could imagine Ti-Bish's face as if it had been yesterday. She could see his large round eyes, the thin and pinched expression. He had looked up at her with a worship-filled gratitude, as if her kindness touched his very soul.

She would see him again, and look into his eyes as she drove some sharp pointed weapon between his ribs and through his foul heart.

What turned you into a monster?

She might even find that answer before she was finished.

A dead Guide is a false Prophet. Lookingbill's words drove her forward.

She wound through a stand of spruce, smelling the sweet scent of the trees, and turned onto the trail. Making better time, she continued at a fast walk.

The sounds of the fighting had vanished behind her, sealed by distance and the breeze in the trees.

"You there!" a sharp voice called.

She turned, fear leaping within, and saw four winded warriors trotting down the trail; two were already fanning out, ready to cut off her escape.

She focused her frightened eyes on the lead warrior. Yes, she knew him: one of Kakala's warriors. He had marched with them on that long walk up from the Nine Pipes camp.

"I am Skimmer," she called, trying to muster courage. "The Guide wishes to see me."

The warrior approached warily. He carried only one dart, and it was nocked, ready to be cast. Then, unexpectedly, he glanced worriedly over his shoulder.

He's as scared as I am!

"I take it the fight didn't go well?" she asked, trying to ignore the frightened beating of her heart.

He turned his attention back to her, making a hand signal to the other warriors. "No, it didn't go well at all."

The second warrior muttered, "I say we just kill her. After what we just survived, I'm ready to pay them back any way I can."

"No," the first replied. "I was in the Council chamber with Kakala and the Guide. He asked about Skimmer."

"So?" the second demanded.

Skimmer watched the remaining warriors close in from the sides; like the first man, each had only one dart left to him. They looked like they were more than eager to use them on her. She tensed every muscle in her body to keep from shivering.

"Are you a fool?" the first demanded. "If we go back to report Kakala's destruction, just who do you think is going into the cages? After what just happened at Headswift Village, Brookwood is nothing!"

"That's right," Skimmer said, fighting to think clearly. "But, well...say that you captured me before the fight. Say that Kakala sent you back with me. You'd have no part in what happened later, would you?"

The lead warrior tilted his head, running the idea through his soul. He rolled the long war dart in his fingers. "You would agree to that story?"

She nodded, hoping they didn't hear her dry swallow. "Let's just say that it has a certain appeal when the other option is being raped by four warriors, and then having my throat cut."

The warriors looked back and forth.

Then the first nodded. "You're a smart woman."

She smiled, trying to keep her voice from breaking. "And you four would be even smarter by delivering me directly to the Guide. Last time, that fool Nashat almost killed me."

The whistling sound of clubs shattering bone lived in her memory.

The warrior took a deep breath, shooting another worried look over his shoulder. "You may not be so glad you found us, woman. I have no idea how many warriors are following our trail. You're going to have to run like you never have before."

"I—I'll do my best." Then, in what she hoped was a firm voice, she added, "But the four of you had better remember that without me, you're headed for a miserable couple of moons in the cages."

"Oh, you can bet on that," the leader replied. "Now, let's see how fast you can run, woman." Skimmer looked down. Her hands were trembling.

Come, Skimmer. You can do this.

Chapter Six

Keresa dusted off her cape and looked up at the rocks over her head. Between the gaps in the boulders, she saw the gray gleam of dusk. There were still men out there, moving around. She could hear them talking.

She shouted, "I want to talk to Windwolf!"

No one answered.

"Where's Windwolf? Tell him Deputy Keresa must speak with him!"

Whispers rose, as though they were discussing it; then she heard nothing but silence.

A short time later, a sliver of Windwolf's face appeared in one of the gaps. "What is it, Deputy?"

"Let's talk."

"I'm listening."

"I should think that telling you we surrender is a little ridiculous, but if you need to hear it—"

"I don't."

She exhaled hard. "What can I do to save the lives of the rest of my war party?"

Windwolf hesitated, and it occurred to her that he was about to tell her "nothing."

He asked, "How many warriors can the Nightland clan Elders gather to attack us?"

She stared up, confused at first, until it occurred to her that he was already thinking five steps ahead: *What will happen if I don't kill them? The Nightland Elders will catch wind of it. What will they do? They'll probably order Deputy Karigi to attack the village and free the hostages. What if they decide to make a full-scale assault? How many warriors can they muster?*

Keresa replied, "More than you can defend against, Windwolf. Even if Deputy Silt arrives with your warriors. Even if you manage to coerce every child into carrying a stick. You cannot win. Our warriors are coming, in overwhelming numbers."

Fish Hawk stood to Windwolf's left, watching.

The famed war chief looked dead tired, drained of every shred of the strength that had kept them alive over the past few hands of time. His dark eyes were dull, lifeless. He propped a trembling fist on the rock, and said, "You've just helped me make a difficult decision, Deputy. I thank you. I was actually considering letting you live."

He got to his feet and walked away.

Keresa shouted, "Windwolf! Windwolf, wait! Talk to me! *Talk to me!*"

Confusion

I sit with my back against the ice wall and stare at the dark form five paces away. Against the faint gleam of the fiery lake, he looks tall and massive, almost blocking the tunnel when he spreads his wings.

In a very small voice, I say, "I don't understand."

"You don't have to. Just tell her."

Raven Hunter might stand right in front of me, but his voice sounds far away, like the distant rumble of thunder.

"Will she understand? About the feather?"

"Better than you know."

"You're sure she's alive?"

"Oh, yes."

I toy with the fringes on my cape for a few moments before rising to my feet. "I'll tell her as soon as she arrives."

"I know you will."

The blackness retreats down the tunnel, heading for the fiery lake, growing smaller and smaller, as though flying.

33

The scents of water and algae rise powerfully in the backwash of his wings.

I take a deep breath and watch until Raven Hunter is gone, and the pale gleam of the lake returns to waver over the ice walls like sunlight off water.

"Feathers and suffering," I whisper to myself. "I don't understand."

As I slowly head back up the tunnel, I wonder why Skimmer would understand when I do not. Is she smarter than I am? I feel a flush creep into my cheeks. Everyone is smarter than I am. Perhaps after I have told her the message, Skimmer will explain it to me.

"Yes, she'll explain it."

Chapter Seven

Silvertip couldn't have explained it—not in words. He was sitting on top of the high boulders that rose over Headswift Village. How he had come to be there was beyond him. He didn't remember. The fact was: He sat on the stone, where he had been sitting, but with no idea of how long he had been there.

Nor could he explain his body. It lay before him, supine, with arms at the side, legs out straight. His hair had been washed, combed, and braided. A beautiful hunting shirt, stained blue with larkspur dye, had been dotted with white, signifying stars on a night sky.

A terrible wound marred the side of his head, and his eyes were opened to slits, dried and gray with death. The gray lips were parted, and he could see the tips of his teeth, starkly white. His belly was distended, swollen with death.

Silvertip studied his corpse, seeing the familiar scar in the web between thumb and forefinger on his right hand. He'd gotten it while learning to knap flint a year before. A long white chert flake had cut deeply, and when the scar slowly healed, left a bright white line on his skin.

How did this happen?

The memory seemed to seep into him, like water through moss.

I had to die.

He looked down at his Spirit hand, opening the fingers, remembering the feel of the stone. How, crazy with fear, he'd ran into the path of the woman warrior and cast the stone with all his might. She had easily ducked it, and he remembered his terrible fear as she charged down on him, shifting her dart and atlatl, reaching for the club.

He had stood, frozen, watching the club lift, how it had flashed in the sunlight. Then, darkness.

And I am here.

He should have been afraid. Worried, or perhaps sad. Instead, he felt hollow, as if nothing were left.

"That is the way of it," a voice said gently.

Silvertip turned, startled, to find a great black wolf, its yellow eyes studying him intently.

"You were in my Dreams."

"The Spirit world lies beside yours. Separate, but touching. Power flows through them both, binding and pulsing. It beats with your heart, lives in the center of the stone, and flows with the sap in the trees. It waves with the grass in the wind. Then, sometimes, when the right kind of soul touches it, it fills a person."

"Like me?" Silvertip asked hopefully.

"Just like you." The wolf raised his eyes. "He comes."

Silvertip followed the wolf's gaze, seeing a dark dot high in the glowing sky. It circled slowly, hanging on the air, floating. As it drew nearer, the long black wings could be seen.

"Condor," Silvertip said at last.

"Condor," Wolf agreed. "The great bird of the dead." Then he added, "Do not be afraid. You must watch to understand."

Silvertip nodded. He'd never heard of a condor hurting anyone. They were shy things, awkward when taking flight from the ground. They much preferred roosting in high places where they could leap out and let the air fill their great wings.

The giant bird circled closer, cocking its ugly head, the brown eye glinting as it studied Silvertip's body.

In that instant, Silvertip understood. "It's coming to eat me."

"Oh, yes." Wolf's great yellow eyes were fixed on him. "And you must fulfill your role in the way of the world. Until you have experienced it, you will never understand."

Silvertip watched wide-eyed as the great bird backed air and settled lightly to the rock. Cocking its head from side to side, it inspected the corpse. Then, with a tentative peck, it looked for any reaction.

Silvertip swallowed hard as his body remained inert.

He wanted to scream, "No!" but his voice was mute with horror.

The great curved beak shot down, neatly plucking one of the eyes from the socket, twisting and pulling to sever the resisting tissue before it gulped the prize.

Silvertip jerked, reaching up, aware that half of his vision had vanished.

"Do not fight it," Wolf cautioned. "You must only be."

Silvertip gasped as the great beak shot down, and then his world was black. All that remained was feeling. He tried to stand, to run, to escape from the sharp beak that now sliced into his skin.

But all he could do was sit there, feeling with exquisite sensation as his body was picked apart, piece by piece. Then the beak sliced into his belly, and he could feel his intestines being pulled, severed, and pulled some more.

Silvertip threw his head back, screaming. But no sound issued from his hollow throat.

Skimmer ran in the middle, with two warriors in front and two behind. They followed the beach trail that led around the western finger of the Thunder Sea. In Sister Moon's half-light, the dark surface of the salt water glimmered as though sprinkled with silver dust. Great bergs glistened with ethereal white where they had grounded off the littoral, stranded by low tide. The smell of the salty shore lingered, exotic in her nose.

She let the soft lapping of the waves soothe her.

Conversations had been brief, to the point. The previous night's camp had been a dreary affair, the warriors splitting up the rations in her pack. When the topic of her escape came up, she'd said, "Sleep. I'm not running away."

"And we are to believe that?" Kishkat had asked.

"My destiny lies with the Guide." Something in her voice had convinced them.

The two warriors in front, Homaldo and Tibo, kept up a steady distance-eating pace that was beginning to wear her down. Soon, she'd be stumbling.

Bless the Lame Bull for several days of rest and good food.

She mouthed a silent hope that Lookingbill and the rest had survived.

She wondered about the battle. What had happened to Windwolf? Had he won? Was Ashes all right? Skimmer imagined her daughter eating supper with Dipper and Silvertip—pretending to be brave while worrying about her mother. Skimmer's heart ached. Ashes had just lost her father, her family, her clan, and village. Now her mother, too, was gone.

I am doing this for you, beloved daughter.

They hit a rocky section of the trail where waves had washed high. Skimmer's steps hammered the ground. She kept gazing out at the waters, looking so peaceful now, but few people lived along the strand. When great sections of ice were undercut by the warm tidal waters, they collapsed. Literal mountains of ice would slam down, sending giant waves to wash up, carrying everything before them.

As she looked out, she could see the cleanly scrubbed land, devoid of trees, with rocks piled here and there; deeply incised drainages had cut where the great waves drained away.

What would it be like?

She imagined what a wall of water would look like, tall, its crest glistening in the sun as it swept forward. According to the tales from the few survivors, seeing such a thing was the most terrifying sight in the world.

They never survived anything like I did.

39

The thought gave her a curious kind of courage.

As they reached a creek, Homaldo lifted a hand and called, "Time to drink."

They came to a halt, breathing hard, and Skimmer dropped to her knees. She dipped the water up in her hands and drank it greedily.

The warriors knelt, bending down to suck up the cold fresh water.

When Skimmer had drunk her fill, she sat down hard in the sand and heaved a sigh of relief. To the north, Sister Moon's gleam shadowed the trail. It resembled a gigantic black serpent winding along the shore.

"Why does the Guide want you so much? I heard that Nashat sent Blue Wing to him, and he turned her away." Kishkat shook his head. "She was a very beautiful woman."

The other warriors chuckled.

Skimmer shrugged. "I was kind to him once. In those days your people had cast him out...called him the Idiot."

Tapa cast a nervous glance over his shoulder. "We shouldn't linger."

Kishkat smiled. "I think Nashat still thinks he's an idiot." He took another drink from his cup and swallowed. "As to myself, I don't know. That night we found him trying to set Kakala free from the cage..." He shrugged. "Well, he just left me confused."

"Nashat is an evil man," Homaldo agreed. "It was his order that placed Kakala in the cage." He glanced at Skimmer. "And, but for this woman, he would have done the same to us."

"We had better hope the woman is enough," Tibo said.

Skimmer frowned. "Then the Guide doesn't issue all of these insane orders?"

"No." Kishkat bowed his head, looking weary to his bones. "The orders come from the Council. I think they come from Nashat. No one sees the Guide." He hesitated, looking at his companions, lowering his voice. "Sometimes I think the Guide is as much a captive as the rest of us."

To Skimmer's amazement, heads were nodding. "Captives? But you're the feared Nightland warriors!"

Tapa smiled wistfully. "I was a hunter. That's all I wanted to be. Then the Council made us 'hunters of men.'" He shook his head. "At first, it was exciting. I think we all got carried away with the glory. It makes a man feel great in the beginning. But then the fighting got harder." He looked at her with hopeless eyes. "My brothers are dead. My best friend, whom I grew up with and loved, is dead." He glanced back down the trail. "Now, even my war chief, whom I served and trusted with my life, is dead."

"We have all lost so much," Tibo agreed. "If I could have anything, I would ask to be the man I was before all of this began. I fear, however, that somehow, I am going to die a miserable death."

"Come." Kishkat climbed wearily to his feet. "What is, simply is. We can't change it. Our only hope is to follow the Guide to the paradise of the Long Dark."

Skimmer got to her feet and gazed out at the silver ribbons of waves rolling in. "Let's go."

The sooner I can find a way of killing him, the sooner all of this madness is over.

Chapter Eight

The struggle had encompassed eternity. Silvertip could remember nothing beyond a desperate obsession with keeping himself whole. As the condor devoured his body, bits and pieces of his soul vanished. Nothing could convey the sensation of having his soul sliced up. One moment he would be frantically trying to retain some kind of hold on his very being, only to have a hole torn out of what remained...until the inevitable. But when had that been? When had the last tattered bits of his soul simply given up?

What remained of his body were bones. Little more than the scattered fragments of his soul, and then that, too, began to slip away as one by one, the ligaments rotted, and fingers, toes, legs, and arm bones rolled off the high stone, to drop...where?

Nothing remained to scream as Silvertip's loose jaw fell away to tumble down the rock. The skull finally slipped loose from the spine, clattering hollowly...falling...

Moonglow filtered between the boulders, shooting a sliver of light across Goodeagle's face. He rolled uncomfortably to his back and struggled to sleep. Cramped between two warriors, he could barely stretch his legs to their full length. Worse, the constant low hum of distant voices chewed at the edges of his dreams like rodent teeth. Every time he drifted off, he heard Windwolf's soft baritone. Would he never escape Dreaming the nightmare of Walking Seal Village? After an eternity of restless tossing and turning, he finally sat up, and slid back to lean against the wall. Weariness clung like a granite cape around his shoulders.

Stop torturing yourself. You did the right thing.

He braced his forehead on his drawn-up knees and closed his eyes. His breathing finally melted into soothing rhythms. The voices faded...

...In the dream Goodeagle was back, standing in the great ceremonial lodge at Walking Seal Village. He could see the startled expression on Kakala's face, hear Keresa's bitter curses. Bramble lay naked, bitten, and raped, her eyes widening as she recognized him.

"Goodeagle!" Bramble sobbed. "Goodeagle...oh, no, get out!"

That was the moment his soul died, and with it, all that remained of the man once called Goodeagle.

In a tight voice, he said, "Kakala, you told me you wouldn't hurt her."

He couldn't tear his eyes away from hers as she looked up at him through stark horror, pain, and fear.

"Goodeagle?" Bramble called, as though he were suddenly the only thing she had to hold onto. The instant she figured it out, it registered as a change in her eyes—a single frozen heartbeat of time. Her fear turned to hatred.

He backed up until he hit the wall. Why hadn't he realized Karigi would do something like this?

Through tear-blurred eyes, he saw Kakala's jaw harden.

"Deputy Karigi?" Kakala asked in a weirdly calm voice Goodeagle had never heard. "Why is she still here?"

Goodeagle remembered only Karigi's insolent smile. The words buried in the hatred that seemed to shoot from Bramble's eyes.

Kakala's barked order had penetrated Bramble's spell. "Tell your warriors to get out."

Karigi blinked. "What? Why?"

"Do it!"

Karigi took a step back, ordering, "Terengi, take your men and bring me Windwolf's head."

Glancing at each other, they filed out, striding past Goodeagle as if he didn't exist. He remembered Kakala, still and quiet. Karigi fidgeting, shooting nervous glances at Bramble.

"War Chief, I intended..."

The rest had been lost as Kakala drove a hard fist into Karigi's stomach. Goodeagle had watched in disbelief as Kakala kneed the man, lifting him clear of the floor. Karigi had dropped to his knees, his war dart flying.

As Kakala vented his wrath, Goodeagle had watched the dart, seen Bramble's desperate gaze fix on it.

As though his eyes were disembodied, he'd stared at the dart, vaguely aware of Kakala and Karigi ramming together, their screams of rage disjointed and unreal as they kicked, slugged, and abused each other.

Goodeagle's remote eyes followed Bramble as she edged a foot toward the dropped dart, toes questing for the shaft.

"She's after my dart!" Karigi's shout echoed in Goodeagle's soul. *Yes, use it, Bramble! Kill him. Kill me!*

A shout came from outside; Keresa knocked him sideways as she hurried to stare out the doorway.

Bramble screamed.

Goodeagle's heart seemed to stop.

When he looked back, Karigi's dart was sticking out of Bramble's chest.

Goodeagle stumbled back against the wall, watching Kakala and Keresa race by, leaving him alone. For the last time, he looked at Bramble.

"I didn't know he'd do this, Bramble. I swear."

Faintly, almost inaudibly, he heard a voice plead, "Goodeagle?"

He took a fumbling step toward her—then blindly turned and ran.

Running. Running. I'm still running.

Goodeagle jerked bolt upright, panting.

"Just a...a dream," he whispered.

Shuddering as though from deadly cold, he folded

his arms tightly over his aching stomach. Breath rushed in and out of his lungs in huge desperate gulps.

From the darkness, Washani said, "Yes, just a dream this time. But Windwolf is going to come for you."

Goodeagle tipped his head back against the cold stone wall, and breathed, "...I know."

Ashes looked up at the black ceiling, pretending to be asleep. Silvertip's cries had wakened her many times last night, but this time his soft whimpers twisted oddly in her belly.

She'd been in the middle of a Dream. The last image still lingered in her soul: She'd been crawling through a black tunnel on her hands and knees. She could hear the people in line behind her whimpering in fear. Silvertip had reached back and grasped her hand, holding it so tightly it ached.

"Ashes," he'd whispered, "I can't find the way, and I — I'm afraid. What should I do?"

"The Wolf Bundle," she'd whispered. "Ask Wolf Dreamer. He knows the way."

When Silvertip didn't respond, she'd reached forward and found his face. Tears dampened his cheeks.

"I'm gone," Silvertip whispered, barely audible, so no one else would hear. "Even the bones have been picked clean. I don't know what I've done..."

And then Silvertip's cries had wakened her and she'd found herself staring at the ceiling. The sharp damp scent of the deep tunnel still clung in her nose.

Most of the night she'd Dreamed about her mother,

wondering where Skimmer was, and if she would ever see her again. Loneliness made her feel like she had to throw up.

She slid a hand down to rub her belly and stared at Silvertip. Even the Healer wasn't sure if he was alive or dead.

They had placed the Wolf Bundle atop his chest. His body now twitched, as though his soul were walking through a horrifying land.

She wondered if he was still crawling through the darkness, lost and frightened.

From right beside her ear, a deep voice whispered, *"Yes, he's always gone when you need him, but I'm right here, right here, Ashes."*

She tried to scream, but no sound came out of her mouth, so she dove under her hides, and lay there shaking, waiting for him to speak to her again.

Throughout the night, she jumped at every sound, but she never heard the voice again...just Silvertip's soft suffocating gasps for breath.

Chapter Nine

The pale lavender gleam of dawn filtered through the boulders, bleaching the faces of the warriors sitting around the chamber.

Keresa ran a hand through her long hair and paced back and forth. All attention was focused on Kakala.

The big war chief tossed and turned, writhing beneath his sweat-drenched cape, reaching pleadingly for people who weren't there. All night long he'd shrieked and wept.

"Hako?" Kakala had cried. "Hako? Where...where are you? Tanta, where is she? Is she..."

Degan looked up at Keresa and said, "Hako sounds like a woman's name."

She nodded. "Yes, it is."

She'd never heard Kakala speak Hako's name with such desperation.

Degan said, "Have you known him to be with a woman named Hako?"

"She was his wife once, before—"

Kakala screamed, "You're dead...*dead!* Tanta get down! What...what are you...doing?"

The echoes of his voice rang through the chamber, almost covering the grating that came from above as one of the boulders was rolled aside.

Dawn light poured into the chamber. Keresa looked up. Against the brilliant background, she couldn't see any of the warriors' faces. Smart of them. Peering down could get the looker a dart through the face.

"Deputy Keresa," a voice called. "War Chief Wind-wolf has granted your request to speak with him."

"Thank the gods," she muttered. "Can I climb up?"

"After you remove all your weapons."

Keresa untied her weapons belt and let it fall to the floor; then she pulled out the stiletto she always kept in her right legging and dropped it. "I've pulled my teeth."

"All right, climb."

Keresa climbed up, hesitated just below the scar in the rock where she had dodged death several days earlier. Nerving herself, she lifted her head, half expecting to duck another dart. The warriors just beyond the periphery of her vision were armed, alert, but none was set to skewer her. She pulled herself the rest of the way into the light. Eight warriors encircled her. A short burly man stepped forward.

"I am War Chief Fish Hawk. I need to search you."

"Of course." She spread her arms and legs and waited while he ran his hands over her body. To her surprise, he was thorough, but took no inappropriate liberties.

Fish Hawk nodded sternly. "Be careful not to do anything foolish. We have more Sunpath refugees here today. They will not be happy to see you. One wrong move and we might just let them have you."

"Fish Hawk, you've never met a more careful warrior than me."

From the depths of their trap, they'd overheard the warriors who'd guarded them talking about Windwolf. The tone of voice would have been more appropriate to Old Man Above than a human war chief.

She looked around at them, at the glow in their eyes. *They've made a mystical Spirit out of the man.*

According to the story Windwolf had personally gone to speak with the refugee chiefs and clan Elders, asking questions, assuring them they were safe here. It was said among the guards that many had fastened themselves to his legs, pleading for his leadership.

Is there anything we can do to use that against him?

Keresa started forward, but Fish Hawk's hard hand on her forearm stopped her.

"I think it's better if you follow me. Windwolf is concerned about your safety."

Fish Hawk had said Windwolf's name with such reverence, she ground her teeth. And why not? Her own warriors were starting to speak of him the same way.

Fish Hawk stepped out in front of her while the other two warriors fell in behind. Her spine prickled, knowing they had their darts centered on her back.

They followed the trail over the top of the rockshelters that composed Headswift Village. Below, she heard children talking, and the voices of elders. A dog barked happily.

Fish Hawk led her around the base of the boulders and straight through the Sunpath village—if it could be called a village. When the people saw her, they ran forward to stare and call insults. Her knees trembled, but she kept her head high.

As she rounded a corner, groans and sobs filled the air. Many people wore bandages. Black bloody tatters of hides wrapped heads and legs. One old man—with a face like a weather-beaten mountain—gazed at her through hate-filled eyes, watching her every movement.

As she passed, an old woman with a missing eye spat at her, crying, "Nightland *filth!* You killed my family. You killed my *whole* family!"

Keresa's heart skipped. Had she been on that raid? There had been so many.

Memories rose of a Hunting Horse camp they'd attacked in the early days. After they'd burned it to the ground, they'd gone down to inspect what remained, and she remembered too clearly the multitudes of orphaned children wandering among the ruins, crying, searching for family they'd never find again. Kakala's eyes had possessed a haunted gleam for days.

She said, "You have *many* more refugees."

Fish Hawk replied stiffly, "Karigi and Blackta are still attacking Sunpath camps. The people who can make it here, do."

With this many mouths to feed, they'll be running short of food soon.

Fish Hawk led her around the boulders and onto the path in front of the rockshelters.

They had placed the dead Nightland warriors in a pile at the bottom of the hill. Looking down she could see they were naked. Had they stolen even the clothing? Many of the bodies had been brutalized—objects of the hatred these people lived. Two guards now stood to protect the dead. Blood trails marked the paths where they'd dragged the bodies. The Lame Bull dead must be in the ceremonial cave, being ritually prepared for the journey to the afterlife.

Fish Hawk stopped. "Wait here." He ducked through a low oblong opening.

She leaned against the stone wall, pressing her hot cheek against the cool rock while she fought the overwhelming urge to vomit. The two warriors stared at her with cold eyes.

Pull yourself together. You can't let Windwolf see you like this.

Arranging this meeting had been nearly impossible. Through two long days, she'd begged every person who'd stood guard to let her speak with Windwolf.

Think, rot you! You don't have time to feel sorry for yourself. Look, learn, plan.

As she forced herself to study the village, something struck her as odd. The two guards at the corpse pile were barely more than boys. Eight men guarded her people. Where were the rest of the warriors? Surely some of the Sunpath refugees had been warriors? When mixed with the Headswift Village warriors, there should be many men and women with atlatls and darts walking around. She tallied a total of ten. Then she noted an eleventh, down working with a group of older boys and girls, training them how to use a war club. *Children?*

Fish Hawk ducked out and held the door curtain aside. "Go in. He's waiting for you."

She rubbed her sweaty palms on her cape, called on all of her courage, and ducked beneath the leather curtain.

Inside she stood face-to-face with the one man she'd feared for most of her adult life. Their eyes met: that same challenge crackling between them as it had when they'd tried to kill each other just a few days past.

He wore a clean blue war shirt painted with red buffalo on either breast. Then she looked closer. His eyes might have struck fire, but his face was haggard, lined with fatigue. His muscular legs were locked the way a man did to fight exhaustion. Black hair clung to his forehead in clean wisps, as though he'd just bathed.

"Deputy, please sit down." He gestured to the hides around the fire hearth where a small blaze burned.

She walked to the hides, but remained standing. The firelight cast a pale amber glow over bare rock walls. The chamber spread about four paces across. He apparently had few belongings. His atlatl and a stack of darts—many of them having once belonged to her warriors—leaned against the wall. Beside the fire a tripod with a hide bag stood. Wooden cups rested near the hearthstones. A rolled buffalo hide had been shoved against the wall to her right.

Windwolf went to stand in the middle of the chamber, and the heavy weapons belt he wore clattered. He gestured to the bag hanging on the tripod. "You must be thirsty. Please fill yourself a cup of tea."

She crouched, picked up a cup, and dipped it into the tea bag. The tea, made of rosehips and dried berries, smelled sweet and warm.

She straightened and studied the knives, stilettos, and two war clubs he carried. "I assure you, War Chief, I'm in no position to be dangerous. They forced me to leave my weapons in the chamber."

"I don't meet any Nightland warrior unarmed. You in particular. You're dangerous no matter what."

Her stomach cramped threateningly. She tipped her cup up, drained it dry, and dipped it into the bag again.

She might not get anything else to drink for days—or forever.

Through the laces of his shirt, she could see his chest was streaked with deep cuts. Hurt and tired. Could she find a way to use that? Wring information from him he wouldn't ordinarily reveal?

She knelt on the hides.

A brief expression of relief crossed his face. He lowered himself across the fire from her and stifled a weary sigh.

"War Chief," she began, "thank you for agreeing to meet with me."

He nodded. "How is Kakala?"

"Delirious. As I'm sure your spies have told you. He keeps reliving old battles. All night long he called for Hako and Tanta, and screamed things about Brookwood Village."

Windwolf reached over and dipped himself a cup of tea. As he swirled the liquid, he said, "He was placed in a cage as punishment, wasn't he?"

"Yes. Our Council of Elders ordered that every warrior involved in the battle be locked in a wooden cage. Since War Chief Gowinn was killed in the battle, Kakala, his deputy, was singled out for punishment. They tortured him for two moons. When he was finally freed, he crawled out of his cage a changed man, they said. He spent several moons living alone in the mountains."

Windwolf sipped his tea and casually said, "Why did the Nightland Elders do that?"

She lifted a shoulder. "If you punish people for losing battles, they won't lose as many."

"If you escape, will they do that to you?"

A cold sensation filtered through her, as though ice water had just been poured into her veins. "Let's...let's talk about something else."

He slowly shook his head. "Once, before the coming of Nashat and the Prophet, the Nightland People were envied. Your people harvested the waterfowl, fished the Thunder Sea, hunted the seasonal migrations of the caribou, and stored their wealth of food in the ice caves for winter. You crafted the finest artwork, conducted the most elaborate rituals. Your Dreamers charted the paths of Father Sun, Sister Moon, and the Star People. You made the finest boats out of wood. We traded north in return for your dressed hides, paintings, and shell jewelry."

She sat silently, remembering.

Windwolf clapped a weary hand to his knee. "And now your Council orders its finest warriors placed in cages." His gaze bored into hers. "I have just learned that they had Kakala locked in a cage again because he failed to take Headswift Village with ten and six warriors. How he was returned to leadership is a little hazy, but tell me, are your chiefs mad?"

She caught herself on the verge of speaking, and bit her lip.

"I thought so," he added, reading her expression too well. "Tell me, how did Kakala get out this time?"

"On the Guide's orders."

"He didn't order him placed there?"

She gave him a narrow-eyed glare.

"Nashat," Windwolf guessed.

At her silence, he asked, "What do you think of this Guide of yours?"

"He will lead us to the paradise of the Long Dark." It was a safe answer.

Windwolf stared at her for a long time before saying, "Kakala is interesting, isn't he? After the Spruce-bell massacre, did he really send runners to the surrounding Sunpath villages telling the chiefs to be ready for the survivors?"

"He did."

"Thoughtful of him, considering that the Nightland Elders might have had him killed for it."

"He knew that."

"Then why did he take the chance?"

"To save a few worthless Sunpath lives."

Windwolf ran a hand through his damp hair. "That's difficult to believe, considering the tens of tens he's taken in the past few summers. But I'm sure he has his reasons. I've promised myself that after I've had a thick buffalo steak and slept for three days, I'll think about it."

She lifted a brow. "Why don't you just ask him? When he gets better."

"If he gets better. I really was trying to kill him."

Just like I tried to kill you.

She clamped her jaw and watched the way the dim light shadowed his forearm above his wrist. His hand shook slightly from exhaustion. "You're not very subtle."

"But I'm a good host. Your cup is empty. Please fill it again. Some of the refugees killed an elk on the way. They would think poorly of me were they to learn, but you are welcome to the piece offered to me." He raised his voice. "Fish Hawk?"

"Yes, War Chief?"

"Could you bring that roasted elk to me?"

"Of course."

She dipped her tea, thinking, *Keep him talking on friendly terms; think of something.*

"That was a crazy stunt you pulled at Jayhawk Village."

He looked at her curiously, aware of the change of subject. "You were holding my people hostage. What did you expect me to do?"

"Something saner. You rushed a heavily armed camp with six warriors to rescue *two* people?"

"I liked them."

"You must have. Your escape at Star Tree Camp, however, was brilliant." She gave him a small smile.

He smiled back, as though he saw right into her soul. "I didn't know you were so devoted to me, Deputy."

She lifted a shoulder. At Star Tree they'd had his warriors boxed tight in a narrow valley, outnumbered five to one. Rather than surrendering like any sane war chief who knows he's lost, Windwolf stationed eight warriors in strategic locations, then stampeded a herd of buffalo right through the middle of Kakala's camp. When their warriors scattered in every direction, Windwolf's people had picked them off like wingless ducks.

"You killed ten of our warriors that day," Keresa said.

"I'm disappointed. I thought it was more."

"Hopefully Wolf Dreamer heard that and will make

sure your soul becomes a homeless ghost, wandering the forests forever."

He tilted his head and smiled. "Wolf Dreamer, Deputy? I've heard that you follow a different Spirit."

She ground her teeth. She'd always had what Kakala called "a noxious interest" in Sunpath beliefs. "I'm not a disbeliever."

Windwolf laughed softly. "You're a surprise, Deputy. Though I don't see what that has to do—"

"Your vision is very limited, isn't it? Yours and Goodeagle's. Is that a Sunpath trait?"

He set his cup on a hearthstone and looked her over in detail.

At that moment, a boy, perhaps eight summers old, entered with a bark plate on which a thick section of elk backstrap rested. The aroma drifting off the hot meat sent the juices flowing in Keresa's mouth.

"Bless you, War Chief," the boy said in awe. "We saved the best for you." Then he shot a worried glance at Keresa and fled.

She took another long drink, letting the warm tea wash away her sudden craving for the meat. It didn't work.

Windwolf extended the bark plate, setting it before her. "Oh, go ahead. If you're going to escape, destroy me with the handful of warriors you have left, you're going to need your strength."

She lifted the piece of meat, tearing into it, trying not to look like a starved wolf, but failing, as the twinkle of amusement in Windwolf's eyes communicated too well.

As she ate, he said, "Deputy, let's discuss what you and I are doing here. I'm trying to protect both Sunpath and Lame Bull People from the brutal orders your Prophet, Council, or whoever has been giving. I'd lie, cheat, steal, do anything, say anything, to kill him and every one of your clan Elders. I—"

"Leave the Guide out of it!" She cursed herself as that look of understanding glinted in his eyes.

He continued. "I've watched tens of tens of my people die under your darts, Deputy. Do you know what it's like to witness old men, women, and helpless children running in terror before they're slaughtered by warriors from the far north? Do you have any idea..."

Desperate rage smothered her. Unthinkingly, she rose to her knees and slammed a fist into the tripod, sending the tea bag splashing across the floor. "You just murdered two tens of my warriors, Windwolf! They're lying in a pile, naked, hacked, and stabbed. Don't be so righteous!"

He leaned forward tiredly, and his blue-painted shirt rustled in the sudden quiet. "And you've destroyed seven of our bands since last summer, Deputy. We kill warriors, not babies. Didn't you ever feel a twinge of conscience murdering children?"

She sank to the hides again, hearing her own words in his mouth. "No warrior enjoys killing children."

"Well, maybe the Nightland warriors are human after all. Some of my people have begun to whisper that you're evil Spirits straight from the Long Dark that your Prophet preaches about."

She gripped her cup hard and took another long drink. "Windwolf, what are you going to do with all the refugees here?"

"Find some way to feed them."

"And then?"

"Explain."

"I'm no fool. I suspect your warriors, what's left of them, are on their way here right now." *Are they?* "When they arrive, are you going to use me and my warriors as sacrificial offerings in the stead of our clan Elders?"

"Sunpath warriors have souls, Deputy, despite what you've heard."

"Does that mean your men won't rape me and torture my people?" -

When she'd said the word *rape,* he'd flinched. Thinking about Bramble, no doubt.

Through a long exhalation, he said, "As to torture, that depends on whether or not you tell us what we need to know."

She shook her head, picking up the meat again. Her stomach had started to ache; perhaps filling it would help. "We're not going to tell you anything."

"Then what are you doing here? You asked for this meeting."

"I..." She squared her shoulders and took a deep breath. "I need your help."

His dark eyes glittered as though he was wondering how she had the guts to ask.

Keresa swallowed the last of the succulent elk. When she looked up, she found him watching her like a cat at a mouse hole. "We need water. We drank all that remained in our water bags yesterday."

He thumped his finger against his cup. "And what will I get in return?"

Keresa swallowed hard. "I'll order my warriors to lay down their weapons; then I'll turn the weapons over to you."

"All of them? No tricks?"

"No tricks."

A suave brutality tinged his voice when he asked, "And will your warriors obey you?"

Keresa glared. "Yes."

He smiled as though intrigued by the entire conversation. "Let me make certain I understand. I'll give you water, and you'll willingly become my prisoners. Is that it?"

"Willingly? I said we'd give you our weapons, not our hearts. We'll fight to the last to kill you and escape. We'll just have to use our hands to do it."

"These are the kind of warriors the Nightland Council would put in a cage?" A small smile touched his lips. "I agree to give you water."

She bowed her head in relief. "One other thing."

"Yes?"

"Kakala...I fear he may be dying. While I know this may not disappoint you, it does me. If there is a Healer in this village, I would appreciate—"

"If I send a Healer to care for him, what will I get in return?"

"What do you want?"

He drummed his fingers on his cup, as though trying to decide. "A map of the Nightland Caves."

The boldness of the request made her laugh. "Is that all?"

"No. It's just the beginning." His face showed no more emotion than a dead panther's.

"I can't do that," she said. "And my map wouldn't be much good to you anyway. I—"

"If it wouldn't be any good, what's the harm in giving it to me?"

"I've been in the caves a few times, but I know only the main passageways. There are tens of tens that I've never seen. You don't want a map from me."

He looked regretful. "Then I can't send a Healer."

Fear soured her belly. She wasn't sure Kakala would survive without a Healer. Nor was she sure he'd survive with one. Windwolf's blow may have crushed his skull, and he was already dead; his body just didn't know it.

She said, "I'll draw you a map of the main passageways. After the Healer treats Kakala."

"A true map. No tricks?"

"I give you my word." She frowned before saying, "I won't have to worry about the Healer murdering Kakala in his sleep, will I?"

"I'll make certain the Healer understands that will be my privilege, and mine alone."

Bizarrely, that made her feel better. "I thank you for the food and drink."

She rose to her feet, and he quickly got up to face her.

He takes no chances...

He reeled slightly before he caught himself. Even in exhaustion, his physical presence was daunting. He moved with a leashed power that made her wish she had her war club in her fist.

As she walked for the mouth of the rockshelter, he said, "I have one question for you."

She stopped and turned. "What is it?"

He stared at her, and it went straight to her soul.

"Is Goodeagle in the cave with you?"

She blinked, surprised.

That means there are other caves where my warriors are trapped? How many?

She remembered Goodeagle screaming at her, asking her what they were going to do. "No. I don't know where he is."

She couldn't read his expression when he said, "That must mean he's dead." Then he called, "Fish Hawk, the deputy is leaving."

Fish Hawk drew the curtain aside and said, "Come with me."

Before she exited, she looked at him. Their gazes held.

Just beneath that calm confident surface...he was as terrified as she was.

Chapter Ten

In an endless gray, Silvertip thought: *I am*.

The sensation was of floating, rising and falling, buoyed by something.

"You are," a voice told him from the gray. "You can only be after you have ceased being everything else."

The odd lack of sensation surprised him. He couldn't feel cold or heat, just being.

"Where am I?"

"Nowhere, lost in the Dream of the One."

"I died."

"You did."

Silvertip let the questions flow away. He could feel a slight pulsing now, a faint sensation of movement.

"You are coming into the Dream," the voice told him. "It will happen slowly. Do not think, just be One."

"One," Silvertip agreed, feeling resistance as his arms spread. The first sensation was of being suspended, as though his arms bore what little weight he had. Then he recognized the rushing sensation, as though he slipped through a delicate resistance.

Wind, he felt wind!

"Just accept," the voice told him. "You are One."

"I am One."

He tried to stop the sudden rising of his arms.

"Do not resist," the voice told him. "Accept. Allow the feelings to flow through you. Become One."

Silvertip steadied himself, aware of his arms rising and falling, but something was odd about his hands and fingers: When he tried to splay them, the air pulled, causing a slight roaring.

"Accept, Silvertip. Simply be."

The soothing words allowed him to relax, feeling the resistance fade. Again he slipped effortlessly through the air.

His arms lifted, stroking down, and experienced the lift, could feel the pressure beneath, the subtle vibrations that quivered in his skin.

"That's right. Learn, allow the knowledge to flow through you."

"I am flying."

"Very good. Accept that."

And he did. Flying. Not arms, but wings.

Awed, he raised the wings, stroking, feeling the lift, the surge forward.

At a sudden gust, his tail shifted, the experience unsettling.

"Accept. Learn."

Silvertip allowed his new tail to adjust and felt the Tightness as he came back level.

Time had no meaning as he tried different movements, flapping, twisting his tail, marveling in the movement of his body through air.

"Where am I going?" he asked.

"Up there."

A faint glow suffused the gray. He focused on the glow, stroking with his wings, feeling air rushing past his body.

"Slowly, Silvertip. There is no need to rush. You are outside of time. Accept."

He stiffened his wings, allowing his beating heart to settle, simply soaring toward the glow. As he did, it grew brighter, the foggy image of clouds appearing. The way it did through mist, the round ball of the sun could be seen emerging above and to the right.

"You are One," the voice insisted.

"I am One. I accept."

He turned his head, glancing down through the silvered mist, aware of patches of trees barely visible so far below. In fascination, he felt himself slip, his body beginning to fall.

"Extend, Silvertip. Do not think. Simply be."

He reached out with his wings, feeling them catch the air, and recovered his balance with a twist of his tail.

"Now, rise."

He took a cautious stroke, then another, feeling the lift. Yes, this was easy.

"Of course it is. But only if you simply accept."

The world below was clearer now, forest and lakes, grassy meadows, the meandering lines of streams like veins upon the land. To his right, he could see the ragged, cracked expanse of the Ice Giants. They looked so odd from up here: dirty, broken, extending to the north in a jumble of peaks, blocks, and dark crevasses. He could see the long inlet of the Thunder Sea, its dark, silty water filled with dots of white ice.

The tundra stretched as a gray-green belt, undulating over hillocks and pocked with holes. Clusters of boulders jutted up, and to the south, the spruce lands of his youth were carpeted with dark-green patches of trees. The great freshwater lakes to the west gleamed a greenish blue. Strips of beach were catching the white froth of waves. Sparkles of smaller lakes and ponds caught the sunlight, glimmering as he soared overhead.

"That is not our goal."

He slipped into complete clarity, the wind rushing past as he sailed out high over the land.

Something caught his eye, just off to the left.

"Do not be startled," the voice told him.

The sense of vision was odd, taking in the entire world as he coasted through the crystal air. A great eagle slipped sideways, dropping down toward him.

"You're an eagle?"

"In the One, yes."

He tried to crane his head, only to lose his balance. But he knew now and corrected. "What am I?"

"Condor."

Memory came to him. "A condor ate my body."

"That is the lesson, Silvertip. Life is the One. You have become what you feared the most. Through death, you live again, in a different form. That is the way of the Dream. We are all the One."

Silvertip took a breath, allowing his worry to dissolve, and cocked his head, focusing with extraordinary clarity on the eagle that soared off to his left. The sky hunter stared at him with a familiar piercing yellow eye.

"You are the Spirit Wolf."

"Sometimes, yes." A pause. "But you will never see me as a Raven."

"Wolf Dreamer!"

"Come, try your wings. I have something to show you."

The eagle flapped great wings, the white tail correcting its flight into a turn.

Goodeagle leaned against the wall, desperately thirsty, trying to catch some sleep. A hornet's nest of emotions hummed inside him. He dropped his face in his hands and watched the memories that ran across his soul.

His thoughts kept returning to the firelit rockshelter near Walking Seal Village.

He and Windwolf had been sitting in the mouth of the overhang, gazing up at the magnificent pines that seemed to pierce Sister Moon's heart. Light penetrated the soughing trees, carelessly throwing moonglow like silver nuggets over the valley. He remembered so clearly, so very clearly, the forest-scented winds that had ruffled their sleeves, the strong handclasps they'd shared.

When had it all gone wrong?

He couldn't quite place the exact moment, but sometime, somewhere, they had stopped defending Sunpath villages, and started attacking Nightland warriors. Blind. Desperate. Hitting hard and running fast.

He'd pleaded with Windwolf to stop and take a good look at what they'd become. But he never did—couldn't, he said. Even now, he could hear Windwolf's deep voice: "The whirlwind has caught us up and twisted us around so much, Goodeagle, the only way out I can see is to fly into the storm."

"But Windwolf..."

The hands pressing against Goodeagle's face trembled. He dug his fingers into his flesh to still the nervous attack. How many innocent people had died while they'd been out attacking Kakala's camps? They'd kept Kakala busy, but that had freed Karigi to wipe out one band after another. If they'd divided their warriors and sent them to guard vulnerable bands, perhaps those people would have been spared.

For a while Windwolf had been satisfied with a life for a life; then it had escalated to two Nightland warriors for every Sunpath killed. Making up for the past murders, he'd said. Then three to one, because they'd lost so many pregnant women and little girls...

"All we have to do is find out what they want!" Goodeagle had pleaded. "If we go on this way, there will be no one left!"

"They *want* our destruction!" Windwolf had insisted.

"But how can we even *ask* if all we do is kill each other over revenge?"

Goodeagle couldn't bear it any longer. When they'd been planning the defense of Walking Seal Village, he'd shriveled in upon himself, so staggered by the anticipated bloodbath he could no longer turn his head.

"You will go to Karigi?" Windwolf had asked. 'Tell him we wish to meet in Walking Seal Village?"

"Yes," he'd whispered hoarsely, knowing he'd planted the seeds of the ambush in Windwolf's mind.

"Good. Bring him here in six days. It will take me four to get our warriors assembled and in position. I will arrive on the fifth, ensuring we have plenty of time to prepare for Karigi's arrival. If we do this right, only a few will ever see their families again."

He'd gotten up from the Council meeting and been sick, sick to death with the horror, the screams that filled his dreams, the terrified faces of little children running, running along trails filled with corpses.

"Windwolf," he'd begged, "let's go talk somewhere alone. I need to talk to you. Let me talk to you!"

Windwolf had frowned, his eyes distant—already lost in springing the great trap, mind weaving the strategy he devised so well. He'd warmly grabbed Goodeagle's shoulder and murmured, "I promised to have dinner with Bramble. We have so little time together anymore. Later? Maybe tomorrow after we've..."

But there'd been no tomorrow.

He whispered, "Why wouldn't you listen, Windwolf? I begged you."

Tendrils of the friendship he'd tried so desperately to kill wrapped around his heart. He hurt as though he'd been bludgeoned.

He brought up his knees and rested his forehead on them.

Why didn't you talk to me?

Chapter Eleven

As night fell, Skimmer followed Kishkat around the last curve in the trail. To her left, the jagged peaks of the Ice Giants rose so high they disappeared into the bellies of the Cloud People. Their mournful groans and squeals echoed, sounding like lost ghosts.

"We're almost home," tall Homaldo called, and gestured toward the orange campfires that bordered the ice. The fires seemed to blink, and Skimmer realized that tens of people must be walking back and forth in front of them.

"Thank Raven Hunter," Tapa said. "I miss my wife and boy."

"At least we'll see them again."

The warriors glanced back and forth, fear behind their grim expressions.

"Remember," Kishkat reminded, "we were sent with Skimmer before the attack."

They trotted straight toward the Ice Giants, and Skimmer saw the black maw that led into the Nightland Caves. Last time, she had been held farther south and never brought this close to the famed cavern. It was a huge opening, perhaps four body lengths across. Passing Traders had told her that once a person went through that maw, the ice tunnels branched many times, flowing out in every direction. One of them was reputedly "the hole in the ice" that led back to the Long Dark where Raven Hunter still lived and breathed.

Her legs had been shaking for the past four or five hands of time. Skimmer longed to sit...

"Stop!" Kishkat called, peering into the half-light. "Who's there?"

The warriors surrounded her, the move almost protective.

For days now, they had traveled together, sharing meals, water, and stories.

When did I begin to see them as friends?

The notion stunned her.

Rocks and gravel scalloped the edge of Thunder Sea. Some of the boulders were three times the height of a man.

Skimmer struggled to see what had alarmed Kishkat. Near the rocks ahead, a human form slipped through the shadows.

"We said stop!" Tapa insisted, and lifted his single dart.

The man kept coming, and finally a soft voice called, "Kishkat? Is that you?"

Kishkat's eyes went wide. He stepped forward and whispered, "Blessed Spirits! Guide? Is that you?"

The warriors fell to their knees, and long-legged Homaldo called, "Guide! We've brought the woman you wanted. Kakala dispatched her when we encountered her on the trail."

The Guide walked gracefully, hands clasped behind his back, apparently deep in thought.

The warriors hissed back and forth, wondering how Ti-Bish had known Kishkat. It was too dark to see their faces.

Homaldo shot a frightened glance at the other warriors and said, "Guide? How did you know it was us? No runner could have beaten us here. No one knew."

"I've known from the moment Skimmer slipped away from the Lame Bull caves," the Guide said.

Hatred and fear burned through Skimmer's veins like a Spirit plant, paralyzing her trembling legs. She could only stare as he walked nearer.

When no more than two body lengths away, he stopped and looked at her. She couldn't be sure in the darkness, but she thought a faint smile curled his lips. He spoke gently, "Raven Hunter said you'd be here tonight, Skimmer. I've been waiting for you for a long time."

"Ti-Bish, I must talk with you. Don't...don't hurt me."

He stepped closer, took her arm, and led her up the trail, as though they were friends of many summers.

The warriors followed a few paces behind them.

"Don't worry. You're safe now." Then he bent down to whisper, "Raven Hunter told me to wait for you here. He didn't want Nashat to see you first."

As the words sank in, a wave of nausea tormented her. "Why?"

"He said Nashat would frighten you."

She looked at his gentle hand on her arm and the kindness in his eyes. "Why would you care?"

In the silver gleam of light that reflected from the Ice Giants, she saw his jaw tremble. "You need me, Skimmer. Raven Hunter helped me see that truth. He wants you close before the first motions of the destruction begin."

"The...destruction? Of what?"

"Oh." He smiled boyishly. "Everything."

Skimmer's stomach threatened to empty itself. She'd walked into the lair of a madman.

Windwolf had been right. She couldn't see this thing through.

Run! Now!

The desire made her shiver. He noticed, turned, and wrapped his arms around her. His bearskin cape felt warm, but smelled of darkness, of things that grew deep underground where sunlight never reached.

"Don't run. Please? You don't know the whole truth yet." He murmured softly, "Come. Let me take you inside where it's out of the wind and we'll talk." To the warriors he said, "Thank you for being so kind to Skimmer on the way here. You may go home to your families. You will be rewarded for your service."

"Thank you, Guide," Kishkat bowed deeply, and backed away.

As the warriors trotted out toward the campfires scattered across the tundra, Ti-Bish led Skimmer through looming shadows toward a small cave. "Raven Hunter wants you to know that your daughter is safe. Ashes is staying with Dipper and Lookingbill."

"How do you know?" Her suspicion burned brightly.

"Because Windwolf won the fight." He waved it away. "It doesn't matter. I think Keresa was Traded for you."

"Keresa?" She frowned, remembering young Silvertip's Dream.

"I don't understand all of the details, but they are fighting over the end of the world."

Of course, the end of the world.

Skimmer pointed to the huge maw. "Aren't we going through there?"

"No. I have a chamber prepared for you in a different part of the caves. No one will know where you are until I tell them. It may take some time before I can teach you some of the things Raven Hunter has taught me. I want you to be happy during that time."

She stared at him. He wanted to keep her all to himself, locked in the bowels of the Ice Giants?

"Ti-Bish, the warriors will tell Nashat I'm here. He'll search the caves until he finds me."

He timidly lifted a hand to stroke her long hair, and she forced herself not to shudder. "He won't find you, Skimmer. No one will."

Chapter Twelve

The Council chamber smelled of sweat and damp hides. Lookingbill smoothed a hand over his bald head and gazed at the warrior who stood guard outside the entrance.

Tens of people walked along the tunnels. The rock-shelters were already packed. Where in Wolf Dreamer's name would they put any more? He thanked the gods that Dipper was making those decisions. After the past few days, he felt hollow, as though his insides had been eaten out.

"I don't know which hole to aim for," Ashes said.

He looked back and frowned at the holes in the floor and the positions of the round stone balls. The goal of the game was to roll the balls into the holes with a flick of the wrist. The stones couldn't be bowled. It wasn't easy.

"You're just tired, Ashes. Would you rather take a nap, like Silvertip?"

His wounded grandson lay on a hide on the far side of the chamber, next to his elderly cousin Loon

Spot. The old woman had been snoring for a hand of time.

He tried not to look at Silvertip. The Healer had drawn sacred designs on his face and forehead, each but a desperate attempt to keep his soul contained in the body. The swelling on the side of the boy's head had finally receded, but the high fever remained.

Old Loon Spot had taken to continually dribbling water between the boy's lips. Any more than a couple of drops at a time, and he'd choke, unable to swallow.

More than once, Lookingbill had feared the boy was dead, but placing his ear to the thin chest, he could hear the heartbeat, frighteningly slow, but there nonetheless.

"No," Ashes said, maintaining the fiction of Silvertip's "nap." "I—I have bad Dreams when I close my eyes."

"What kind of bad Dreams?"

She shrugged. He'd tried to get her to discuss her Dreams since dawn, hoping he could ease some of the girl's terror, but she'd refused.

Lookingbill saw her mouth quiver before she clamped her jaw. "Your mother is all right, Ashes. She's a strong woman, and she knows what she's doing." He hoped.

"I was thinking about my father." She swallowed hard to keep tears at bay. "Wishing he were here."

"When was the last time you saw him?"

"The day the Nightland warriors burst into the ceremonial lodge and started killing people."

No wonder she had no desire to sleep.

Ashes flicked one of the stone balls. It rolled across the hard-packed floor and settled in a hole.

"Good aim, Ashes. Well done."

She didn't look happy, just relieved. "I don't want to play any longer."

"We don't have to play. Would you like to do something else?"

"No, I just—"

Loon Spot woke suddenly—stared at them as though she'd never seen them before—and threw a basket with all her might.

Lookingbill dodged just in time; it went sailing across the chamber toward the warrior who stood guard. The poor man must have thought it sounded like a dart cutting the air, because he dove for cover.

"Loon Spot, what are you *doing?*" Lookingbill demanded.

The willowy old woman had a shriveled triangular face tucked beneath a gray mop of hair. A broad smile creased her lips.

"I Dreamed you were a dog," she said.

Lookingbill scowled and thrust a hand toward the guard, who peered nervously through entrance. "Look what you made the guard do."

She grinned. "He moves fast. That makes me feel safer."

"I wish you'd go find another chamber to sleep in. I'm tired of you *and* your snoring."

With all the dignity he could manage, the guard pulled himself to his feet and straightened his war shirt. Beneath his breath, he murmured, "Crazy old—"

Loon Spot said, "He's not crazy. He's senile. There's a big difference."

"He meant *you,* Cousin."

She gave him a disgruntled look. "Just wait until

you've seen six tens of summers. Your aim won't be so good either."

Ashes smiled, and it warmed Lookingbill's heart. She had a soft, luminous look in her dark eyes, betraying the desperately tired little girl beneath.

"It's good to see somebody around here has a sense of humor." Loon Spot leaned across the floor to pat Ashes' arm affectionately.

"How come you aren't sleeping?" Loon Spot pointed a crooked finger reprovingly. "When I went to sleep, you said you were going to take a nap."

Ashes' smile faded, and she stared down at her rest-lessly twisting hands. "I can't sleep, Loon Spot. My Dreams are bad."

"Well, whose aren't? You should have seen what Lookingbill looked like as a dog."

Ashes laughed, and it made Lookingbill smile. From the instant they'd met yesterday afternoon, Ashes and Loon Spot had been fast friends.

Loon Spot waved to her. "Come here: Tell me about these Dreams."

Ashes walked over and sat down. Loon Spot put a skinny arm around her shoulders and whispered in her ear. Ashes sniffled in response.

Gradually, their two low voices intertwined, barely audible, and he could tell the little girl's fears had ebbed. Her tone grew calmer, brighter. Lookingbill shook his head. Who knew that gruff, sharp-tongued Loon Spot could speak so kindly to anyone?

Loon Spot whispered, "So he came and floated over your bed?"

Ashes nodded, twining her fingers in her cape. "Mother said he was dead. Just like Wolf Dreamer."

"Did he look dead?"

"Only a little. He had eyes like black stones." Ashes' mouth puckered, and tears glistened on her lashes. "Why is he coming to see me? I don't *want* to see him."

"Tell him that; maybe he'll go away."

Ashes toyed with the fringes on her leggings. "I'll try to sleep...if you stay here and watch."

"Oh, you bet I will. Someone bring me another basket. I'll toss it at any nasty raven that flutters close."

A raven? Lookingbill wondered.

Ashes curled up on the hide and closed her eyes. Loon Spot gently kissed her forehead. It seemed only moments before the girl was sleeping soundly.

Lookingbill whispered, "You two get along too well to have been strangers only yesterday. Are you sure you haven't been giving her gifts in secret?"

"I don't have to buy friendship. You're just jealous because you've never had a way with women."

"For once in your life, you're right."

They sat in silence for a time; then Ashes moaned.

Loon Spot waited until the girl's face slackened, then she whispered, "Did you know Raven Hunter was speaking to her in Dreams?"

Lookingbill's breathing stopped. "That's what she told you?"

"That's why she doesn't want to sleep."

"Blessed gods." Lookingbill massaged his brow. "I'm so tired. It never occurred to me to ask why—"

"Of course you're tired," she interrupted. "A few days ago you were sitting around enjoying the sun on your face. Now you're in a fight to the death with the Nightland Elders."

He lowered his hand to his lap. "I had to help the Sunpath People, Loon Spot. Someone had to."

"Dipper says the food stores down in the ice caves will be gone by the next quarter moon."

"She's right." He gave her a dull appraisal. "Windwolf has been meeting with the chiefs. He's preparing the refugees to head west. They're to leave in small groups, escorted by warriors. He thinks that in small bands, traveling by different trails, many can make it to safety in the Tills."

"How soon do you think the Nightland Elders will find out Windwolf defeated Kakala and took him captive?"

Lookingbill picked up one of the stone balls and tossed it toward a hole. He missed. It kept rolling until it hit the wall.

"Two or three days, if we're lucky. Then they have to gather warriors, depending on where Karigi and Blackta have gotten to. Windwolf calculates that it may take as long as a moon to assemble the number necessary."

"And then?"

He gave her a sad look. "By then, we'll be a quarter moon's travel west of here, making the best time we can toward the Tills."

Chapter Thirteen

Kakala weakly pushed the hide off his chest and rolled onto his side, blinking at the hazy ceiling. His flesh burned with fever. Thirst plagued him. Dim silver light came from somewhere.

How long had his soul been out wandering? Days? A moon?

He took a deep breath, and the room swirled around him. "What a...headache."

His skull throbbed agonizingly. Gently, he tried to push up on one elbow to reach for his blurry pack, but the effort sent his soul tumbling, thought after thought, memory after memory. From the corner of his eye, he saw someone move. He blinked and fell back to his sweat-soaked hide. Closing his eyes, he struggled to control the cascading images.

"Are you finally awake?" Keresa asked.

"You don't...sound happy about it."

He pried an eye open; even that hurt. A blue spot wavered in the direction of her voice.

"I am happy. Now I can stop wasting my strength cursing you."

"Glad to...to finally be of some use. How long...how long has it been?"

"Since the battle? This is our fifth night here."

Keresa cautiously stepped over sleeping warriors to reach him. He closed his eyes and listened to her quiet movements.

"Where...are we?"

"In a rotted hole beneath Headswift Village."

He opened his eyes and saw the blue spot hovering above him. He squinted and thought he could make out the shape of her face. Her eyes looked more red than brown.

"You look terrible," he commented.

"Probably because I've been slaving to keep our warriors from killing each other while worrying myself sick about you."

He smiled. "Is there...water?"

She made noise, and he heard water splashing into a cup. Keresa sat beside him, slid an arm beneath his shoulders, and gently lifted him. Then he felt the cup touch his lips. He drank greedily. Liquid spilled from the corners of his mouth and ran coolly over his chest. He finished it and let his head fall back against her arm.

"Better?" she asked.

He nodded, but as she pulled her arm from beneath his shoulders, his mind tumbled again, confused memories flying close, then soaring away.

"Wh-where am I?"

Suddenly, he couldn't remember. He shook his head, struggling to recall. In the background he heard the shrill whine of the Ice Giants...didn't he?

"Kakala, are you all right?"

"Hako?" Hope burst his heart. He reached out for her.

"No, War Chief. It's Keresa."

Images of lightning-filled skies pulsed behind his closed eyes. He could smell the vile odors of blood and torn intestines. Hako looked at him in utter terror.

"Hako, I told you to run! *Run!*"

Darts cracked on the rocks all around them. Someone screamed...

"War Chief. Do you remember that Windwolf captured us at Headswift Village?"

"Windwolf ?" His mind struggled to sort images of many battles. "He...he what?"

"There was a battle. We lost. He took us hostage."

Not Hako. *Hako's dead. Dead for too many summers.*

He shuddered, twining fingers in his damp hide. The battle at Headswift Village...Windwolf bashing him with his war club...Trap, ambush...Keresa's hard voice demanding, "Kakala? Kakala, hold onto me! We have to get out of here!"

"I remember...Keresa."

"Good. Lie still. A Healer will be coming to check on you. He's been here twice."

"Healer? What Healer?"

"A man from Headswift Village. I don't know his name."

He threw her a questioning look. "Search him...before he touches me, all right?"

"Forget it. Windwolf assured me he wanted to finish you off himself."

He felt like laughing, but figured it would kill him. "How are our warriors?"

She exhaled hard. "Not well. In order to get a Healer to come and see you, I had to order them to turn over their weapons. No one is happy about it."

"But they...did it?"

"Of course. I threatened to kill each man who hesitated."

"Keresa? What do the warriors...think...I...?"

Even in his haze and pain, he'd been worried to death about that. Surely the ones who'd lost friends would be blaming him, praying he'd die. When he was able to take control again, would they obey his commands?

"Some have misgivings. But most of them are with you. I'm with you."

"I...I know that."

With hushed violence Keresa said, "The world out there has gone mad, Kakala. There are tens of refugees crawling all over Headswift Village, and more appear every hand of time. Windwolf's forces are growing rapidly."

He sucked in a deep breath. "Have we...heard..."

"We've heard nothing. Windwolf must have ordered the warriors who guard us to keep their mouths closed. At first I heard many interesting things, but since then, nothing."

"What about Goodeagle. Did he...did he survive?"

She stopped pacing to stare down at him. "Did you want him to?"

"Not really. I just...thought he might suddenly...be of use."

Keresa laughed, but it was a strange, near-desperate

sound. Since he felt the same way, he chuckled with her — and instantly regretted it. His head shattered like a block of ice dropped from a mountaintop.

She said, "Windwolf did say something that made me think he might be alive."

"What?"

"He asked me if Goodeagle was in this chamber with us, which made me think he meant there were other chambers where our warriors were being held."

"Keresa...when possible...try to find Goodeagle...Get organized."

He thought he saw Keresa run a hand through her hair, but it was a splotch-on-splotch movement so he couldn't be sure. Her voice came out soft, strained. "I've missed you, Kakala."

He smiled. "You...scared?"

"Terrified."

"Don't be. Windwolf may have taken...us hostage, but he can't...can't hold us. We'll escape."

"I think you're right. If he keeps taking in more and more refugees, it won't be long. When the people here are going hungry, tensions will rise. He'll have his hands full just managing his own refugees' quarrels. And it won't be long until the Nightland Elders realize we haven't returned from this raid. We might be dead before they get here, but surely—"

"No we won't."

She took a deep breath and spread her feet, looking like she'd just braced herself for hand-to-hand combat.

"You have more faith in our Elders than I do." A treasonous tone invaded her voice.

Why did she do that to him? It set him on edge, and she knew it.

He lay still, thinking until he felt the silence so desperately he knew he had to get up—get the warriors organized.

He pushed up on his elbows, and a sharp pain nearly fragmented his skull. He fell back weakly, thoughts rolling, jumbling, pieces of images swirling, slips of different voices shouting...

Keresa watched him writhe; her fists knotted in futility. She should have let him sleep. But she'd needed to talk to him, to bolster her own flagging spirits.

Many of her warriors were awake now. Their eyes gleamed in the faint slivers of light that fell through the boulders.

"Hako?" Kakala called. "Don't...don't leave me." He feebly lifted a hand, reaching out.

Keresa felt like she intruded on some private memory, but she knelt and...

Footsteps grated on the rocks above, probably warriors changing watches, but in Kakala's soul they were enemy warriors.

"No!" he screamed. "No! Don't! Oh, gods, not...our fault!" He raised his hands to his head, squeezing hard as he tossed from side to side.

"Kakala," she called. "It's Keresa. You're here with me. You're safe!" What a lie that was.

"Safe?"

"Yes."

He shook his head, as though clearing the feverish fog. "No. Even if we...Hako?"

He turned toward her, and the soft pained look in

his usually hard eyes made her feel like he'd ripped her guts out.

"Kakala," she assured him, "Calm down. Try to sleep."

"No, I...I'm frightened, Hako. I—I don't...Hold me?"

He weakly lifted his arms to her. She sat down and let him wrap his arms around her.

Warriors whispered, and she didn't like the sound of their voices.

"You're safe, Kakala. Get some sleep."

He tightened his arms around her back and feebly pulled her against his chest, tenderly rubbing his chin in her hair. "Never safe...no...never."

Drained from his outburst, he blinked wearily and drifted off. His arms slowly slid back to his sides.

Keresa got up and looked around the chamber, her eyes squinted. "Any warrior here who thinks what I just did makes me weak had better never turn his back on me."

Laughter rose. Some of the tension eased.

Footsteps grated above her again, and this time there were voices.

She looked up as one of the boulders was rolled aside.

Windwolf loomed tall and hard-eyed in the moonlight. A shorter man stood behind him, a bag beneath his arm. "Deputy," Windwolf greeted. "How's the war chief?"

"Bad."

"I've brought the Healer, Flathead, again. Just like last time, before he comes down I want all of your warriors to gather on the far side of the chamber."

She turned. "Do it."

Her men rose and moved to the rear, muttering unpleasantly to each other. They should be used to it by now.

A pine pole ladder was lowered into the chamber; then an old man descended one step at a time. He had a small pack on his back. The Healer immediately went to Kakala's side and put a hand to his fevered brow.

"Now, Deputy," Windwolf said, "I want you to climb out."

"Me?" Keresa asked.

"If you're no longer deputy war chief, I'll take your successor. Someone has to keep a promise you made."

The map of the caves...

Keresa glanced nervously at her warriors. "All right. I'm coming up."

She climbed and stepped out onto the boulders. Eight warriors surrounded the entry to the chamber. Four clutched war clubs; four held nocked atlatls. Just in case any of her people escaped.

She heard Kakala whimper; then the Healer said something soft.

Windwolf crouched over the opening and looked down.

"Hako?" Kakala called feebly. "No...no. Reach... farther. I can almost touch...Don't! I—I need you. I—"

"It's all right," the Healer soothed. "You're going to be all right."

"No! Please...please no more. I can't..."

Keresa shifted uncomfortably. Windwolf had no right— *no right!*—to see Kakala like this. She tried to impale him with her fiery glare, but he kept looking thoughtfully at Kakala.

He rose suddenly, said, "Come with me," and walked away.

She followed. Two guards fell in line behind her.

What had he felt? His expression had betrayed deep, grudging emotion.

By instinct, she studied the high points, noting every place a warrior stood silhouetted. Frowning, she looked again. No good warrior would allow himself to be seen so easily. And these warriors looked very slender, and short.

When Windwolf turned around and caught her scrutinizing the high points, he said, "Deputy, I would prefer that you walk beside me. We can talk on the way to my chamber."

Chapter Fourteen

W indwolf almost breathed an audible sigh of relief when Keresa finally followed him into his chamber. Once he had wondered how the Lame Bull People could live in these holes. Now he felt distinctly uncomfortable out in the open—especially with so many refugees filling the valley.

Most were just reverent, but too many insisted on crowding around him, reaching out to touch him, demanding his attention. The look in their eyes left him shaken; each and every one believed that he could save them.

By Wolf Dreamer's sacred breath, it will be a relief when the first groups leave tomorrow.

Too many things disturbed him these days. As he had watched Kakala, his heart had saddened. Why would his old enemy's suffering bother him so? Was it just the things he'd learned? That Kakala had tried to kill Karigi for what he'd done to Bramble? Or that somehow, he'd gone from a heartless butcher to a vulnerable captive?

I can't afford sympathy for a man who'd love nothing more than parading me into the Nightland Council.

But what about Keresa?

He studied her as someone down in the camps started playing a wooden flute. The mournful lilting notes made him stop and listen. It was too beautiful for this time and place.

She stood by the fire, arms folded tightly across her chest. Her red doehide war shirt conformed to her body, accenting every curve. He couldn't keep from staring at her, wishing so desperately that this able woman was anyone but his foe. Something about her manner, the way she handled herself, spoke to his loneliness. How long had it been since he'd spoken to anyone as frankly as he did to her? If only...

"Those acorn nut cakes smell wonderful," she said, breaking the spell and pointing to the basket that rested beside the hearth.

"I'm sure they do, since you haven't had anything but water for two days. Please, eat some."

She didn't waste any time, but knelt, unfolded the hide wrapping, and pulled out one of the cakes. She gobbled it down as fast as she could and reached for another.

Windwolf walked across the chamber and picked up the hide he'd chosen earlier. As he walked back, he asked, "Do you like them?"

Crumbs had fallen onto her dress. She didn't take any time to brush them away. Around a mouthful of food, she replied, "Wonderful."

"They were made for me by a woman who once lived in Walking Seal Village."

She stopped chewing.

Well, that tells me something about your conscience.

He sat down on the opposite side of the fire and watched her.

She swallowed, and said, "I'm grateful for the food."

"You're welcome."

She finished the cake, sank to the floor, and exhaled slowly. "May I dip myself a cup of tea?"

"Please."

As she did, he unrolled the deer hide and found the piece of charcoal he'd been saving from the fire.

She shifted positions, brought one knee up, and propped her cup on it. From this side view she seemed all the more slender. It touched something inside him, some illogical masculine need to protect—as if this warrior needed anybody's protection. Nonetheless, it softened his guarded responses to her.

"Windwolf, will you tell me something?"

He lifted his brows, expecting something unpleasant. "Go on?"

"Why is it that Sunpath People keep plotting to kill our guide? We've wiped out one nest of conspirators after another, but more spring up immediately."

He listened to the lilting note of the flute. If he let himself, he could almost feel as though he'd stepped backward in time, and Bramble was still alive. He could hear their son laughing...

"Your Guide preaches the extermination of anyone who believes in Wolf Dreamer. What do you expect my people to do?"

"Some have converted. Like the Seadog band."

"Yes," he said. "I remember. It was the first day I took my son into the forest and started teaching him how to throw a dart and swing a war club."

93

In a graceful motion, she made a sweeping gesture to Headswift Village. "So, he owes all this to you? Is he grateful in his praise?"

He lightly stroked the fine hairs on the deer hide. "My son is dead."

Her stony expression melted. "Forgive me. I didn't know." After a few heartbeats, she added, "The earlier a boy learns to fight, the better. You were clearly a good father."

She looked like she wanted to ask him what had happened, but restrained herself.

He was thankful for that. It might have been one of her darts that had killed Lion Boy four summers ago. The fight had been swift and hot. Nightland warriors had struck the Hunting Horse camp fast and hard before they dashed away into the forest like cowardly dogs.

In the fireglow, her hair had shaded golden, as though a glistening web of real summer sunlight netted her head. He fumbled with the piece of hide, suppressing an ache for the family he'd lost, for the scents of wet dirt and wildflowers, the rustling of wind through pines around the Hunting Horse camp.

"What have we done to ourselves?" she asked softly.

He said, "That almost sounded friendly."

"Did it? I must be exhausted beyond good sense. But I'm not blind, Windwolf. My angle of vision is just different from yours. I've seen the Sunpath People kill many of our children, too."

"*I've* never killed your children."

She smoothed her fingers down the side of her cup. "No, you haven't."

Thoughtfully, he rolled up the hide, then unrolled

it again. "Deputy, I know some of the stories of the Nightland People. Do you any Sunpath stories?"

"I know about the Exile and the climb through the hole in the ice to this world of light. I know about Wolf Dreamer, and his battle with Raven Hunter." She smiled wistfully. "They used to be our stories, too."

"There are others. Every time my people got settled into a nice comfortable place, something went wrong, and we ended up running for our lives. It was as though Wolf Dreamer had abandoned us. So we dedicated ourselves to seeking the One. We..."

She put a hand to her mouth to cover a yawn, and Windwolf said, "Am I boring you?"

"No, it's not you. It's just...I've never been this exhausted in my entire life."

He unrolled the hide again. "Draw this map for me and you can go."

He started to rise; to hand her the hide and charcoal, but she reached around the fire to touch his sleeve. He could feel the chill of her delicate fingers through his shirt.

"I'm sorry; it's not you." She laughed, as if amused at herself, eyes softening. "Odd, isn't it? Here I am, facing my enemy, and I feel at ease." She hesitated. "Can we talk while I draw?"

He lowered himself back to the hide. "Of course."

"For just this one moment, can we forget who we really are?"

He lifted a shoulder noncommittally. "What would you like to discuss?"

"Only things that don't matter. Tell me..." She drew a line on the hide and shrugged. "If you could have one wish, what would it be?"

"To be left alone." He looked down at his hands. "The problem with life is that you never know what to miss until it's gone."

She nodded sympathetically. "And your favorite food?"

"Nothing you'd like. It's a plant so spicy almost no one but me can eat it. It's called beeweed and comes from the far west."

"How do you get it?"

"From the river Traders. One summer they brought a sack of beeweed to our camp in the Hunting Horse territory. That's the only time I've had beeweed, but I remember the flavor."

She smiled, a true gesture, not one of those carefully contrived to ease tension. It made him feel better. She drew a black curving line on the hide. "The Waterthrush People make an acorn bread that they serve with bumblebee honey. That's my favorite."

He leaned forward. "I'll have to try it the next time I'm there."

She smiled, white teeth flashing behind her lips. "Do. You'll like it."

They fell silent, gazing across the fire at each other.

Who is this woman?

As he looked into her eyes, it was as if to touch her soul. He could sense her fear and the worry that chewed away at her. For that moment, she wasn't deadly, didn't mask her insecurity in the face of the future. In the firelight, he watched her pupils expand, her lips part. Then, self-consciously, she took a breath and went back to drawing.

A long silence stretched.

"Windwolf..." She pressed her lips tightly together.

"I'm sorry that all this..." She bit it off, averting her eyes, irritated with herself.

"You did what you had to, Deputy." He smiled wearily. "We all do."

He watched the fire dance over her smooth cheeks, wondering why no man had devoted himself to her.

As if in defeat, she murmured, "As Kakala says, we have to be Nightland warriors."

"You sound like you'd rather not."

"Like you, I'm tired of it." She met his eyes, that curious vulnerability calling to him. "Do you believe in what you're doing?"

He made a helpless gesture. "If I don't save my people, who will?"

"Can't they save themselves?"

He shook his head. "I don't know. Think about what we were: loosely knit bands of hunters and gatherers, moving our villages from place to place. All anyone wanted was enough to eat, to watch our children grow, to appease the Spirits of the animals we hunted and the plants we ate. Most of our time was spent squabbling with each other over trivialities." He paused, staring into her eyes with a desperation of his own. "Now it all seems so silly."

She broke the connection, frowning as she bent down to trace another line, scowled, and spit on her palm to rub it out. "Tell me...do you ever long to just ran away? Maybe travel south to the nut forests, or out to the grassy plains?"

"More than you could know," he said sadly. "Were it not for my responsibility to save my people, I would be gone." He rubbed the back of his neck, feeling curiously uneasy. "There's nothing left here now. Only painful memories of my wife and child, dead friends, and a happy life that is lost."

She nodded, lips pursed. He decided he liked the pouting frown in her forehead.

"Do you and Kakala wish to run away, too?"

"I do. Kakala..." She looked up, slightly startled. "No, Kakala and I aren't like that. It's hard to explain. We're..." The frown was back, a minor for her own confusion. "Closest friends." She gave a dismissive gesture. "There's no man in my life."

"Are they all fools?"

She laughed, genuinely amused. "No, and I guess that's the problem. You'd have to be a fool to want a woman like me. Few men can stand a woman who runs faster, throws harder, or hunts better."

"Some do." He glanced down at his hands again. "Once, I had a woman like that."

"I know." She shook her head, voice dropping. "Bramble was my friend."

"Then you know what they did to her?"

She nodded. "Karigi." She swallowed hard. "When Kakala saw..."

"Go on." He felt his chest tightening.

"If you hadn't attacked, Kakala would have killed Karigi. I've never seen him in such a rage. He was in the process of beating him to death. It wasn't just that Karigi had disobeyed orders."

"Why?"

She looked up at him, eyes liquid. "Because Kakala liked and respected Bramble. It takes a great deal to earn Kakala's respect. But Bramble did. Seeing...It wounded him." She rolled the charcoal in her fingers, staring into his eyes, the corners of her lips twitching.

"What was Kakala's plan at Walking Seal Village?"

"He thought if he could take Bramble, hand you a crushing defeat, it would be an incentive for your people to leave without more killing. If the Sunpath just went away, left, the Nightland would have only the Lame Bull to convince. With no enemies, the Council would have no reason to send out war parties. No one who believed in Wolf Dreamer could follow us when the Guide took us into the paradise of the Long Dark."

"A quick way to end the killing?"

"Kakala sometimes has grand notions." She returned to her drawing.

Windwolf frowned, thinking back. Bramble had broached the subject of leaving. He had even been considering it before Walking Seal Village. Now, summers later, what was he doing, but sending parties of refugees west to the Tills?

Kakala tried to kill Karigi? Would have, had Silt and I not arrived when we did?

"Have you ever thought about changing sides?"

She lifted a brow and laughed softly. "Don't be ridiculous. You're doomed."

"We could use you."

"I'm intrigued by your faith in the future." She laughed again and shook her head, as though she doubted his sincerity, while she drew several more curving lines. "But I'll keep it in mind."

"I'm serious."

Something about the softness of her expression touched him. He wanted her to stay, to talk, to just let him look at her.

He pointed at the map. "How are you doing?"

"I'm finished." She handed it to him.

When he reached for the map, he accidentally grasped her hand where it held the hide. Time seemed to stop. Conflicting emotions danced across her beautiful face: a magnetic attraction to him, fear, confusion. They might have been frozen, the physical contact lasting for five heartbeats, then ten. Her cool skin under his sent blood rushing in his ears.

Finally, Keresa gently pulled her hand back and said, "That's the best I can do."

Windwolf looked at it, pulse pounding, short of breath. "Is this the eastern entrance to the caves?"

"Yes." She tapped the map. "And this is the western entrance."

She'd drawn many more passageways than he'd thought she would, and based upon his own explorations, they looked accurate. It told him something very valuable about her sense of honor.

Her dark eyes fixed on his. He could see the question there that she dared not ask.

"Yes?" he prompted.

"About Kakala, back at the cavern. You shouldn't have stared like that."

He sighed. "All these moons I have wanted him dead. And now..."

"Go on."

He shook his head.

"May I go now?" She refused to meet his eyes, but he could see the pulse racing in her neck.

"Of course." He went to the entry to hold the curtain aside for her.

She ducked outside and was gone.

Chapter Fifteen

S ilvertip fought his way through a thick haze of gray, images of the Dream living within him.

Each of Wolf Dreamer's words remained fresh and clear, as though they had become a living part of Silvertip's soul.

He blinked his eyes open and winced at the grating feel, as if sand had been poured behind his lids. He reached up with a feathered wing, oddly surprised to find a very human hand at his control. It took a moment to remember how to work his fingers as he rubbed his dry eyes. His tongue stuck to the roof of his mouth, and a terrible pain filled his head.

Unlike his Spirit body, this one hurt; his bones ached. His bones, the same ones he'd seen slowly bleach and fall away. Making a fist, he savored the miracle of muscle, tendon, and bone. He felt stiff, but he was whole.

When he turned onto his side, it wasn't with a simple twist of his tail, but the more ponderous movements of a dull and clumsy body.

It took a moment for his eyes to focus. Then he knew where he was: the Spirit Chamber.

Glancing at the door, he determined it was night. The fire in the center had burned down to coals. Grandfather Lookingbill lay wrapped in his buffalo-hide. Loon Spot sat just to his side. Her head drooped at an odd angle, mouth open to expose a few peglike teeth, a rasping snore rising from her wattled throat.

I'm back.

He looked down at his small body, so poorly human. But in his soul, the magic of flight still ran through him like a beam of morning light.

Tears brimmed in his eyes, silvering his vision. He blinked at them, and sniffed, a profound grief welling within. The sense of loss grew, encompassing a sorrow he didn't know his breast could contain.

"Give me back my wings. Please, Wolf Dreamer!"

In the middle of the night, Keresa heard a familiar voice. She sat up and rubbed the sleep from her eyes. All around her, warriors lay stretched out across the floor with their capes tucked closely about their bodies for warmth. Kakala whispered and whimpered, lost in some dream.

The familiar voice came again, and she realized it wasn't coming from this chamber.

A thrill went through her.

She got to her feet and picked her way between the sleeping men to the blocked tunnel. The debris, composed of several large boulders and tens of small rocks, felt icy cold.

Two voices: both soft, but familiar.

Why hadn't she heard them before? Voices carried farther at night, especially when it was as quiet as it was tonight. There was no wind. The warriors above her were silent.

She used her hand to dig out some of the gravel and dirt that filled the space between two of the large boulders. It crackled as it hit the floor, but none of the sleeping men seemed to hear it.

When she'd created a hole as deep as her arm was long, she pressed her mouth into a gap and called, "Washani?"

The voices stopped.

"Washani?" she called again, as loud as she dared.

Silence.

Then Washani called, "Deputy Keresa? Is that you?"

She leaned her forehead against the wall and smiled.

Skimmer lay on the thick pile of buffalo hides and stared at the utter blackness. She had no idea where she was, but she had to be very close to the beating hearts of the Ice Giants. Their cries and groans seemed louder here, more grief-stricken.

She rolled to her side and tried to sleep.

Ti-Bish had led her through the dark tunnels for hands of time, feeling the way. At each fork, he would sniff the air, as though the tunnels had a distinctive scent. She had funneled all of her concentration into the task, but had no more chance of retracing her path than she did of flying.

When they'd finally arrived here, he'd taken her hand and placed it on the items in the cave: the sleeping hides; a water bag; a basket of pemmican, consisting of a length of intestine stuffed with meat, berries, and fat; and wild rice cakes.

Then he'd left her alone.

The darkness pressed on her eyes and ears as though it had heavy hands.

"Did Windwolf really win?" she whispered, and her voice seemed to ring in the silence, bouncing back from the ice walls. Ti-Bish had assured her he had, and that Ashes was safe. But how could he know for sure?

If Windwolf had lost the battle, what had happened to Ashes? Had Lookingbill gotten her out before the end?

Horrifying images flashed: Ashes being raped by Nightland warriors...Ashes being herded northward with the other orphans to become slaves in Nightland villages...Ashes lying dead in the Spirit Chamber with her head bashed in...

"He won," she said sternly. "Windwolf won. He killed Kakala and destroyed his war party to the last warrior."

She had to believe it.

But whatever had happened, she still had a terrible task ahead of her.

She had to kill Ti-Bish. Perhaps in the chaos afterward, Windwolf would be able to storm the Nightland Caves and force their Elders to halt the attacks on the remaining Sunpath bands. Or, with the Guide dead, maybe the Nightland would simply lose heart, their warriors withdrawing meekly to leave her people alone.

A strange tapping began. It echoed from some distant tunnel. She listened, hoping it was Ti-Bish returning with a lamp. The tapping turned into a forceful thudding, and she realized it was water.

Had a new crack opened in the bellies of the Ice Giants and allowed a pool of meltwater to escape?

Would it flood her cave?

Is this how I'll die? Drowned in ice water, here, deep in the darkness?

She bent her head, tears of despair streaking down her cheeks. She sobbed, wishing for sunlight, air, and the feel of wind on her face.

The Ice Giants let out an ear-splitting groan, then trembled, shaking the floor beneath her...and the thudding stopped.

Skimmer clamped her jaw to keep her teeth from chattering.

Pain

S he doesn't know I'm here, sitting just outside her chamber.

Raven Hunter told me long ago that I needn't fear the darkness; that I walked with Death every instant of my life, and if I could just keep staring at it, I would never be afraid again.

But I worry about Skimmer.

She is a creature of light and warmth.

Raven Hunter tells me that I must force her to live in perpetual darkness for at least one moon. That she has to get used to it, because it is the nature of Raven Hunter's world, and the sooner she learns what that means, the better.

I haven't the heart.

She's tearing herself apart in there. Her breathing is rapid and shallow. She keeps whimpering as though she can feel the hands of monsters stroking her body.

Doubt consumes me.

I asked Raven Hunter today why it was taking so

long, why he couldn't just show me the hole in the ice
and let me lead our people back to that paradise.

For the first time, he grew angry. The earthquake
that followed his outburst lasted for nearly three tens of
heartbeats. I was terrified that the Ice Giants were going
to collapse around me, burying me in the darkness
forever.

He told me he was struggling to assure that everything happened at the right moment and ordered me
never to question him again.

I won't.

Skimmer has started crying.

I am afraid for her.

And for me, if I don't obey Raven Hunter.

Chapter Sixteen

Windwolf leaned against the mouth of the rockshelter and stared out at the boulders that created Headswift Village. In the sunlight, they gleamed wetly with the morning dew. Down the hill—at the base of the outcrop—Sunpath People went about their morning duties, cooked breakfast, and played with their children. A pack of dogs raced through the village, barking.

He sighed heavily. Two camps had already headed out on the trail west, but another three had arrived. It was an awkward way to move people. Those who came north to Headswift Village might have a couple of days of recuperation, only to be sent off west, knowing they had to ford the great river at the western edge of Loon Lake. They could have saved a moon's travel or more by simply traveling straight west along the southern margins of the lakes.

But Karigi and Blackta were out there, somewhere.

"I do not understand," Fish Hawk said. "I just told you that we heard boulders being moved in the chambers where we've trapped the Nightland warriors. Doesn't that disturb you?"

Windwolf kept his gaze on the Sunpath villagers. "I know my orders sound...unusual, but I have my reasons."

"Please help me to understand them."

A boy ran down the trail in front of them. His dog, a puppy, trotted happily at his heels. Windwolf waited until they'd passed.

"Deputy Keresa needs to speak with her people. Let her."

Fish Hawk studied him curiously. "They'll be plotting against us."

I'm counting on it. I'm also counting on their growing desperation."

Fish Hawk propped his hand on his belted war club. "If they work hard enough, they may open a tunnel connecting the chambers."

"If they do, pretend you don't know about it."

Fish Hawk's brows knitted. "They'll think we're fools."

Windwolf nodded. "Perhaps. But desperation grows with numbers. I want them all sharing each other's doubts."

"Then...you want Kakala's warriors all in the same chamber?"

"Now you're getting the idea."

Fish Hawk shook his head as though he hadn't heard right. Long black hair fell over his shoulders. "If I were making the decisions, I would be trying very hard to keep them separated. The warriors in the new chamber must still have weapons. We don't know how many there are, but if they get together, they are much more powerful. They'll be plotting to escape, and if they escape, they will surely kill some of us."

Windwolf pushed away from the wall and stepped out into the sunlight. Cold wind gusted up the trail and flapped the collar of his buffalo coat. "That's a chance I'm forced to take."

Fish Hawk held his gaze. "Why don't we kill them?"

"Because the longer we hold them, the more time they have to think, to lose hope. They know the cages are waiting for them. As soon as I know how the Nightland Elders will respond to our hostages, I'll explain my bizarre orders." He clapped a hand on Fish Hawk's shoulder. "In the meantime, I must ask you to trust me."

"Well," Fish Hawk said through a long exhalation. "I hope you're being brilliant, not stupid. If they escape, Kakala won't rest until he kills you."

Windwolf tightened his arms over his chest and gave Fish Hawk a tired smile. "Then, we had best not let them escape."

"I'll bet you want to kill Keresa," Ashes said as she knotted fibers cut from spruce roots. Her nimble fingers were occupied making a net bag.

"No," Silvertip told her as he clutched the Wolf Bundle to his chest. He mostly kept his right eye closed, since it was hard to focus. And the headache didn't make talking easier.

"Why not? She tried to kill you."

Silvertip pursed his lips, giving her a squint-eyed appraisal. "She only did what Power wished."

Ashes gave him the sort of look she'd give the

demented. "Power wanted you to have your head bashed in?"

He glanced around, seeing none of the adults close. "I had to die."

"Well, you came pretty close."

He gave the slightest shake of his head. "No. I died. I saw my dead body. Watched as a condor came down and..." He pressed the Wolf Bundle against his stomach, remembering the sensation of the condor's beak pulling out his guts. "I had to watch until my bones fell away."

"Why?" Her eyes were wide, the partially finished net bag forgotten in her hands.

"To learn to fly," he said wistfully. "It was the only way I could become Condor."

"Condor?" She hesitated. "Did you eat dead things?"

"It's not so bad." He gave her a somber look. "What was wonderful was Dreaming the One. And don't ask. I can't explain. It's a...harmony. A sharing of life and light." He clamped his eyes shut. "If I could only go back."

"Go throw another rock at Keresa."

He smiled, but it hurt. "It's tempting. But I have things to do."

"Like what?"

He stared into her eyes. "The voice you hear in your Dreams is Raven Hunter's."

Her interest was replaced by suspicion, and not a little fear. "Loon Spot told you?"

"No. I saw us. In the future."

Her expression had turned wary. "In the future?"

"After our world is destroyed."

"You're starting to sound like the Prophet."

"He is Raven Hunter's tool. Wolf Dreamer was lost

in the One, Dreaming the harmony. He didn't understand. Opposites crossed. There's great Power in that.
Harmony and order must be crossed with chaos and
creativity. Life must be balanced by death. Only when
male and female are joined can new life be created.
Wolf Dreamer didn't understand. The battle between
him and his brother was just beginning."

"He's not the only one who's confused. You're
sounding peculiar yourself."

"The Ice Giants are melting."

"Tell me something that I don't know."

"You've heard of the great lakes beyond the Southwind People's lands?"

"Of course. The Traders tell how the whole
southern rim of the Ice Giants is one endless lake after
another."

"Water runs downhill."

She laughed. "That was a good bump on the head.
If you didn't know that before, you needed it."

"And all that holds it back is a narrow dam of ice."

She stared at him, thinking. "But the Ice Giants are
melting."

"As Condor, I flew over the last dam. I looked down
at the cracks and tunnels. Wolf Dreamer and I saw it. In
the One, I watched it give way." He looked down at the
Wolf Bundle, hearing its soft whispers and feeling its
growing warmth.

"You have to warn people."

He nodded. "Many will listen. Others won't believe
a boy who was hit on the head. They will say I'm too
young to be a Dreamer."

"Then what will you do?" She was giving him a
serious look that he would come to love.

"I'll take you with me."

"But...what about my mother? She'll come looking for me here."

"That's just it, Ashes. There will be no 'here' left." He looked around. "All of this, it will all be washed away."

She gave him a skeptical look. "And what if I don't go?"

"Then you will never become my wife, and our children will never struggle to find the balance between Wolf Dreamer and Raven Hunter."

Chapter Seventeen

S kimmer...Skimmer...Skimmer..."
    She jerked awake at the sound of her name being repeated over and over and stared up into Ti-Bish's worried eyes. He carried an oil lamp with a moss wick. Two long braids framed his boyish face and hung down over the front of his bearskin cape. In the fluttering light, the tiny black ravens painted on the cape seemed to move, to be flying.

"Is it morning?" she asked and sat up.

"There is no morning here. Are you hungry?" He lifted the basket in his left hand, and she smelled the distinctive aroma of roasted fish.

"Starving."

Ti-Bish started for the mouth of the cave. "Come, I want you to see something. We'll eat there."

Skimmer rose, swung her cape around her shoulders, and followed him out into the tunnel. The endless moaning of air flowing through the crevasses and tunnels mixed with the low groaning of the ice.

Her mouth dropped open at the size of the winding

irregular passage. She'd had no idea when she followed him here in the darkness. This stunned her. The tunnel arched three body lengths over her head and spread five wide. Sand and gravel dotted the floors and walls. Occasionally a massive boulder jutted out through the ice.

"I thought the Nightland caves were pure ice," she said.

"The ones near the surface are," he replied softly, but his voice reverberated from the walls, almost as though he'd shouted. "Here, in the lowest tunnels, the Stone People live with the Ice Giants."

The tunnel forked. Ti-Bish took the passageway to the left, the one that slanted sharply down. Skimmer was happy for the gravel in the floor; it kept her moccasins from slipping.

"It's not much farther," he said.

"Where are we going?"

"To my secret place."

She kept her eyes on Ti-Bish. He had a gawky walk, like a blue heron hunting shallow water.

In another six tens of heartbeats, the tunnel seemed to fade, but as Ti-Bish carried his lamp closer, she saw the truth.

Ti-Bish stepped out onto a gravel shore and looked up. A pained howl rose from the bellies of the Ice Giants and shook the world.

"Blessed gods." Skimmer had to brace her hand against the tunnel wall to stay on her feet. When the tremor stopped, she walked out behind him...and her breath caught.

The water rippled in the aftereffects of the quake; it spread before them like an endless ocean. An ocean of living light. Tens of fish swam near the surface, driving billows of light with their heads and, in their wakes, leaving milky veils behind. As far as her eye could see, the water had a faint glow; and the ice ceiling above—scalloped and sculpted by eons of water—gleamed.

"It's...unbelievable," she whispered. Her heart began to pound. "No one could ever Dream such a place."

Ti-Bish knelt on the gravel and set his basket down. "Grandmother Earth is alive, Skimmer. The mountains have souls. The trees Sing late at night. Grains of sand can speak. It's just that no one listens."

Her gaze followed a sinuous trail of light created by a very large fish. She had heard elderly Traders speak of the far oceans as living seas of light, but she'd never imagined this. "Where are we, Ti-Bish?"

"Beneath the Ice Giants."

"You mean..." Terror killed her voice. In a bare whisper she said, "You mean that massive bulk of ice sits on top of us?"

"Yes. This lake is their tears. Every time they cry, the water level rises." He pointed to the ledges that had been carved into the ice from the rising and falling water.

"Do they know we're here?" she whispered.

"Oh, yes, they called me here—to this very spot—ten summers ago." That mad gleam had entered his eyes again.

"Called you?"

"Please, sit beside me. Let's eat and talk." Ti-Bish laid out shell bowls. With care he unwrapped four roasted fish and divided them into the bowls. Finally, he drew out two wooden cups and handed her one.

Skimmer took it and sat down cross-legged.

Ti-Bish pulled out a water bag and filled his cup as he said, "The water here is salty, so you can't drink it."

"How can it be salty when it's melted ice?"

"Because it's part of the Thunder Sea. At high tide, saltwater rushes in, and fresh water drains out at low tide. Those are ocean fish. And sometimes I see seals and walrus in here."

Skimmer let him fill her cup from the bag and drank. It tasted good. "This must dazzle everyone you bring here."

He gave her a hopeful look and softly said, "I have never brought anyone here."

For the moment the awesome vista overwhelmed her hunger. He picked one of the bowls up and handed it to her.

Skimmer set her water cup down, took the bowl, and rested it in her lap. When she took a bite, she found the fish still warm, the meat flaky and delicious.

Ti-Bish said, "I come here when I'm afraid or worried. When I'm here none of the terrible burdens of being the Guide weigh my soul down. I feel like I've already gone through the hole in the ice and returned to the sanctuary of the Long Dark."

Her thoughts shifted briefly to Headswift Village, and worry began to nibble at her heart. She ate more of her fish, trying to force the thoughts away, but when she looked up, she found him studying her anxiously.

"I'm glad you're here, Skimmer."

The air around her shifted, as though moving in response to the wind outside, and the faintest of ripples brushed the shore. "Why, Ti-Bish?"

"I need to be with you. To pray with you."

She gave him a hard look. "I thought you wanted me for other reasons."

"What other reasons?"

"As a man wants a woman. The way Nightland warriors usually do with women captives." She watched his eyes widen as she added, "If that's the price I must pay for my people, I will lie with you."

"You would..." He looked completely stunned. "I...I..." He swallowed hard, turning his eyes away in embarrassment. In an oddly squeaking voice he barely managed to say, "I only want to pray with you."

"Pray?" she asked, confused.

His eyes widened. "Yes, you...you're important. To me, and especially..." His excited voice stopped suddenly as though he'd been hushed by invisible Spirits.

"Yes, Ti-Bish?"

"You would..." He blinked his eyes, as though suddenly tortured. "I *can't* lie with you."

She sighed relief, ate another bite of fish, and swallowed. "We live in a terrible world, Ti-Bish. I'm sorry I—"

"Terrible?"

She blinked. "Filled with rape, sadness, and death. Suffering is the heart of everything."

Ti-Bish pulled a long strip of crispy skin from his fish and ate it before he replied. "Fortunately, there is darkness to kill that terrible light."

She frowned. "What did you say?"

"Sadness and death are but sharp daggers of light that blind the soul. Darkness eases the pain." He spread his arms to the dark womb that held them. "Raven Hunter's black wings make it go away."

He inhaled the scents of the darkness as though they soothed him.

Skimmer finished her first fish and tossed the bones into the lake. An eerie glow expanded in its wake.

She watched it fade before she started on her second fish. "Do you actually see Raven Hunter?"

He smiled and bowed his head. "No one believes me. But, yes, of course I do."

Fascinated, and frightened, she asked, "What does he tell you?"

"Oh, things I'm too stupid to understand. A few days ago, he told me that Wolf Dreamer has touched the Spiral and it's twisting down into nothingness. Like a child's top, winding down."

Hesitantly, he reached over and caressed her hand. The warmth of his skin, the tenderness of his touch, made her turn her palm up so they could twine fingers. He gripped her hand tightly and heaved what sounded like a sigh of relief. Then he closed his eyes as though drowning in the feel of her flesh against his.

"What's wrong?" she asked.

"I..." He lifted his gaze and shyly said, "I need to talk with you."

"Then talk."

He gazed at her through dark eyes that glowed with a haunted light. "Do you remember when I brought you the feather?"

"I remember."

"You laughed, but you had tears in your eyes." He hesitantly reached out and touched her hand where it rested in the sand, caressing her fingers. "I asked you why beauty made you cry."

She didn't remember any of this. "What did I say?"

For an instant, his heavily lidded eyes reminded her of deep dark holes. He dropped his gaze to examine the twig of driftwood. "You said that beauty died."

"Why did my words about the feather bother you, Ti-Bish?"

"Because"—his voice sounded pained, unsure—"it has a bearing on our lives, doesn't it? I mean, if you believe that all beauty dies, then you're never happy."

The hollowness in Skimmer's breast seemed to boom. She said nothing.

He pressed. "Why do you think there's so much suffering?"

"You're the holy man. You tell me."

Ripples undulated across the surface like swirls of luminous frost.

"I asked Raven Hunter." He gazed up at her with childlike innocence, but his eyes seemed haunted. "He told me it's the fault of the Sunpath People."

"Our fault? Why?"

He tenderly stroked the long black hair that fell down her back. After the consternation her offer to bed him had caused, she allowed it. "Because you believe in Wolf Dreamer."

"Well, the next time you see Raven Hunter, tell him there is one fewer believer."

"You...you've stopped believing in Wolf Dreamer?"

"He's just a story our Ancestors created to entertain children."

Sounds from the lake drifted to them: a fish jumping, water dripping, the deep aching groans of the Ice Giants.

Ti-Bish looked at her through eyes filled with so

much sorrow that she felt wounded. "Oh, no, he exists, Skimmer. He's just wicked."

A curiously empty sensation invaded her. "If he exists, I agree with you."

And there's no sense in telling you what I think about Raven Hunter. Not after what I survived in the pen that night.

Ti-Bish reached around and pulled the basket onto his lap. As he unfolded the hide that had kept the fish warm, he said, "This is for you."

He handed her a beautifully painted bundle.

Skimmer took it and examined the designs. The paintings looked ancient. In many places the colors had flaked off, leaving gaps in the picture, but she could still make out the two men hurling lightning bolts at each other. "Where did you get this? It's very old."

Ti-Bish wet his lips and stammered, "I—I found it. I've never opened it, though, and I don't think you should either. Just...keep it. As a gift."

A strange phosphorescent fog formed on the far side of the lake and moved toward them, as though being pushed by Wind Woman's breath.

Ti-Bish said, "Father Sun has risen. He's warming the sea outside."

Skimmer stared at the fog. "Do people come in here in boats?"

"No. You can't see the opening from outside because the Ice Giants have fallen into the water, blocking the way for boats. But I think once, a long time ago, people rowed their canoes in here. I've found skeletons on the shore."

"Skeletons? Of people?"

"People and animals. Some of the monsters are frightening. They're huge, and their bones are rock."

A fluttering like bats overhead sounded, and Skimmer looked up. The ice vault shimmered, but nothing alive flew around up there.

Ti-Bish abruptly got to his feet, picked up his oil lamp, and said, "I have to take you back to your chamber now."

"Why?"

"It's necessary."

Skimmer clutched the bundle as she rose. "I hate the darkness, Ti-Bish. Could you bring me a lamp?"

As he led the way back up the tunnel, he said, "Not yet. Soon, I hope. Raven Hunter says you need the darkness right now."

"Why?"

"To smother the spark of Wolf Dreamer that lives in your soul."

There is no spark of Wolf Dreamer left, Ti-Bish. He is as dead in my heart as Hookmaker is.

As they walked back toward her chamber, the darkness grew heavy, leaden, weighing down her shoulders like a granite cape. The worst part was the fear...

Chapter Eighteen

Silvertip sat with his legs dangling over the sharp edge of a boulder that perched high on the slope overlooking Headswift Village. Below him, yet another of the Sunpath camps was packing up their few pitiful possessions. The two warriors who would lead them west were talking to the Elders, pointing at this and that.

They are the lucky ones. But how can I tell them that by having lost everything but their lives, they have gained a future?

Craning his head, he could look out over Thunder Sea. In the distance, across the gray water, the Ice Giants shot their cracked, piled, and tumbled heights into the sky. No human could cross that.

But I flew.

He longed for the sensation of wings.

"What a gift, just to have known it."

He could hear the soft whisperings of assent from the Wolf Bundle where he clutched it tightly in his lap.

Wind tugged at his hair, sending cold fingers past his hunting shirt and along his skin.

To feel is to live.

He heard Ashes as she climbed up and immodestly seated herself beside him. She looked out at the camps, then turned her eyes west, where the faintest rim of Loon Lake could be seen.

"Why do you think I even want to be your wife?"

He smiled, knowing full well that she'd been puzzling over that.

"Because you and I are matched by Power. After what happened to you in the Nightland pen, you have no illusions about this world. After I died and Dreamed the One, I have no illusions about the Spirit World. Both of us were changed, Ashes. We have both lost everything, and gained everything."

She gave him that probing look. "Your family is alive. You have people who still love you."

"You've never Dreamed the One, only to lose it." He closed his eyes, savoring the memory. "I had wings, Ashes. *Wings.*" A tear crept past his cheek.

She was silent, considering that. Finally, she said, "Well, what about Mother? You said you'd seen the future?"

He nodded. "She will come back to you." He paused. "But you won't know her."

"That's silly. Of course I'll know her. She's my mother!"

"She's Raven Hunter's. As I am Wolf Dreamer's."

"But you said that I'm Raven Hunter's, too."

"You are. But he will never own your soul like he does Skimmer's."

"I don't understand."

"She has no balance. You have me, and I have you. I will bring order and peace to your life, while you bring chaos and creativity to mine. Together, we will balance our Power, and lay the seeds for a new world."

"Don't bet on it." Wind teased strands of her black hair across her face. Her eyes were fixed on the distance to the south where spruce gave way to pine, maple, and oak. "Somewhere out there are warriors who wish nothing more than to kill us."

"But we can Dream a new way."

"Only if you have the darts to back it up." She shrugged. "My father was like you. He thought that if we left the Nightland alone, they'd do the same to us."

"But your mother wanted to kill the Guide."

"Mother dragged Father into that kicking and screaming. Up until the end, he thought he could keep his world the same." She glanced at him. "It doesn't work that way, Silvertip."

"No," he whispered, "it doesn't. And you're right. As much as I dislike the thought, we will have to have warriors who protect what we create. But unlike the Nightland and Sunpath, we can't forget that Power fills the world."

She shifted on the rock. "It must have been a wonderful thing...to fly."

"The world looks different from up there." He raised his eyes to the sky, seeing a hawk gliding on the thermals.

"Well, what if I really do love you? Among my people, Dreamers avoid women. In the myths, it was love that killed First Woman. If I slip into your blankets some night while you're Dreaming, are you going to lose your soul in the One like she did?"

He reached out, taking her cool hand in his. "Nothing comes without a price, Ashes. I agreed to that when I came back. To do what I must, I can't Dream the One again. Not like I did."

"Good," she answered simply. "Because I remember how it was between Mother and Father. They thought I was asleep, but they liked coupling." She grinned. "They used to have this look, something special in their eyes before they sneaked off to lie together. I think I'm going to like coupling when I'm finally a woman."

He laughed. "I'll do my best to keep you happy."

"I suppose you've seen it?"

He nodded. "But that's all right, because I already know you've imagined it."

She punched him playfully in the shoulder. "I've imagined a lot." Then she sobered. "But for a while, during that terrible night in the Nightland pen, I thought they were going to kill me."

He searched her eyes, seeing the wounded soul behind them. "Then you know, as few others do, that every moment is a blessing

Goodeagle sat in the near darkness with his jaw clenched. Scents of wet dirt, human feces, and sweat tainted the air. Kakala and Keresa had been taking turns questioning him for over a hand of time. Keresa's questions confused him the most. She kept asking things about Bramble: How did she wear her hair? Did she tilt her head in a certain way when she smiled? What sort of hand gestures did she use? He felt crazed, on the verge of violence.

As soon as Kakala had crawled through the recently opened tunnel, he'd ordered his warriors, and Goodeagle, to remove and pile all of their weapons in the far corner—out of sight, but within reach. Then he'd told his people to leave. They'd crawled into the adjacent chamber and Goodeagle had heard them guzzling water from water bags, laughing and joking with their friends.

He would have given anything for one sip of their water.

"Why is he leaving us alive down here?" Kakala asked. The side of his head looked terrible: cut, swollen, and scabbed with dried pus.

"I—I don't know, Kakala."

The war chief sat on the floor, looking ill. Blood-matted hair hung in greasy strands around his scarred face.

"You are truly worthless. Windwolf is asking questions about the Nightland caves, and you haven't any notion of what he might be up to? What's he doing?"

"I *don't* know. Leave me *alone!*" Discussing Windwolf made his stomach cramp. He kept seeing the man's eyes, and he couldn't shake the remnant of old and abiding friendship.

Goodeagle glared up at Kakala and Keresa. Every word he spoke to them made him feel like he was reliving that terrible day at Walking Seal Village when he'd first made the deal with Karigi to betray Windwolf. His stomach cramped again. He bent forward in agony.

Kakala looked at Keresa, then tilted his head toward Goodeagle. She walked lithely forward.

"Goodeagle," she said, "let's lay out what we know. Windwolf has totally reorganized this village. He's ordered the Elders to stay inside and posted guards around them. He's set up a warriors' training school for young boys and girls. Nearly all of the true warriors here, both Lame Bull and Sunpath warriors, seem to be missing. He's kept a few critical people—like War Chief Fish Hawk—but his own green child warriors are currently standing guard on the high points. What's he doing? Is this a ruse to distract us from something else? Is it possible he's already sent warriors to attack the Nightland caves?"

Goodeagle examined her from head to toe. She'd said "Windwolf" with a hint of softness in her voice.

He ran a hand through his moist black hair and forced himself to respond. "Windwolf would never dispatch a war party to the Nightland caves unless he was leading it."

"What about the missing warriors?"

"I suspect they're involved in finding food for the refugees." He looked up and smiled gloatingly at Kakala. "You already told me they've looted the dead."

Kakala's nostrils flared. "I would do the same thing. Let me ask you this: Is it possible Windwolf is planning on exchanging us for some of the hostages Karigi is holding? Or perhaps the Sunpath slaves at the Nightland caves?"

Goodeagle chuckled. "If somebody corners him, he'll try arranging an exchange—your people's freedom for his. If that doesn't work...well, you won't have to worry about anything ever again."

But then, even if they were exchanged, they only have the cages to look forward to.

Goodeagle paused. Was Windwolf counting on that?

Kakala's gaze drifted to Keresa. She wandered

slowly around the edges of the chamber, grimacing at the walls and floor. Goodeagle's eyes narrowed. He'd watched her go about her duties for moons; he knew her style: brusque and honest. What was this new feminine allure? He shook his head, fighting against the clear similarities between her graceful movements and Bramble's. Did they affect Windwolf in the same way? He felt suddenly numb—the thought like a stiletto driven into his soul.

Perhaps her newfound allure reflected exactly what she knew Windwolf liked? Or was it his direct, if subtle, coaching?

Whose side are you on, beauty?

He had to know, and fast.

"I'm worried," Keresa said. "I think the missing warriors are on their way to the Nightland caves, and if we don't get out of here to warn our people—"

"Really?" Goodeagle gave a low laugh that made his own blood run cold. "Did Windwolf tell you that? In personal discussions? He's a rare man, isn't he? Gentle, willing to bend over backward to compromise so he doesn't have to hurt you. Yes, I can hear it now, 'Keresa, just help me and I'll guarantee the safety of everyone you love. Help me, Keresa.'"

She seemed to stop breathing. He leaned forward. "And he has a reputation for being an expert beneath the hides. Oh, I'll bet you like that, don't you? Did he promise you riches as well?"

Kakala glanced at his deputy, and Goodeagle could see the lurking doubts surface. Kakala suspected it, too.

In a warning voice, Kakala said, "Goodeagle, if I were you, I wouldn't—"

"You're not me! And this is too amusing. Don't you

disapprove of treason, Kakala?" He thrust a hand out toward Keresa. "Blessed Ancestors, I've seen this so many times!" he lied, pushing, trying to force her cool confidence to break. He ignored the slight shift of her body, the cold glare she gave him. "Seducing women warriors is a game with Windwolf, he—"

In a graceful dancer's whirl, she kicked out. Her right foot slammed into Goodeagle's shoulder and sent him sprawling. He struggled to his knees, but she kicked him down on his stomach, landed on top of him, and her arm tightened around his windpipe. He gasped for breath.

From the corner of his eye, he could see her smile. "You're dead, Goodeagle."

"Keresa," Kakala said sternly. He tried to pull her off, but her arm just constricted tighter.

"Keresa! Let him go! We're all crazy from the tension. Don't let this—"

"You'll back me, won't you, Kakala? Goodeagle was obviously suffering from a bout of Sunpath conscience. He was trying to escape...to go warn Windwolf about our plans."

Kakala hesitated, then nodded. "Make it quick and clean; I don't want any noise."

The cool way Kakala had spoken left Goodeagle reeling.

"Wait!" he rasped. "The Nightland Elders promised me sanctuary! Kakala, you can't—"

"No, but I can." Keresa smiled again, speaking to Goodeagle in a caressing voice as she lessened the pressure. "Let's have a final talk, shall we? If I get the right answers, you might even live. Hmm? What do you say?"

He twisted to gaze up into Keresa's icy eyes. "What — what do you want to know?"

"Details. Just minor details of the Walking Seal Village battle." She toyed with him, smoothing her deadly fingers down his neck like a lover's hand. Every muscle in his body went rigid. Kakala looked on as though bored.

May the Spirits curse him! He's a Nightland war chief, and the Council promised me sanctuary!

He blinked at the pressure at his throat.

But that's not why I did it. No. No!

"For example," Keresa said in a silken voice. "We had Walking Seal Village surrounded. When Windwolf's warriors ambushed us, it was a terrible battle. But in the midst of all the killing, he ran straight for the ceremonial lodge— abandoning his warriors. Why?"

Goodeagle's breathing came in shallow gasps now; sweat stung his eyes. If he could get to his knees, he might be able to take her. He considered it. No, no, even if he managed to take Keresa, Kakala would probably kill him out of some bizarre sense of loyalty to his deputy. "To rescue Bramble."

"I don't believe that. He's too good a war chief to endanger his warriors simply out of—"

"You're a fool, Keresa." Goodeagle shook his head, chuckling hysterically. Maybe he could talk his way out. "I'd have thought you'd know this by now! Windwolf has some fundamental flaws. He's a cool calculating war chief only up to a point. He can recover from any surprise, but if he takes a blow to the heart, he stumbles. He *loved* her!"

"Let's discuss Bramble. Try to imagine, Goodeagle. Try to see what her last discussion with Windwolf must have been like. He let her go into a situation where he knew she might die."

He shook his head. "I—I never really liked her. I don't—"

Her arm pressed coolly into his windpipe. He swallowed convulsively, belly threatening to empty itself. "He...He probably said something about how dangerous it was. And...And she told him he was too valuable to risk...that she was the right choice."

Keresa asked, "Would she have discussed you? Women tend to be more perceptive about people than men. She had suspicions you weren't the loyal friend Windwolf thought, didn't she?"

"Bramble and I never got along. She was always so fanatically dedicated to Windwolf that it sickened me. I couldn't even have a decent argument with him without her tongue—"

"But he *let* her take the risk?"

"You didn't know Bramble like I did."

"And how was that?"

"She was strong-willed like a man. How he could love a woman like that..."

Keresa released him and stood. She glared down, disgust and hatred marring her normally composed face. Her full lips pursed as though she wanted to spit on him. "I've heard enough."

Kakala nodded. "Go. I need to question him for a time longer."

She briskly strode away.

Goodeagle collapsed to the floor, gasping for breath and rubbing his throat. "Kakala, if you push Windwolf, he'll head straight for the Nightland Elders. None of them will be alive when he leaves."

"And how will he accomplish that feat of magic? Did the two of you ever plan such an attack?"

"Yes. Many times, and in great detail." Goodeagle rolled to his stomach and wiped sweat from his eyes, trying to catch his breath. "But before I tell you, I need water. Bring me some water!"

A few heartbeats later, a water bag sailed through the tunnel and thudded on the floor.

Chapter Nineteen

ashat rolled his hips, enjoying the pressure of Blue Wing's pubis against his. The woman had her long legs wrapped around his buttocks as he had instructed the first night he'd taken her. Some deep-seated comfort filled his chest, augmented by the sensations of his shaft moving inside her. He liked full-breasted women and pressed his chest into hers.

When the tingle began in his loins, he stiffened, eyes closed. As waves of pleasure spasmed, he gasped, "Gods, yes, Keresa, yes!"

He lay spent, then lifted himself on an arm, looking down at the woman.

"I am Keresa again?" she asked emotionlessly.

"It's an expression among my people." He rolled off her, then watched as she stood, wiped herself, and listlessly pulled a dress over her head. He watched her breath fogging in the cold, wondering if it reflected the disgust in her soul, and added, "I would take it as most inappropriate if I heard that you made mention of such things among the slave women." He smiled. "And I will know."

She nodded, the defeated expression on her lovely face sharpening.

"Oh, come, Blue Wing. At least you're fed...and alive."

"Is that what I am?"

"Would you rather have remained in the pen with the others? I hear the wolves have even taken the bones."

She gave him a dull look, as if she didn't really know.

And to think the Guide just told her to go home?

He dressed as she ducked out through the hanging. He shivered, stepping over to the woodpile and tossing three pieces onto the coals. Would he never be warm again? Glancing at the pile, he noticed how low it was. What were the slaves doing on their half-moon-long trips down to the forests and back to keep him supplied?

He heard someone clear his throat beyond the hanging. "Yes?"

"The warriors you requested are here. Councilor."

Nashat straightened his long war shirt, hung a string of shell beads with an intricately carved ivory pendant about his neck, and slicked his hair back. "Enter."

He watched as a nervous Kishkat and Tapa stepped in, wary eyes taking in his opulent surroundings. Neither one seemed to have any idea what to do with his hands.

"Ah, Kishkat, Tapa, how nice of you to accept my summons."

"Thank you, Councilor," Kishkat said, trying to mask the deep-seated fear behind his too-quick movements.

Nashat stood, fingering his chin, letting them stew as he gave them a half-lidded glare.

The pressure got to them. Kishkat stammered, "C-Can we help you, Councilor?"

"Imagine my surprise when I learned just recently that you were at home with your wives and families instead of on the war trail with Kakala."

Tapa looked like a trapped hare. "Is...is that a problem, Councilor?"

"Why don't you tell me?" he asked pleasantly.

Kishkat spread his arms. "We brought the woman, Skimmer! Under...under War Chief Kakala's orders." He swallowed too hard.

"Skimmer is dead."

"Oh, no, Councilor," Tapa protested. "We...we found her just outside Headswift Village. On...on the trail." He looked pleadingly at Kishkat. "Isn't that right?"

Kishkat took a breath. "Yes, Councilor. Kakala, in accordance with the Guide's orders, sent us here with the woman."

"With a dead woman."

"But she's not *dead!* Kishkat insisted. "We delivered her to the Guide! Go ask him."

Nashat narrowed an eye. "Just where did you do this?"

"Beyond the caves!" Kishkat swallowed hard. "He was waiting for us in the dark. Skimmer told us he wished to see her. And we brought her. He took the woman and told us that we should go home, and that we'd be rewarded."

"We just did what the Guide said, Councilor." Tapa's voice sounded like something squeezed out from under a rock.

Skimmer is alive?

Nahsat frowned, taking a couple of paces before the fire. Shooting a glance at the warriors, he could tell that that much was true.

"Why didn't you come to tell me this?"

Kishkat spread helpless arms. "We...we serve the Guide."

"We *all* serve the Guide," Nashat snapped. "At least in our own way." He took a deep breath, the tension he'd shed lying with Blue Wing rebuilt in his chest. "Where is the woman now?"

The two warriors glanced at each other and shrugged. Kishkat said, "Wherever the Guide took her, Councilor."

Skimmer has been with Ti-Bishfor several days? And I've heard no word of it? By Raven Hunter's breath, is the Idiot still alive?

"And what of Kakala? I have heard no word."

Kishkat took a deep breath. "I can honestly say that I have no idea what has happened to the war chief."

Nashat gave him a nasty smile. "Then tell me dishonestly."

Kishkat blinked. "What?"

"What was he doing when you saw him last?"

Tapa had sweat beading on his brow. "P-Preparing to attack Headswift Village."

"Did you know that Skimmer was plotting to murder the Guide?"

Both warriors looked stunned.

Kishkat shook his head. "They talked like friends.

Nor did Skimmer say anything unkind about the Guide during the days we were on the trail with her."

Nashat could feel a headache coming on. "Go. Get out of here. And if the Guide is harmed in any way, you will bear the blame."

They bolted headlong from the chamber.

He reached for his cloak, calling, "Guard! Prepare me a lamp."

Of all things, he hated climbing down into the dark ice tunnels like some sort of misbegotten rat.

Ti-Bish, you idiot, if you are dead through this foolishness, it is going to really complicate my life.

War Chief Fish Hawk called, "Windwolf? Are you awake?"

Windwolf blinked, yawned, and tried to shed fragments of his Dream. In it, Bramble and Keresa kept merging together: sometimes one, sometimes the other. An odd mixing of grief and hope left him muddled as he stared around his stone-lined chamber.

He wearily threw off his hides and rose to his feet. As he reached for his buffalo coat and slipped it on, he called, "I'm awake, Fish Hawk. What is it?"

"Deputy Keresa wishes to speak with you."

He frowned. Why would she request a meeting at this time of night? He blinked at the firelight that flickered over the stone walls. How long had he been asleep? If the fire was still burning, not long. "Is she with you?"

"Yes. She told me it was urgent."

"Let her enter, Fish Hawk."

The curtain was drawn back, and she ducked under it. Her red doehide war shirt looked faintly orange in the dim glow of the fire. She wore her long hair loose about her shoulders. The style made her seem more frail—an illusion he dared not fall prey to.

He gestured to one of the hides on the other side of the fire. "Sit. May I get you a cup of tea?"

"Yes, thank you."

"What may I do for you?"

"You may set me and my warriors free."

"Try as I might, I can't quite talk myself into believing that's a good idea." He paused. "Assuming, that is, that they wish to continue attacks on my people."

She walked over and stood beside him as he dipped the cup. He gave her a sidelong look. In the fire's gleam, her tightly clenched fists shone starkly white. He examined her more closely. She was fighting to keep her breathing even, but it wasn't working. His brows lowered. Either the stakes were uncommonly high—or she wasn't particularly practiced at this. Maybe both. Was she covering for someone? Kakala? A moment of panic set his heart to racing.

He stood and handed her the cup, noting with interest how long she allowed their fingers to touch before taking it. The touch sent a small tingle through him; just as she'd intended. Interesting.

"Did you decide not to sit down?" he asked.

"I think I'll stand."

He eyed her speculatively as he sipped his tea. "What can I help you with?"

"The tension among my people is growing. Fights

are breaking out over nothing. Just moments ago one warrior was very tempted to choke another to death."

He lifted an eyebrow. "And I should think that's a bad idea?"

"Nevertheless—"

"I suppose I could climb down and give them a lecture on the intricacy of good manners while awaiting the inevitable."

"I think..." She paused. "That might make things worse."

He nodded amiably. "What do you suggest we do about it?"

She gave him an uncertain glance. Were his suspicions that plain? Or was she just uncomfortable with the role of trickster? Lifting her cup, she finished it to the last drop, and handed it to him for a refill.

He dipped another for her. "Is this discussion difficult for you?"

"Not yet."

"Do you expect it to be?"

"I don't know."

"Really? I'm disappointed."

"Disappointed?" She gave him an irritated look that he thought completely charming.

"You're a warrior. You should have had your strategy worked out before you came in."

She fixed him with a penetrating but uneasy stare. "What do you mean?"

He shook his head and tossed more branches onto the fire, stalling; giving her time to stew.

Silence stretched; she started to fidget.

He relented. "Tell me something. How distracted am I supposed to be? Enough to forget myself completely?" He brazenly looked her up and down. "I hope you're not counting on my sense of honor."

"I've already heard about your honor when it comes to women." Her cheeks turned a rosy hue. She exhaled haltingly and ran a nervous hand through her hair.

My honor when it comes to women?

He smiled. *Goodeagle!*

"I think you are one of the most attractive and capable women I have ever known, Keresa, but don't count on me losing my senses just because I find you fascinating."

"Counting on you in any manner seems risky."

He scrutinized her unmercifully. She stood quietly, staring into her tea cup, as though vaguely embarrassed.

"Do you wish to tell me what we're really discussing?"

"Not particularly."

"Then why don't you let me start?" He took three steps to stand directly in front of her. "Let's discuss how Kakala is plotting to escape."

"We've tried. It's impossible. We can't—"

"No good war chief ever gives up. And my old adversary is a very good war chief."

She opened her mouth to say something, then thought better of it. He took the opportunity to refill his cup. As he straightened again, he ordered, "Sit down, Deputy. It's not working."

She stood defiantly for a moment, then knelt across the fire, eyes sharp as if to see into his soul. "If it's not working, why don't you throw me out?"

He grinned. "I like you."

"Is that supposed to ease my tension?"

"Not particularly." Toying with his tea, he asked, "So

Kakala's finally decided he needs Goodeagle's knowledge?"

"Goodeagle's dead. You said it yourself."

"Goodeagle knows the rules too well to be dead. Surely he'll fill you in on all of my plans. It's in his interest to get out and as far away from me as he can get."

She let out a frustrated breath. "I don't understand you, Windwolf. Why are you just sitting here? Good-eagle— assuming he's alive—can *hurt* you."

A small thread of warm emotion tinged that last. He noted her flushed cheeks, the anxious movements of her hands around her cup. She was good.

"Maybe I'm foolish enough to believe in old friendships."

"You're going to let him work his poison? Just like he did at Walking Seal Village?"

His control crumbled. She'd done that deliberately, taking charge of the conversation.

"Careful," he advised. "Be very careful. What are you getting at?"

He saw the change in her eyes, as though she'd come to a difficult decision. When she lifted her head, her tanned skin gleamed in the firelight. "At Walking Seal Village, you knew he was off plotting behind your back, didn't you? Surely someone tried to tell you that your best friend—"

"Bramble tried to tell me. Didn't matter. I trusted him."

"Like now? If you lose this gamble, they'll *kill* you!"

His gaze drifted slowly from his cup to her piercing eyes.

Blessed gods, does she know what I'm doing?

She was a shrewd warrior. Had he misread her motives? The possibility struck him like a blow to the belly. "What are you trying to say?"

She rubbed both hands over her delicate face as though in disbelief. "Nothing, I—I've lost my wits."

"Are...are you trying to help me, Deputy?"

She stared down at her hands, slowly shaking her head. "I don't know what I'm doing. I don't know what you're doing. If you think that because you and Good-eagle were friends once...well, don't! There is no redemption. Not in his worthless soul."

She looked suddenly weary, weary beyond exhaustion. After peering interminably at the floor, she lifted her right hand—her throwing hand—and opened the palm to the soft light. A somber expression came over her face. She stared at it, then slowly closed it to a tight fist and shook it at some inner foe. He understood that gesture better than any of her spoken words. Tens of times in battles, he'd cursed fate with that same soundless ferocity.

She said, "I hated you for summers. You killed so many of my friends."

A familiar ache swelled in his chest. He stared at the fire, letting her finish.

"But as I watched what you did, I came to grudgingly admire you. You were so perfect. Every move was clean, precise, no emotion."

"That's how it looked from the outside?"

"Yes, and I suggest you continue the practice. You're in an impossible situation. What are you going to do? Nashat may already know what's happened here. He will combine Karigi's and Blackta's war parties, and together they will overrun these caves." She thrust her arm out. "All of those faithful camps out there are going to be' destroyed, the people murdered. And you're just sitting here like..."

She closed her eyes, a look of defeat on her face.

"Then, what would you suggest?"

"If you wish to stop these attacks, you have to do it at the source: our Elders. But you'll have tens of warriors waiting for you at the Nightland Caves. You can't—"

"Maybe I can."

"Windwolf, think! No matter how well these children fight, they'll never be good enough to match Nightland warriors. And you sent all of the other warriors away, didn't you? All of the adults? So they're waiting, expecting orders to attack the Nightland Caves. But what if Karigi locates them in the meantime?"

He blinked at the question. "Shall I tell you all the details of my plan?"

She met his gaze with a severity that stopped him short. "I'll know soon enough. Your best friend, Goodeagle—if he's alive—will undoubtedly tell Kakala exactly what he expects you to do. And here you are—"

"Being far too honest with a woman I like far too much."

Their gazes held, and he noticed how hers softened. He shook his head sternly. "You should go. Otherwise we'll both make fools of ourselves."

"Don't hate me for asking about your strategy. I figured you needed help."

He chuckled softly, unsure now if she really cared, or if they were still sparring for advantage. "As a matter of fact, I do. Tell me how Kakala plans to escape."

His heart pounded at the look on her face. She

paused almost as if she wanted to. A ploy? It was a good one. He would do anything to help her step across that silken bridge of loyalty to his side.

Her voice was little more than a whisper. "Were I to stay with you, help you, would there be a way that Kakala and my warriors could leave in peace?"

"Could they promise me that none of them would ever lift a weapon against my people again?" His heart began to pound. Was this the way?

"I don't..." She shook her head. "No. They fear the Council too much. Doing that would mean a worse punishment than the cages."

"Keresa, just tell me..."

She shook her head miserably. "You're right. I have to leave."

She rose and walked toward the door, a defeated slump in her shoulders.

"Keresa?" He saw her turn, eyes moist. "There has to be a way out of this. Help stop the killing. Some way, any way, that turns good people like you, me, and Kakala back from being the monsters we've become."

He stepped toward her, taking her hand in his. He rubbed his fingers over the smooth skin, his desperate gaze boring into hers. "If we follow the same old path, there will be nothing left for any of us."

She pulled hard against his grip. He refused to let go. They stood eye to eye for ten heartbeats, and he could feel her pulse increasing until it raced as rapidly as his own.

He reached up with his other hand, gently running it down her long hair. What had she done to him? How had she worked her way into his heart?

Her lips parted, eyes widening. The telltale pulse in

her neck was throbbing. Abruptly she seemed to melt against him, her body conforming to the hollows of his. She tightened her hold, as though he were the last thing she had left to cling to. A surge of warmth flooded Windwolf's veins.

In the back of his mind a voice whispered: *A game. This is all a game. We'll both use whatever leverage we can, but what harm is there in soothing each other for a few moments? What harm...?*

He slowly disengaged himself and backed away. She was watching him, tears rimming her large dark eyes. Her breasts rose and fell with each rapid breath.

"Keresa," he said in a strained voice, "tell Kakala that Goodeagle's right about one thing: If I can't find a way out of this, I won't leave anything alive in the Nightland Caves."

She hesitated for an excruciating amount of time.

"Windwolf, if I..."

He balled his fists. "I need you, Keresa."

Without a word she ducked beneath the door curtain and disappeared. He caught a glimpse of Fish Hawk's curious face before the curtain fell closed again.

Keresa walked down the trail with Fish Hawk at her heels. The warrior followed a good pace behind her.

The sensation of Windwolf's strong arms around her had stirred feelings that terrified her.

Too deep, she'd gotten in too deep. How had that happened? How had she let it happen?

The game was going awry...

After Keresa and Fish Hawk had passed into the darkness, Silvertip emerged from the cleft between two rocks. The shadow had been deep, black, and the crack that led under an overlying boulder had allowed him to slip close enough to hear most of what had been said in the war chief's quarters.

Now he cradled the Wolf Bundle and stared after the dark forms. "We all have our parts to play. I hope that you have bargained well, Wolf Dreamer. If we all Dreamed the future, would any of us find the will to live?"

He ducked back into the shadows as Windwolf emerged to stalk down the trail like a man with a purpose.

As the War Chief's footsteps faded Silvertip looked up into the night sky. He could hear Raven wings gliding through the dark air overhead.

Chapter Twenty

Kakala slept soundly, dreaming of the pleasant lazy days of his youth...

The sweet pungent scent of tundra blossoms drifted on the warm wind. Hako was stretched out at his side beneath a huge boulder. From their vantage overlooking the Thunder Sea, they could hear the soft singing of the Ice Giants. Gulls flew overhead screaming. Pilot whales, six of them, were coursing among the bergs just offshore. A warm southern breeze was blowing across the land, driving the black flies to cover. The rock's soft shadow smoothed Hako's triangular face, and jet-black hair hung like a cape around her shoulders. She gave him a reproachful look.

"Kakala, you're the best warrior in the village. You can throw a dart farther than anyone else. Swing a war club harder. But when it comes to finding your way back from Little Lake, you get lost."

He chuckled in amusement. "I'm only good at useless accomplishments. Killing people and—"

"Someday, when you're the high war chief, you're

going to regret that your deputy has to lead every war party."

"Then I'd better pick you as my deputy. You can always find your way. I don't understand it."

Her laughter reminded him of warm winds through autumn-brittle leaves. He cherished it, engraving it in his memory to hear again and again. When he thought he could bear no more of the horrors of war, or the futility of command, recalling her laughter soothed him.

Somewhere, down deep in his soul, scenes of her death struggled to rise, flitting like butterfly wings through the Dream. Desperate to avoid them, he looked into her mischievous eyes.

"Hako," he said. "I love you. I wish we could—"

Faintly, he heard the boulder above him being rolled away. Hako's face began to fade. He fought against it, not wanting to wake up. The ladder thudded as it struck the floor, and all around him warriors leaped to their feet cursing.

Kakala rolled to his back and grimaced at everything in the chamber: the warriors backed against the walls; silver streaks of moonlight painted the floor; the hated ladder was like a lance through the heart of his domain.

He noted Keresa's strained expression as she dropped to the floor. He knew that stiff posture, and the thunder reflected on her lined brow. Something had her terribly upset.

His spine went stiff when a deep voice called from above, "Kakala? It's Windwolf."

Kakala pulled himself to his feet. "What do you want?"

Windwolf stepped into the gap and looked down.

Behind him, Sister Moon's face gleamed, giving the air a silver sheen.

From the corner of Kakala's eye, he saw Keresa hug herself.

Windwolf coldly said, "I need to speak with you, War Chief."

"I have nothing to say."

They held each other's gaze like two bull mammoths during the rut. Windwolf yielded first, shifting his attention to one of the warriors who stood guard. Windwolf said something that Kakala couldn't hear, but he understood when two armed warriors climbed down the ladder. Six others stood over the opening with their darts aimed down.

The tall warrior said, "Climb up. Now."

Kakala looked at his own warriors. None of them seemed to be breathing.

Keresa said, "Just go, Kakala. Find out what he wants."

Kakala muttered a curse and climbed. When he stepped onto the boulders, two men took particular pleasure in searching him.

Windwolf said, "Tie his hands."

One of the warriors pulled out a twisted hide rope and tied Kakala's hands in front of him.

"Do you see that flat boulder up the slope?" Windwolf pointed.

Kakala turned to look. It was perhaps three body lengths long and two wide. "I can see it just fine, thank you."

"Walk Toward it."

Is it my time to die?

He smiled grimly. For days, he'd been trying to

figure out why he was still alive—now he wished he'd enjoyed them more.

When he reached the flat rock, Windwolf ordered, "Sit down."

Four warriors surrounded him, taking up positions eight body lengths away—which he found interesting. Windwolf must have told them he wanted privacy. Another warrior placed a basket on the rock, then trotted back toward the village.

Kakala took a moment to appreciate the stunning view. To the north, the peaks of the Ice Giants glowed in the moonlight as though lit from within. Thunder Sea looked liquid silver. A fringe of dark spruce trees rimmed his high perch, resembling a buffalo's beard curving beneath a pristine stone face.

"If I have to tell you to sit down again, you'll be standing up for the rest of the night," Windwolf said.

Kakala eased down onto the rock. In the moonlight, Windwolf looked haggard, his eyes red-rimmed from lack of sleep, but he wore a clean blue war shirt, painted with red buffalo, and he'd bathed recently. His short black hair shone.

For that alone, Kakala detested him.

He'd actually been dreaming of taking baths in rivers, pools, waterfalls, even the icy Thunder Sea. Anywhere to wash away the blood, grime, and stink that clung to his body.

Windwolf spread his legs; the weapons clattered on his belt. "That basket contains food and water. The Healer, Flathead, said you needed to eat."

Kakala studied the basket, and his mouth started to water. For two days, he'd felt like his navel had melted into his spine.

He held up his bound hands. "How am I supposed to eat with my hands tied?"

"A clever man like you? I'm sure you'll discover a way."

Kakala slid over, grabbed the basket, and brought it back to his lap. As he unfolded the hide inside, the smell of roasted arctic hare rose. He pulled it out, delighted with an entire rabbit roasted on a skewer.

He lifted it to take a big bite, but stopped, letting the hare hover right in front of his teeth. By Raven Hunter's breath, that would be a cruel twist, wouldn't it?

"Oh, I see," Windwolf said irritably. He walked up, pulled off a strip of meat, and ate it. "Feel better?"

"I will in another six tens of heartbeats. I'm sure you'd only use the best poison."

"Of course I would. Why would I want you to suffer for days? After everything you've done for my people, I'd want your death to be quick and painless, wouldn't I?"

The irony in his voice made Kakala's skin creep. "Your cunning in war is legendary. Your sense of humor needs work."

Kakala took a big bite of the juicy white meat and swallowed it whole, barely chewing. Then he attacked the carcass.

Windwolf squared his shoulders, standing rigid as a wooden statue.

With a greasy hand, Kakala gestured to the far side of the flat rock. "Why don't you sit down? You look like you need to."

Windwolf just stared at him.

While Kakala ate, Windwolf meandered around

the boulders, glancing frequently back to make sure Kakala still sat eating his hare. The night breeze was sharp with the scent of spruce needles.

Kakala asked, "Have you already sent warriors to the Nightland Caves?"

"No."

Kakala laughed condescendingly. "You should run there right now and throw yourself at the feet of the Guide to beg for mercy. If you surrender, he might spare your life."

"And after two botched attacks on Headswift Village, maybe Nashat would show the same leniency to you. Why don't we go together?" He paused. "Or we could ask Karigi what punishment he would prefer."

At the thought of Karigi—and the disaster at Walking Seal Village—Kakala's belly soured. He took another bite, but it didn't taste nearly as good.

Windwolf wandered to the far side of the flat rock, and his gaze settled on Kakala's cape, the red war shirt visible through the open front. A strange expression tensed his face. He pointed to the painted sash that belted Kakala's waist. "That's from the Star Tree band, isn't it? It looks like their painting style."

Kakala took another big bite of his hare and, as he chewed, looked down at his sash. "The Star Tree painters were some of the best anywhere. I always appreciated their work."

Windwolf studied the sash. "Just when did you develop this appreciation? Before or after you killed every living thing in Star Tree Village?"

A chilling tingle filled Kakala's breast, like icy ants crawling around inside him. "Insults between us are useless at this point, Windwolf. Why did you wish to speak with me?"

Windwolf inhaled a deep breath, as though preparing himself for a lengthy conversation. "Your warriors are holding up better than I'd have thought. You trained them well."

Kakala wiped his mouth on his sleeve and eyed Windwolf speculatively. The compliment sounded honest—a gesture from one war chief to another. It made him even more uneasy. "Keresa kept them together while I was ill. She deserves the credit."

"We could all wish for so talented a deputy."

Kakala gently rested the hare bones on the rock beside him. A curious light gleamed in Windwolf's eyes at the mention of Keresa's name. Kakala noted it, then pulled out the gut water bag that rested in the basket and took a long drink.

"Come and sit down, Windwolf. You make me nervous pacing around."

He continued standing. "How are you feeling?"

"Concerned about your skill with a war club?"

"A bit. You should be dead."

"I've had a great deal of practice fighting with you. It's made me fast on my feet."

Windwolf actually chuckled. "Me, too."

"Flathead is a good Healer. I'm doing better. How are your refugees?"

For several painfully quiet moments, Windwolf bowed his head. "Several are dying. Some with agonizing slowness. Others too swiftly for their families to mourn. Why do you care? Worried about your skill with an atlatl?"

From some crack in Kakala's soul, hysterical voices

rose, pleading with him not to kill them. "I've never liked attacking defenseless people."

"No? You've certainly done it often enough. When did you decide you didn't like it? Somewhere between ten children and ten tens? Perhaps it was the women who bothered you? Not enough of them to rape and mutilate?"

"Let me know when it's my turn. I have a few things I'd like to tell you, too."

"Yes, I'm sure you do."

Windwolf walked back and forth in front of the rock with his brow furrowed. "You've never enjoyed murdering my people, or trying to take our lands? I'm glad to hear it. Perhaps you wouldn't mind, then, telling me what other orders you've received lately regarding Sunpath bands?"

Kakala laughed incredulously. "You're bold."

With unsettling silence, Windwolf walked over and seated himself. He stared hard into Kakala's eyes. "Let's discuss your last couple of days in the cage."

Kakala barely moved. "Why?"

"I assume it's bothering you."

His gut tried to tie itself in knots. "And?"

"I'd rather it didn't."

Kakala stared his disbelief. "Why would *you* care?"

"How can I keep that from happening to you and your warriors?"

Kakala shook his head as though he hadn't heard right. This had to be some ploy to gain leverage. "What's this? Don't tell me you've started to believe the rumors circulating among broken Sunpath refugees that you're the promised Dreamer sent to save the world from the coming cataclysm?"

"If I let you go, Elder Nashat will certainly order you captured and hauled off to cages—"

"Not...Not certainly." *Which was a lie Windwolf had to see right through.* Blood had started to surge deafeningly in Kakala's ears. "Why are we discussing this?"

Windwolf's face fell into stiff lines. "Because I thought if we could solve that problem, you would be able to make decisions more clearly."

"Which decisions did you have in mind?"

Windwolf looked up without moving a muscle. "Decisions regarding the Sunpath People and the Lame Bull People."

"You think I have any influence on that?"

They stared unforgivingly at each other for a time, each silently trying to guess the other's strategy.

In cynical amusement, Kakala asked, "Why don't you just tell me what you're offering? If I betray my people, you will...what?"

Windwolf bowed his head and stared at the smooth surface of the rock. In a curious voice, he asked, "After the attack on the Sprucebell band, why did you send runners to the neighboring Sunpath villages telling them to expect survivors? I've heard you did the same thing at other places."

Kakala frowned. The man changed subjects as quickly as a cougar could its charge. Was it designed to fluster him? He studied Windwolf's bland expression.

In a mockingly conspiratorial voice, he said, "Perhaps *I'm* the promised Dreamer who's going to save the world."

Windwolf stiffened. "Let me know when you decide to talk to me as one leader to another." Then the man rose, turned his back on Kakala, and walked away.

Over his shoulder, he said, "Get some sleep, War Chief."

The guards trotted forward. Kakala took another long drink from the water bag before he rose unsteadily to his feet.

"Walk," the tall warrior ordered.

Distress

The slave girl, Pipe, is dead. That beautiful little girl torn to shreds by some mad Spirit. I found pieces of her scattered through the lower tunnels. I buried her head at the fiery lake. My heart aches so much that I can barely force myself to keep going. Raven Hunter says it's Wolf Dreamer's work.

I don't believe it.

I told him yesterday that she loved Wolf Dreamer and didn't wish to return to the Long Dark—that she had vowed to serve me well until the time came for us to go, then she begged me to let her return to her own Sunpath band.

Ancestors, forgive me. I didn't know how insanely desperate he has become.

Now I fear he'll do anything to keep me believing.

Chapter Twenty-One

Sunrise remained hidden behind the high ridge to the east, but a luminous halo arced over the horizon and turned the bellies of the drifting Cloud People a glittering gold.

"Very well, let's begin," War Chief Fish Hawk said, and started swinging his war club. He'd twisted his black hair into a bun at the nape of his neck and wore a tattered deer-hide shirt that reached to his knees. From his cord belt a variety of weapons hung: a stiletto, atlatl, and shining black chert knife. "First, a warrior must loosen his shoulder muscles."

Silvertip followed Fish Hawk's moves, swinging his club back and forth with his right hand, then switching it to his left hand. Two tens of boys and girls, including Ashes, circled Fish Hawk, all swinging their clubs.

As he swung it upward in an arc, Silvertip studied his club. It had belonged to his dead father. Beautifully crafted from hickory, the shaft, as long as his arm, had been carefully thinned and polished. The warhead was fashioned from a splinter of mammoth's tusk, the ivory ground to a sharp point, then grooved and attached to the hickory shaft with green sinew. As the sinew dried, it had shrunk, binding the tusk and wood together. Immediately below the warhead, his father had embedded a large finely flaked quartzite spike. It glinted as he swung the club up and around, now making circular motions.

From the corner of his eye, Silvertip glimpsed Windwolf. The war chief sat near a fire at the edge of the Sunpath lodges, talking with two men. New lodges filled the forest. More Sun-path people had trickled into the village last night. Many were wounded. Their cries rode the cold morning breeze.

Ashes leaned sideways and whispered, "Who is Windwolf talking with?"

"Just before I ran down here to practice, Grandfather told me his name. He's Chief Sacred Feathers."

"What band is he from?"

"Moon Rock. I don't know where their territory is."

Ashes said, "It's far to the west, on the border between Sunpath and Southwind lands. Was it attacked?"

Silvertip nodded. "Karigi."

In the middle of the circle, Fish Hawk perched on the balls of his feet and began weaving and feinting, leaping from foot to foot, shifting his club from hand to hand, twirling it faster and faster. Silvertip tried to do it, as did the other children, but no one was having much luck. In one final leap, Fish Hawk launched himself into the air and landed in a crouch. His club flashed down to within a hair's breadth of the ground.

As he rose, Fish Hawk said, "I don't expect you to be able to do that today, but keep practicing. You must train your muscles before you'll be able to control the club."

Silvertip balanced on the balls of his feet, as Fish Hawk had done, and listened to his club whir as he spun it from one hand to the other, then pirouetted and slashed down.

The other children made surprised sounds and pointed at him. Fish Hawk grinned. "Very good, Silvertip. If you keep that up, you will master the club before you become a man."

Silvertip smiled and ducked his head at the praise. Next summer he would have been initiated in the Men's Lodge. A summer that would never come.

Fish Hawk called, "I'll return shortly. In the meantime, continue practicing."

Ashes walked closer to Silvertip and asked, "Can you teach me to do that?"

He nodded. "It's easy. I'll do it slowly. See if you can follow."

She concentrated on his movements, trying to duplicate them.

"That was good, Ashes. Now, you just have to do it faster."

Silvertip spun his club again, pirouetted, and landed in a crouch while he slashed down with his club.

Ashes did it, but lost her balance at the last instant and fell over. She laughed and said, "I need a lot more practice than you do."

"You will do it. Better than I. You will make it like a graceful Dance, swift like a striking falcon, but balanced, like a cougar that leaps and lands with total control."

She gave him that sober look. "Sometimes, when

you talk like that, it sends shivers down my spine." She glanced warily around. "Why haven't you told anyone about your Vision?"

He straightened, and his gaze drifted again to where Windwolf sat talking with the two men. "When they are ready."

Ashes gave him an askance look, rose to her feet, and watched Windwolf for a time before she whispered, "You cried a lot last night."

He bit his lip, and to hide it, began twirling his club. "It's the only time I can weep for the people."

She watched his club for a time, then said, "This is really going to happen, isn't it?"

Silvertip let his club swing to a stop and propped it over his shoulder. Throughout the night, the Ancestors had slipped through the walls and walked around his bed as though he didn't exist. As the ghosts murmured to each other, he'd heard other things: mammoths trumpeting; giant buffalo roaring like lions, the way they did in the rut; and a young man talking. He thought it was Wolf Dreamer's voice, but wasn't sure.

He said, "It will happen. Just as I said. Before I came to bed, I watched part of the future unfold. Just like Wolf Dreamer showed me. Windwolf met Keresa, and then he went to speak to Kakala."

She cocked her head. "Why?"

Silvertip exhaled hard, and his breath condensed into a frosty cloud. "They are struggling over the future."

As Father Sun rose higher into the morning sky, more and more people came out of their lodges. The aroma of breakfast cooking carried on the cold breeze.

The other children drifted farther away, meandering down the slope as they practiced with their clubs, until Silvertip and Ashes stood alone.

Ashes reached up to touch her earlobe, and Silvertip's eyes went wide. As she rubbed it, she flinched, and he could see that she'd cut off the bottom of her lobe. A person did that as an offering to the Spirit World. Usually it was done for success in Trading, or in hopes of curing a sick relative, but often people made the offering in mourning.

He gestured to her ear. "Did you do that for your father?"

"No." Ashes pulled her hand down, frowned, and looked away. "For Mother. You said she would never be the woman I knew. If I admit that now, it won't hurt as much later."

Though she tried to blink them away before he could see, tears filled her eyes.

Silvertip gently said, "I have already come to love that practical way of yours."

She wiped her eyes on her sleeve and gazed down the hill at Windwolf. As he listened to the Elders, the muscles in his massive shoulders corded and rippled beneath his cape. "They must be saying terrible things. Do you think the raiding is going to get worse?"

Silvertip lifted a shoulder. "Karigi and Blackta are soulless."

To the north a dire wolf barked, then howled. The deep-throated sound echoed through the forests. Moments later another answered. Silvertip listened to them.

"It's almost time now."

He had no sooner spoken, than a scream rent the air. He turned, having seen it, just this way. Bear Boy lay sprawled, his war club off to one side. Little Crow stared in horror, first at Bear Boy, and then at his club. He dropped the weapon, crying, "I didn't mean it!"

Windwolf was on his feet, sprinting. The children that had gathered made way for him, watching as he lifted the boy, staring grimly at the side of his head.

"Help me," Silvertip said as he started forward. "Keep them from interfering." He stopped only long enough to retrieve the Wolf Bundle from where it lay on his coat. Then, Ashes, behind him, he walked up to the crowd, calling, "War Chief? I can help."

Windwolf looked up at him, Bear Boy's head still cradled on his lap. "I don't think so, Silvertip. I've seen head wounds before. He's not breathing, and the heart isn't beating." .

Silvertip crouched, staring into Windwolf's eyes. "You have asked many people for their trust in the last couple of moons, War Chief. Now I will ask for yours."

"Silvertip, this isn't a game. Let me call the Healer."

"I am here," he said simply. "Please, lower him gently. Someone, bring a wolf hide to lay his head on. His spirit is still close. There is time to call it back."

One of the girls hesitantly pulled her wolfhide coat over her head, extending it, then wrapped her arms over her bare chest against the cold.

Silvertip met Windwolf's piercing gaze with his own, then watched the war chief lower Bear Boy, carefully resting his head on the folds of the wolf coat.

Silvertip bent, looking into Bear Boy's vacant, half-lidded eyes. Bear Boy's tongue lolled behind parted lips.

I have seen this look. When I lay dead on the high rocks, before Condor came.

Silvertip closed his eyes, lifting the Wolf Bundle.

The Song rose in his throat. He willed his soul into it, digging down into himself, believing, willing the Power to flow down from the Wolf Bundle. He felt it, growing, prickling. Like a warm rush of water it coursed through him, Singing with him, its Song mixing with his.

In that instant, Silvertip felt wings, and he stretched out, the familiar feel of them bringing a brimming ecstasy to his body.

Bear Boy's soul hovered above the body, dark, frightened, and poised to flee.

Gently, so as not to panic him, Silvertip closed his wings around the Spirit.

"Go back," Silvertip coaxed. "This is not your time. We are here, loving you, calling for you. Go back, Bear Boy. Your body needs you. Do not fear; you will live. We all need you."

He could feel the confusion, and curled his wings tighter, willing his love and warmth into the soul.

Slowly, carefully, he eased it down with his mighty wings. Felt it slide back into the body, and pressed down. keeping it there while it seeped into its familiar shell.

"Live, Bear Boy. Breathe, Feel the beat of your heart, and let the blood flow through your veins."

The gasp came from somewhere distant, as though heard through a thick fog. The sense of lightness swirled around him, and he looked up, seeing the sky filled with color.

"Silvertip!" Windwolf s barked command broke the trance.

He blinked, almost crying out as he felt the wings slip away. He tried to make sense of the blurry face above him. Windwolf!

"Stay back!" Ashes was saying. "He's Dreaming! Are you fools? Don't disturb a Dreamer when he's sending his soul to the Spirit World."

"Silvertip?" Windwolf asked again.

"Tired." He groaned and sat up, the Wolf Bundle warm in his hands. "Bear Boy?"

"He's alive," Windwolf told him. "But, I think he'll have a headache for a while."

"Yes. Me, too."

Silvertip was vaguely aware of Ashes, still haranguing people to stay back.

"You Dreamed the One," Windwolf said reverently. "How long have you been doing this?"

"Since I died, and Wolf Dreamer showed me the way."

"And you told no one?"

"Who would have believed me?"

"Come, let's get you back to your bed."

Silvertip stood on wobbly legs, his vision still swimming. He could make out Bear Boy, tears running down his face as his mother dabbed at his head with the hem of her dress. Ashes looked like a warrior, brandishing her war club, keeping people back. Then he noticed the expressions, people in the crowd staring, struggling to believe what they had just seen.

Silvertip almost made a full step before he bent double and threw up.

Chapter Twenty-Two

Windwolf glanced across at Dipper; she hovered beside Silvertip's bed, a stricken look on her face. Then he glanced at Lookingbill. The old man's lined expression and distant eyes reflected sober thoughts. Ashes looked oddly cowed as she sat with her war club across her lap.

Outside, Fish Hawk said yet again, "The chief is in Council with Windwolf. You may not go in. We will send news when they have finished."

More questions were called, to which Fish Hawk replied, "Silvertip used the Wolf Bundle to Dream the boy's soul back into his body. Beyond that, I don't know."

Windwolf ignored it, turned his attention to the roast haunch of beaver, and took a bite. With this new development, who knew when he'd get to eat again. He chewed the sweet dark meat, swallowed, and looked at Ashes.

"Tell us the whole story. How long have you known?"

She glanced nervously at him and then Lookingbill. "Since the night he woke up. He was different."

"We thought that was due to the wound," Lookingbill said. "People are often introspective after such a blow to the head."

"Tell us everything," Windwolf coaxed.

"He says he died." Ashes fingered the handle of her war club. "That he watched his body laid out on the high rocks, and then Condor came and ate him." She made a face. "He told me it was horrifying as it pulled out his insides and swallowed them. Then, when the bones were picked clean, he watched them fall apart, and then everything went gray. That's when Wolf Dreamer came to him and told him he was dead."

Lookingbill nodded. "Great Dreamers often have to die to be reborn. What did Silvertip come back as?"

"Condor. Wolf Dreamer taught him how to fly, and then they flew west, along the Ice Giants. He saw big lakes, and then, the biggest of all, somewhere beyond the Southwind People."

"I know the lake," Windwolf said. "A huge thing. To skirt it takes moons of travel."

Ashes nodded. "Silvertip saw a great ice dam, a place where the water is backed up." She looked up at him with a piercing stare. "He says the ice is melting. Sometime soon, this entire country is going to be washed away."

Lookingbill frowned. "That's impossible!"

"Our world is ending," Ashes snapped. "I believe Silvertip."

"But Raven Hunter whispers in your Dreams," Lookingbill snapped back.

"We are opposites." She narrowed an eye. "Silvertip

and me. That is what is going to make our marriage so Powerful."

Windwolf raised a hand, stilling Lookingbill's response. "Your ear is bleeding. Did that happen this morning?"

She shook her head. "It's for my mother."

"But you don't know she's...Did Silvertip tell you she's dead?"

Ashes pursed her lips, then shook her head. "He said that she would come back, but the mother I knew wouldn't be there." She raised her eyes. "By offering for her soul now, it won't be as hard when she comes back."

"So you're saying she survives this flood?" Lookingbill asked skeptically.

"Silvertip does."

"What about the rest of us?" Windwolf asked. "Did he tell you anything about the people?"

"Only that they have to go west. Some will follow him to safety; others won't."

Windwolf nodded. "What about me? What does he say I'm supposed to do?"

Ashes shook her head. "I don't know. He just said that you, Kakala, and Keresa were struggling over the future. Something about bargaining between Wolf Dreamer and Raven Hunter."

"I see."

"Well, I don't," Lookingbill muttered. "He's just a boy!"

"One who carries the Wolf Bundle," Windwolf corrected. "And apparently speaks with it." He took another bite of his breakfast. Swallowing, he added, "I was there this morning. Bear Boy was dead. What I felt..."

"Yes?" Lookingbill prodded.

Windwolf shrugged. "I've never been what you would call a strong believer in Power, Chief. But I felt it. Silvertip called to him, and then, I'd swear, I saw great wings."

"Raven Hunter?"

He met Lookingbill's eyes. "Condor. I think the boy called his Spirit Helper and used Power to save Bear Boy's life."

Lookingbill shot a worried glance at his grandson, now sleeping soundly on the hides. "But he's still a boy. What do I do?"

"Begin preparing your people to travel west, Chief. Until Silvertip wakes, we're not going to know how much time we have left. Meanwhile, I need to hear what the new refugees have to say."

Keresa sat with her back to the stone, as far as she could get from the others. She had pulled her cape tightly around her shoulders, attempting to keep some sort of warmth around her body, because her soul was most definitely shivering.

She glanced up at the thin spear of light shining down from the mouth of their prison.

She gave Kakala a warning glance as he stepped over and lowered himself beside her. He had a puzzled look as he draped his hands on his knees.

In a kind voice, he asked, "How are you doing?"

"Confused," she admitted.

He made a halfhearted gesture toward the high opening. "Kind of them to lower food down this morning. But it was almost a fight to ensure it was portioned out fairly."

"Half of a yearling caribou." She rubbed her face. "It was generous, considering the mouths he has to feed."

"How many camps?"

"The hollow below the hill is filled with them. Too many, Kakala. He could have found plenty of reasons to ignore our wants."

Kakala grunted assent. "I'm beginning to understand how he wins the hearts of so many." He glanced at her. "What happened last night? When you came back, you looked terrible."

She shot a look at the warriors, thankful they knew enough to give their war chief and deputy privacy. "I don't know. That's why I'm so confused. But I can tell you now, the ruse of playing Bramble isn't a good idea."

"Oh?"

"Kakala? Do you trust me?"

"With my life." He smiled. "I'm sorry you thought you had to ask."

She lowered her voice. "I offered to stay with him last night if he would let you and the rest go. He said he would, provided you swore never to raise your hands against the Sunpath or Lame Bull again."

He studied his hands, flexing his fingers and watching the tendons work under his scarred skin. "I think he offered me that same option. He asked if there was a way we could go back without ending up in the cages. I thought it was some sort of trick."

She shook her head. "I don't think it's a trick."

"Why?"

"Because he respects us. Isn't that odd after the things we've done to him and his people?"

"We did as our Council ordered. Nothing more, and as it turns out, often less." He gave her a knowing appraisal. "I've watched you since you've been meeting with him. I was curiously affected when you tried to kill Goodeagle yesterday. This offer to stay, was it more than just acting for the rest of us?"

She felt her soul tumble. "I would love to lie and tell you it was a calculating move to enable you to escape." She stared at her hands. "But I am drawn to him as I have been to no other man I've ever met."

"I see."

"Do you?" She searched his face. "I feel torn in two, Kakala. I don't know what's right anymore."

His lips curled in a faint smile. "I know you, Keresa. Perhaps better than I have ever known anyone...even Hako. You need a man who is your equal."

She gave him a sidelong stare. "No jealousy?"

"A little. But not like that. We share our souls, our trust, and hopes. I depend on you. But our lives are separate." He met her gaze. "If you can find more with Windwolf, take it." He glanced away, "Though, Raven Hunter knows, it might be short and miserable. The Council has no doubt learned what has happened to us by now. Karigi will be coming, and this time, not even Windwolf can stop him."

"And when Karigi frees us?"

"You and I both know the penalty for failure." He swallowed hard, a shiver tracing down his spine. "I won't...can't..." She saw his great muscles knotting, swelling the war shirt under his cloak.

"There is a sickness in our people," she said bluntly. "It began with the return of Nashat, and has grown worse with the rise of the Guide."

"Who do you serve, Keresa?"

"You, and these warriors here." She gestured toward the huddled men who now used stones to smash the marrow bones of the caribou. They lifted the fragments, sucking out the pink delicacy. "Who do you serve, Kakala?"

His voice was wistful. "I don't know anymore."

She stared at her hand, remembering Windwolf's touch. She had gone to his arms willingly, and for that one blessed moment, her soul had been at peace.

"I'd almost think I was witched. Could that be it?"

"It was that way with Hako and me." He smiled, remembering.

"I don't even know him."

"Oh, yes you do. You just can't find it in your soul to trust him. He's fed us one bitter meal after another each time we've tried to kill him." He lowered his head. "And then there's "Walking Seal Village."

"It haunts him."

As it haunts us.

She couldn't help but shoot a glance toward the back, where Goodeagle sat, his eyes focused on the distance.

Kakala placed a hand gently on her shoulder. "It's a terrible problem, isn't it? No matter what we choose, we will condemn ourselves in the end."

She nodded, glancing back at Goodeagle. That was the price of betraying one's people.

But if I help Kakala kill Windwolf, I will never forgive myself.

Chapter Twenty-Three

Windwolf leaned forward to warm his hands over the flames. In the slanting afternoon light, the crude lodges thrown up by the Sunpath refugees resembled dark round dots scattered through the forest. Tens of new lodges had appeared overnight. As soon as he'd stepped out of his chamber at dawn, he'd sent a runner to arrange a meeting with the village chief, a man named Sacred Feathers. They had barely begun their discussion when Bear Boy was struck down.

Sacred Feathers sat across the fire from Windwolf and next to his grandfather. Sacred Feathers had seen perhaps three tens of summers. His grandfather, Drummer, had seen at least two tens more.

"So you think the boy is a Dreamer?" Drummer asked.

"You saw what he did." Windwolf studied the old man. "I was beside him; *I felt* the Power."

"We couldn't get close," Sacred Feathers muttered.

"That little girl would have broken our knees with that war club she was swinging around."

"I have heard the boy's story." Windwolf shifted. "I saw his body after the fighting. I thought he was dead. His recovery is as much a miracle as his saving Bear Boy this morning."

"It is the talk of the camp."

"The Wolf Bundle speaks to him," Windwolf added. "Chief Lookingbill gave it to him for safekeeping during the attack. Silvertip belongs to it now."

"Then perhaps the prophecy is true?" Drummer mused.

"Perhaps. We will see. But for the. moment, I need to know what happened at your village. Tell me everything."

Drummer nodded, thinking for a moment. "I told my grandson people were missing from the surrounding camps. He wouldn't believe me."

His face had a skeletal appearance. Every bone stuck out through the thin layer of skin, which made his deeply set brown eyes look cavernous. Two long gray braids fell over the front of his worn cougarhide cape. He shook a fist at Windwolf. "Old Woman Rust never missed the meetings we held every full moon to worship Wolf Dreamer. First she disappeared, then Coal Lion vanished. I knew something was happening."

"They were old and from nearby camps," Sacred Feathers pointed out. "I thought maybe they'd gotten sick or hurt, or just couldn't make the walk any longer."

Windwolf said, "What happened to them?"

Sacred Feathers waved a hand in a helpless gesture. "We found out that just before Deputy Karigi attacked their villages, he sent warriors in to kidnap a few of the Elders."

Sacred Feathers had a birdlike face with closely set eyes and shoulder-length black hair. "He used them as hostages. He told people to put down their weapons or the Elders would be killed. Many people did." Sacred Feathers' head fell forward. He stared blindly at the fire. "Then he killed everyone."

A cold breeze blew through the spruce trees, fluttering the lodge door curtains, and carrying the aroma of roasting grouse.

Drummer glared at his grandson. "They did the same thing to us."

Sacred Feathers crossed his arms over his yellow-painted cape. "I thought if we just did as Karigi said, we'd be all right. For many summers, I've been telling my people that the Nightland clan Elders are not monsters. They're human beings, just like us. I hoped that if we treated them with dignity, they would leave us alone."

"Fool!" Drummer's wrinkled face tensed. "The Nightland People are monsters straight out of Raven Hunter's Long Dark."

Sacred Feathers pointed to an old woman sitting in front of a lodge scraping a fresh deer hide. She used her hafted chert scraper to carefully remove the last bits of flesh, preparing the hide for tanning. "The morning before our band was attacked, a Nightland warrior ran through, gave her a freshly killed snowshoe hare, and ran away. I thought it was kindness. A gesture of—"

"He was a *spy*! It got him into our camp so he could look around. I told you we should have killed him before he could run away."

Sacred Feathers threw up his arms in exasperation. "Grandfather, Nightland warriors have been traveling through our territory for many summers. They stopped, they Traded, they told stories. Most Nightland warriors are peaceful!"

Drummer leaned forward and squinted an eye malevolently. "It's a lot easier to kill people when they still think you want peace."

Windwolf watched the conversation with an ache in his chest. He'd heard these same words so many times. There was always a peacemaker and a warrior. And depending upon the circumstances, each might be right.

"When did Karigi strike?" Windwolf asked.

Sacred Feathers threw another branch on the fire and watched the flames. "Two moons ago. We didn't know what to do. We just crept northward, hunting, fishing, hiding by day, hoping to find sanctuary in other Sunpath territories." He hung his head. "Most of them had already been abandoned."

"What brought you here?" Windwolf said.

"We met other fleeing people on the trails. They said Chief Lookingbill had promised sanctuary. And we heard you were here."

Windwolf let out a breath. "You are safe here. For the moment. But you can only have a couple of days to regain your strength. I will appoint a couple of warriors to escort you west. We are building a new home in the Tills."

Sacred Feathers ran a hand through his hair and shook his head. "I don't know. This is the land of our Ancestors.

I've always believed that we could negotiate with

the Nightland People, establish agreements for Trade, or the use of certain hunting or gathering grounds, but now...now, I don't know."

Drummer banged his foot on the hearthstones, as though to get everyone's attention. "The only time talk has ever helped the Sunpath People was when Windwolf rammed it down their throats with a war party at his back."

Windwolf nodded in gratitude, but deep inside him, a voice asked, *"There are fewer Sunpath bands now than when I started protecting our people. Have I helped them?"*

Drummer continued, "The only reason Karigi didn't capture me is because I was afraid to return to my lodge. After the snowshoe hare was delivered, I walked all day to get to Walnut Creek Camp, spent one day there, and moved on. I just kept moving."

"How did you hear about the attack?" Windwolf asked.

Drummer extended a hand to his grandson. "The great chief, Sacred Feathers—his tail stuck between his legs— and a handful of survivors came running into the village where I was staying."

"Oh, Grandfather." Sacred Feathers exhaled the words.

Windwolf interrupted. "I need you to help me understand what Karigi is doing." He pulled his stiletto from his belt and started drawing in the dirt around the firepit. "These are the bands I know he has recently attacked." He poked holes into the soil. "Do you know of any others?"

"Yes," Sacred Feathers said. He used his fingers to

poke two more holes. "Both of these. We met survivors on the trails."

"The survivors were not headed here?"

Sacred Feathers shook his head. "No. Many people do not believe that the Lame Bull Elders will keep their word when Karigi finally arrives here. But they haven't heard you are here, either. Or that you've trapped Kakala."

Why do they have such faith in me? I've failed them all.

"Given what you've heard, where is Karigi now?"

Sacred Feathers seemed to be thinking about it. Finally he said, "He could be on his way back to the Nightland country. He's moving very fast."

"How many warriors does he have?" Windwolf 's stomach muscles clenched in preparation.

"Six tens, maybe seven tens. We didn't have time to count."

Six tens? With Hawhak and Blackta's warriors, plus any others the Council can scrape up, they could hit us with more than ten tens.

Were it he, he'd attack with two tens of warriors coming from five different directions. There could be no defense.

But Karigi 's moving fast. His men will be worn out.

Down the slope in the village, a little girl let out a shriek, then broke into tears. Sacred Feathers whirled to look.

Windwolf followed his gaze. A girl, perhaps eight summers, ran up the trail, whimpering. Tears streamed down her face.

Sacred Feathers opened his arms, and the girl ran

straight to him and climbed into his lap, sobbing, "Father, he *hit* me!"

Sacred Feathers examined the scrape on his daughter's cheek. "Oh, Elk Leaf, what happened? Did you get into a fight?"

She nodded against his shoulder, trying to suppress her tears.

"You didn't hit first, did you?"

"No, Father, no."

"All right. Hush, now." He stroked her back tenderly and kissed her forehead. "Did you say something you didn't mean and somebody—"

"No, I don't know why Little Calf hit me! But Tusk Boy hit him back."

"Good for Tusk Boy," Drummer muttered furiously. His ancient face had taken on the alert, dangerous look of a wolf on the hunt.

Sacred Feathers glared at him. "Elk Leaf, next time Little Calf hits you, you just cover your head with your hands and tell him you're sorry—even if you didn't do anything. He'll stop hitting you."

"I will, Father," she moaned and sniffed, burying her face in his shirt.

From the corner of his eye, Windwolf caught Drummer's enraged expression.

"I love you, Elk Leaf," Sacred Feathers said. "Are you better now?"

She sucked in a deep halting breath and looked up, giving him a frail little-girl smile. "A little."

"Good. Why don't you run down to Aunt Wren's lodge. She made cattail root bread this morning."

"Does she have any left?"

He winked at her excited expression and set her on the ground. "Go see for yourself."

She smiled broadly and ran away down the trail.

Once Elk Leaf had vanished, Drummer violently shoved Sacred Feathers' shoulder, swinging him around to face him. The old man's cheeks blazed. "You want to get her killed?"

"No, I want to keep her safe!"

"You're teaching her to be a mouse. You think she should get used to being a victim? That she should come to like it, maybe?"

Sacred Feathers met Drummer's hot stare with one of his own. "Maybe being a victim isn't as bad as being dead."

The anger drained from Drummer's face. He stood up and straightened to his full sapling-thin height. They stared at each other in silence.

Then Drummer's hard eyes turned to Windwolf. "Tell him, will you? Tell my grandson that all the *I'm sorry's* in the world won't make murderers put down their clubs."

Drummer turned and stamped away down the trail, following behind Elk Leaf.

Sacred Feathers had his eyes closed and his teeth gritted. "He's old," Sacred Feathers said. "He doesn't think as well as he used to."

"I'm afraid he's right, Chief. When your enemy is bent on killing you and taking your lands, you must fight."

"But that is Raven Hunter's way!"

Ashes' words from that morning echoed in his head. "I fear that we have lost our balance."

Windwolf looked out at the village. Sunpath children played in the trees, chasing each other and laughing. Old men knapped out new stone tools in front of the lodges. One of the women sat weaving a basket from strips of tree root: a fine basket, the weave tight enough to hold water.

Windwolf said, "The search for the One does us no good if we Dream it as dead men."

Sacred Feathers frowned at the Headswift Village rockshelters. "Well, you won't have to worry about my people. We will start for the Tills today. And you don't need to provide warriors."

Chapter Twenty-Four

"W hen you bore each of your children, Mother, it was a painful experience, wasn't it?" Silvertip lay back on his thick mat of hides and stared at the firelight playing on the soot-coated rocks above. He could hear the din outside where warriors guarded the entrance to the great chamber. But for them, the room would have been chaos as people tried to get to him.

"Of course," Dipper replied, stroking his hand with loving fingers. She glanced uneasily at Ashes, who squatted to his left, her war club perched on her lap.

"All that pain, and blood, and fluid." He smiled. "In the end, was it worth it?"

"Of course, Silvertip! How can you even ask that?"

"So that you will know that creating a new life, be it a person, or calf, or chick...or even a people, is difficult and painful. For everything, Mother, there is a price."

Ashes nodded soberly, watching him with her now-possessive eyes.

"But why should you—"

He waved Dipper's protest away. "There is no second-guessing Power, or the Dance of the One."

The growing sounds of the crowd indicated some sort of disturbance. He tucked the Wolf Bundle tightly against his left side, feeling the warmth, the rhythm that beat to the time of his heart.

"Make way!" Fish Hawk ordered. "The next person who tries to spit on her will get a taste of my club!"

Dipper's head turned as silhouetted forms blocked the entrance.

"I've brought her, Silvertip. Just as you ordered. But I'll say again, I think it's a bad idea."

"Thank you, War Chief." Silvertip sat up, feeling weak, but somehow rejuvenated. "Come closer, Keresa."

The woman walked hesitantly, squinting in the darkness. Fish Hawk stood close behind her, his war club half-raised to strike at any false move the warrior woman might make.

"You!" Dipper gasped, starting to rise.

Silvertip tightened his grip on her hand. "Mother! No!" He forced Power into his voice. "You will sit, *and listen!*"

Dipper blinked, nodded, and sank back to the floor.

Keresa stopped just beyond the bedding, her surprised eyes recognizing him. "How are you feeling?"

He smiled at her courage. "Very tired."

"Why did you send for me?" She stood tall, head back, her matted long hair falling around her shoulders. He could see the resolve coursing through her like a glowing light.

"I wished to thank you."

A slight frown marred her forehead. "Do not expect an apology."

"You need not apologize for serving the needs of Power, Deputy. You could not have played your part better."

"You *wanted* to be killed?"

"There is no greater gift than the one you gave me. Come, sit." He released Dipper's hand. "Mother, if you would make room for my guest?"

Reluctantly, Dipper scuttled off to the side, her eyes burning with threat as she watched the Nightland woman seat herself.

"You're saying...what? That Power planned this all?"

Silvertip looked into Keresa's controlled gaze. "You served my purpose well."

"Your purpose?" Keresa asked cautiously.

"I had to die to be reborn. The proof of the lesson lies all around us. The cycle of life and death and life is the heartbeat of Power. Yet, distracted by our physical needs, we see, but do not understand."

"I don't—"

"I first heard your name in a Dream, Keresa. One that I did not understand. You are the Wind, Mother of Legends. Kakala is the Fire, and Windwolf is the Water. Together, you act upon the earth."

He watched her eyes narrow the way they would if she were listening to mindless babble. "I see."

Silvertip smiled. "Why is it that you, Mother of Legends, who have so much trouble believing in anything, cannot even believe in yourself?"

He could see the confusion in her eyes. "Mother of Legends?"

"Believe in yourself, Keresa. Step out and place that first step on the trail to your destiny. Stretch your arms wide and gather the winds."

She peered closely, trying to see his eyes, wondering, no doubt if the pupils were the same size.

"I am quite well, thank you." He reached out, taking her hand. At the touch, she stiffened, expression shocked.

When he released her, she might have been frozen, stunned. Her eyes had lost focus, as though her vision was swimming.

When she finally blinked and steadied herself, he said, "I asked you here to thank you for helping me to find the One. As a warrior, it will be counter to everything you believe, but to surrender yourself is to achieve victory."

"You're right. I...I don't understand."

"You will wish to see Windwolf when I am finished with him." He looked up. "Fish Hawk, would you escort Keresa to the war chief's chamber? And when you pass through the crowd tell them they are making way for the Wind."

"Whatever you want, Silvertip."

Keresa had trouble standing, as though her legs wobbled beneath her.

Windwolf peered up in the gathering gloom. The trail was a mass of humanity. If Karigi attacked now, they would kill themselves trying to get down the steep hill.

"Make way for the war chief!" Fish Hawk shouted. "Make way for Windwolf!"

"Windwolf!" came the response from many lips.

The awe, the sudden silence, unnerved him. He climbed carefully through the press, people squeezing aside to make room. Some reached out, touching him, as though he were something precious.

When he could take no more, he turned on them. "What are you doing? By Wolf Dreamer's breath, *get back to your camps!* Go! Now. Or so help me, I'll have warriors clear this whole trail!"

"But the Dreamer?" one old man cried. "He's here!"

"And when he's ready to address you, he will."

They wavered, watching him expectantly.

He pulled his war club, waving it. "I said, go!"

As if herding ground sloths, he bullied them off the steep trail, balking only at the few who cowered before him, willing to take a blow rather than leave their precious Dreamer.

"Wolf Dreamer bless you," one of the guards at the top said. "We've been hard-pressed to keep them back."

Windwolf rubbed his face. "How can you blame them? They've lost everything, and now, suddenly, they have hope."

He ducked inside to find a fire, the pungent odor of spruce smoke thick in the air. He walked back, nodding to Lookingbill. The chief still looked confused.

Gods, aren't we all?

Ashes sat, her war club on her lap, one hand holding Silvertip's. She nodded severely as he walked up. When he looked into her eyes, it wasn't to find a girl. Her captivity, the terrible events in the pen, and the subsequent flight had burned childhood away.

"Windwolf, thank you for coming." Silvertip was seated, his back to a roll of hides.

When Windwolf looked into the boy's eyes, it was to receive a second shock. Something glowed behind that young face, as if the Power were flowing freely through his body.

"I have been talking with some of the refugees. Karigi has a larger force than I thought. We may not have as much time as I had hoped."

"No, we do not," Silvertip replied. "Our people must leave by the quarter moon."

Windwolf settled himself wearily, sighing with relief at the soft hides. "You saved that boy's life this morning."

Silvertip frowned. "I didn't know it would be so draining."

"Ashes told me most of the story. Your Vision about the ice, is it true?"

Silvertip nodded, then glanced at Windwolf. "That you accept Power so easily is unusual." He smiled. "No questions?"

"Hundreds of them. If we survive this, I'll have time to ask each and every one." He paused. "When will you order the people to head west?"

Silvertip's eyes seemed to lose focus. "Soon."

"Then this really is the end of our world?"

"As we know it. Raven Hunter waited, let us fall into the Dream. Now it is his time."

"So, he has won?"

Silvertip reached out, touching the back of Windwolf's hand. His skin seemed to crackle like rubbed fox fur. "You don't understand Power, War Chief. Is day more Powerful than night? Will winter destroy summer? They are equal but opposite, order and chaos, harmony and creativity; they ebb and flow, ultimately opposed, and forever invincible."

"Then, how do we choose?"

"Balance," Silvertip said, reaching out with his other hand to take Ashes'. He looked at Windwolf. "You know the answer, War Chief. You—of all people—have finally found the balance. You are a creature of compromise. Most of all, you dislike extremes. Karigi, you would kill. Kakala, you would save."

He looked up. "Save, how?"

"That is for the Wind to blow:"

"I don't understand."

"You are Water, War Chief."

"Water?"

"Without you, there can be no life; all would be drought and death. And, as you will see, unleashed, there is only flood. Balance is so elusive, and so important."

"And Kakala?"

"He is the Fire."

Windwolf took a deep breath and frowned as if juggling the pieces of a puzzle. "Of course."

"Yes?" Silvertip prompted.

"It's easier when I don't have to look at you. I am unsettled to hear wisdom granted to so few Elders from a mouth so young."

"Opposites crossed, War Chief. As you know so deeply in your soul. Male and female, enemies to lovers...Raven Hunter and Wolf Dreamer."

"Fire and Water."

"You have plans to pursue, War Chief. You may go."

As Windwolf stood, Silvertip added, "I must warn you, nothing comes without a price. What will you pay?"

He swallowed hard. "To save our people? Anything."

Chapter Twenty-Five

K eresa drew her buckskin cape more tightly around her shoulders and paced Windwolf's chamber. Three guards stood outside the entry. She could hear them talking quietly. In the distance, the happy squeals of playing children rose.

Her soul might have been in turmoil after her visit to the boy Dreamer, but her wits hadn't deserted her. She heard plenty, about parties headed west, the Tills, and preparations to leave Headswift Village. Rumors were already passing that the Dreamer would order it.

What does that mean for Kakala and our warriors?

She rubbed her face, remembering the pulse of energy that had run from Silvertip's touch through her body: a sensation of peace and harmony.

Mother of Legends? The Wind? To surrender is to achieve victory?

She shook it off, trying to think. Windwolf's atlatl and quiver were not leaning against the wall where she'd seen them before. His bedding hides lay tangled, as though he'd risen quickly.

Where are you? What's happened?

She walked over and extended her hands to the small fire. The scent of boiled mastodon meat rose from the bag hanging on the tripod. She considered helping herself but decided against it. Instead, she took the opportunity to thoroughly search the chamber. Not that there was much to search. Overhead, a crack between the boulders created a smokehole. Wisps of blue smoke clung to the high ceiling before being sucked out.

She picked up one of his moccasins and sniffed it, finding his scent. "You're being a fool." She cast the moccasin down. "Sniffing old shoes! How could you have let this happen?"

But she hadn't *let* it happen; it just had. She was supposed to be a hard-eyed, ruthless warrior. She had no ability to pretend to be vulnerable. No, she had to *be* vulnerable.

She'd been shocked that Windwolf had responded to her the way he had.

And I responded to him.

She sank down to the hide in front of the fire and drew up one knee. The sooty shadows clinging in the corners wavered in the fire's glow.

Silently, she cursed herself. She could imagine the amusement in his eyes, as though he were watching her. And behind that lay a warm caring.

"You need a man who is your equal." Kakala's words echoed within her.

"Reach out and gather the Wind." She snorted. "I've drawn a storm."

Karigi was coming. Refugees were fleeing westward toward some stronghold in the Tills. If Karigi arrived, Windwolf would attempt to barter his captives. Karigi

191

would accept, but only to parade them through the Nightland villages in disgrace before locking them all in the cages. She didn't have much time for pleasant feelings of self-pity.

She slipped a hand beneath her braid and massaged the back of her neck, easing the tension in the muscles. How could this happen now when everything she'd ever cared about in her life was in danger? They had to escape. And they had to capture or kill Windwolf.

Voices rose outside. Windwolf's deep voice said, "Fish Hawk, I need you to speak with young Silvertip. He will want to address the people. We have to prepare to leave Headswift Village."

"Yes, War Chief."

Footsteps pounded away.

When Windwolf ducked beneath the door curtain, she stared at him through tortured eyes.

Windwolf stood uncomfortably before the door.

As his eyes adjusted to the darkness, Wildwolf clenched his hands into fists. She sat by the fire in the center of the chamber, dressed in her buckskin cape with long fringes. Her braid hung over her right shoulder. Through the lacing on her cape he could see her war shirt beneath.

"Forgive me for not being here when you arrived. Karigi has been very busy. More refugees poured in just a short time ago."

"Which band this time?"

"Moon Rock."

He watched her expression. Her soul must be

following the same trails his was, tracing Karigi's path. The deputy was attacking the southern Sunpath bands, pushing people north toward Headswift Village.

Windwolf quietly walked to the opposite side of the fire. "What's Karigi doing?"

"Clearing the southern territories so that the Sunpath cannot follow the Nightland People to the paradise of the Long Dark." She shrugged unhappily. "Or so we were told."

"Doubts, Deputy?"

"Too many to count. Your Dreamer told me to trust myself, to be the Wind. I'm that, all right. Blown every which way."

He fought the urge to step forward and hold her again, to soothe her doubts.

No, she is still Keresa. Get too close, and she'll split your head open with a rock.

The chamber smelled of fat-rich meat. He hadn't eaten yet this morning. His stomach growled to remind him.

"Fish Hawk told me you no longer wished to be my go-between with Kakala. I'd like to know why."

She crushed the fringes of her cape in nervous fingers.

He watched with amusement as she said, "Kakala is feeling better. You should be meeting with him. He's the war chief."

"We met last night. Somehow we get on each other's nerves."

"It's because you are both so alike."

"Really?"

She smiled. "You've seen buffalo bulls? The big dominant ones? They swell up, step lightly around each other, and then one makes a sound like *Phiisst!* and they both go at each other."

He folded his arms and stood silently, thinking. She expertly evaded his gaze, pretending to have found something fascinating on the floor.

Windwolf absently studied the way the shell beads on his moccasins reflected the firelight. "Keresa, let's be honest. We both know the reason you want me to deal with Kakala. You haven't been able to kill me."

"Is that what you think?" she asked sharply.

He reached to his belt, plucked out a long, bone stiletto, and tossed it at her feet.

She looked away quickly, but not before he caught the buried desperation. Shaking her head, as if angry with herself, she stood in a whirl of fringed cape and strode toward him.

He was on his feet in a heartbeat. "More doubts, Keresa?"

"If not Kakala, then pick another warrior. Degan would be good."

In the dusty radiance of the firelight, her eyes glinted.

"No."

"Why not?" she demanded.

"I want you." Gods, could he say it more clearly?

"You don't...You confuse me." She stalked away. The fire's glow cast her shadow like a huge beast on the far wall.

"Keresa, talk to me. We don't have time for useless games. Tell me why—"

"You are such a fool."

He started to say something, but decided against it. Instead, he propped his hands on his hips, hoping she'd finish that thought and enlighten him. But she clamped her jaws.

A malevolent gleam filled her eyes. "You know, in that position, I could kill you with one swift punch to the throat. You wouldn't know you were dead until you hit the floor."

Uneasily, he glanced down, seeing the bare floor where the stiletto had lain. "I appreciate the warning."

"You should. Two days ago, I wouldn't have given you one."

"Two days ago you wouldn't have needed to."

She exhaled hard, flipping the stiletto into her fingers from where she'd palmed it. "I wish...I wish desperately that you were the monster I used to believe in."

"The Dreamer says I'm a compromise."

"Well, he says I'm the Wind, whatever that means. And you're Water."

"I heard he asked to see you."

"He wanted to thank me."

"For trying to kill him?"

"For getting the job done, according to him." She shook her head. "He touched me. It was...dazzling."

"What else did he tell you?"

"That surrender was the way to victory."

"I think," he said softly, "that to be a good Dreamer, you have to speak in riddles."

A warm, worried expression strained her beautiful face. He walked over to her. The fire cast a yellow glow around them. Keresa observed him quietly. Flickers of gold glimmered in her eyes.

"I heard talk of a great flood. That Headswift Village is to be abandoned."

"Silvertip says this place is going to be washed away."

She suppressed a shiver, and he instinctively lifted an arm to drape it around her shoulders. When he realized what he was doing, he glanced down at the stiletto in her hand. After two or three agonizing instants, she took a small step forward and eased into his arms.

He pulled her close and let himself drown in the fragrance of her hair and the feel of her breasts against his chest. A hot tide flooded his veins. "Keresa, neither of us can afford—"

"No." She looked up at him, and he saw desire and something more in her eyes, soft, fearful. "Between floods and Karigi, we may not have much time. Kakala, himself, said that it might be short...and miserable in the end."

"Kakala said that?"

"He's my friend, Windwolf." She smiled wearily. "My only friend in the world."

"And I am..."

"I don't know yet." She shook her head lightly, as though denying some inner admonition. "But I think I want to find out. Who knows? Maybe after we get past this attraction, we'll decide it was a bad decision."

He closed in upon himself, hiding. Her words echoed around the chasm in his soul, swirling, images of Bramble flashing.

"Don't. Don't need me. Don't care about me. Just...don't."

"I think it's too late." She took a deep breath, stepping back to remove her cloak. "I suppose it's time to put my foot squarely on the path to destiny."

"The path to what?"

"I don't know. Something the Dreamer said." She pulled her war shirt over her head, flipping her braid back to stand naked but for her moccasins. "Kakala says I need a man who is my equal."

Windwolf's breath came in short gasps as he fixed on her body. "He does?"

"So," she asked brazenly, "do we do this with you on your back...or me on mine?"

As the fire burned low, they lay twined in each other's arms beneath his hides. Her forehead pressed against his chin, while her long hair flowed over his chest and arm. He stroked her naked back slowly, letting the silken texture of her skin soothe him.

"You asked about freedom," he murmured. "I think it means being free to fight with all your heart without ever expecting—"

"You mean being free to die for your people, don't you?"

She lifted her head, and he gazed into her eyes. They shone now with a strange warm light.

"There is no greater freedom than that."

She lowered her head and nuzzled her cheek against his shoulder. "Hallowed Ancestors, I think I'm beginning to understand the Sunpath nation."

She'd said it with such a tone of reluctance, his breathing went shallow. "Sorry you stayed?"

"Not at all. I've never been so comfortable with a man. You weren't even timid when it came time to touch me."

"Where's the stiletto?"

"Within easy reach."

"Maybe that's why I dared not disappoint you."

"You didn't." She snuggled closer, resting her long thigh over his belly. "Assuming you can get the people out before Karigi comes, what are you going to do with my warriors?"

"Honestly, I don't know. Your Council doesn't give me many options. Kakala can't go back without a victory to clear his name. I can't let him have one because it means having my people killed. We can't take them with us. Too many people hate them. They'd be rushed with sticks, stones, anything at hand to repay them for dead relatives and the pain they've caused."

"Why do you care?" She ran her fingers down his chest. "We did terrible things."

He smiled thinly. "Because I was headed down that same trail. That was the lesson Goodeagle tried to teach me. His betrayal brought me back...but it took longer than it should have."

He felt her tense. "If we are serious about trusting each other, you have to know. Kakala and I were there. We saw what Karigi did to Bramble."

"I know."

She shifted, raising up to look at him in the dim light. Her eyes were shadowed in the spill of her hair. "I will not have what happened to Bramble lie between us like a thorn that slowly festers. In the end, Windwolf, it was our fault, Kakala's and mine. We trusted Karigi, and we should have known better."

He reached up, cupping her shoulder with his palm. "You said Kakala would have killed him?"

"Oh, yes." She hesitated. "I should have done it

myself. But sometimes things happen so fast we can't understand the implications."

"No. We can't."

"And what are the implications of you and me, together?"

"Difficult." He slid his hand down to envelop her breast. "But if this night is all that we have, I'm going to fill it with you."

Dislocation

He won't come in the day anymore. But at night, he touches me, his ghostly fingers gliding like fox fur over my flesh to wake me. I think...but I shouldn't...if he could hear my thoughts...no, he doesn't care as long as I keep making plans to take our people back to the Long Dark. I...I'm safe. I'm sure of it. And my thoughts are my only refuge.

I'm not sure he's Raven Hunter. He may be an evil Spirit hiding behind the name. Though, Ancestors help me, he's so persuasive. The horror stories he tells about Wolf Dreamer seem true. When I look around me, all I see is suffering.

If I only knew for certain that he was Raven Hunter, I'd go out and challenge Wolf Dreamer myself. I'd ask him why, if he truly could save his people, he hasn't already done it.

Raven Hunter tells me that the only way I can speak to Wolf Dreamer is if I have the Wolf Bundle. It's the door to Wolf Dreamer's Spirit lodge. He says a little

Lame Bull boy has the bundle, and tells me that I should send warriors to get it and destroy it.

I don 'l know. I just don't know what to do...

Chapter Twenty-Six

T
hey know you're here."
The voice seemed to seep from the ice walls and echo around her chamber.

Skimmer sat up in her hides and stared at the utter darkness. It had started to press in upon her like black smothering smoke. If she hadn't experienced it, she would never have believed that mere darkness could become the enemy: a living ominous creature that stalked her. It moved and breathed. It spoke to her in a soft muted voice that rang in her ears.

She called, "Ti-Bish? Is that you?"

Moccasins on ice.

"They know you're here," he repeated from no more than two or three paces away.

"Who?"

"The Four Old Men, the Elders." Ti-Bish shifted uneasily. "The warriors who brought you here have been talking."

Skimmer drew the worn softness of the hides up around her throat. She'd started to shiver. But it wasn't the cold; it was the memory of Nashat's voice coming from just outside the enclosure.

"H-How long have I been here, Ti-Bish?" she asked. The anguish in her voice surprised her. "I can't tell how many days have passed."

"The Elders want to see you."

Why wasn't he answering her questions?

"Ti-Bish...where have you been? It seems like I've been alone forever."

His steps padded closer and he knelt down. "It's not easy to get to. But Raven Hunter showed me the way."

His scent filled the air, something deep and dark, like moss that had been growing in a cave for tens of tens of summers.

"The way?"

He didn't answer.

Tiny flashes of light, like a distant torch reflecting from midnight-colored feathers, surrounded Ti-Bish. She could clearly see the outline of his body as he stood up.

Reflections from the Thunder Sea? This far away?

"We have to go," he whispered. "The clan Elders are waiting."

Skimmer fought to suppress the shudder that climbed her spine. If they killed her before she had a chance to kill Ti-Bish, what would happen to the Sunpath People? To Ashes?

"Ti-Bish," she said as she braced a hand against the wall and rose. "The darkness...has taught me many things."

"Raven Hunter said it would," he breathed, and spread his arms, as though opening them to the black world. "It has become the one ally I can rely upon."

Fear tingled through her. His soul seemed to be loose, flying somewhere far away where it couldn't hear her.

She moved toward him. "You were right. I have seen the truth of Raven Hunter's vision. I *believe* we must go back through the hole in the ice to the Long Dark."

The words terrified her. If the Long Dark was anything like living in this black cave, it would drive her mad. It would drive every normal human being mad.

Ti-Bish took a quick step backward, as though stunned. "Has...has he picked you?"

Nothing he said was making sense.

"Who?"

"C-Come," he whispered. "Let's...let's get this over with. We must prepare for the way."

She shook her head in confusion, but said, "All right. I will try to follow you, but it's difficult. I wish you'd brought a lamp. The darkness..."

Ti-Bish took her hand in a tight grip, and said, "I'll lead you."

As they climbed the sloping tunnels, the Ice Giants groaned and squealed.

Skimmer stopped suddenly when Wind Woman moved around her, blowing her long hair. "Are we nearing the surface?"

"Yes."

The darkness began to recede, and a faint glow lit the tunnels. Ti-Bish still held her hand, leading her up through the maze and around enormous pools of meltwater.

"It won't be long now," he said, and walked around a curve.

As they headed up a steep tunnel, her feet repeatedly slipped on the ice. Ti-Bish kept a tight hold on her hand to keep her from falling. They rounded a bend to find the ice parted, the rough walls split vertically. She stared into the chasm created by the giant crack.

"Is that...?" She sucked in a breath.

"Yes," he said. "There are crevasses everywhere. And more open every summer."

Skimmer tipped her head far back to look up. Sunlight filtered through the fissures overhead. A feeling of ecstasy and freedom swelled her heart. It was as if Father Sun himself had reached down and touched her. For the first time since she'd arrived, she could get a full breath into her lungs.

"That is my *secret* crevasse," he whispered to her, as though sharing a bit of precious knowledge. "Remember it, Skimmer. Someday, you may need to know how to get back here."

They veered left at the next split in the tunnels, and as they continued on up the steep incline, Father Sun faded, but the flickering light of a fire began to waver over the pale blue walls like invisible wings.

The narrow ice tunnels opened to magnificent arched passageways and huge rounded chambers.

When she heard voices, her stomach muscles tensed.

"We're almost to the Council Chamber," Ti-Bish said, and turned to look at her. "Don't worry. I won't let them hurt you."

"I—I believe you."

But she wondered if he had any real authority to stop them.

From within the chamber, she heard laughter, the rustle of hides, and the clacking of wooden tea cups.

She looked down at her soiled doehide cape. The white moons painted around the bottom had grown dim from soot and dirt. She was meeting the Nightland Clan Elders, and she looked like a slave. Using her fingers, she combed her long hair and tucked it behind her ears. It was the best she could do.

Ti-Bish led her into the chamber, and the voices stopped.

The Four Old Men sat around a stone bowl of warming coals with cups in their hands. The tea bag hung from a tripod at the edge of the bowl. Two of the men were bald; two had white hair that hung down their backs in long braids. Each was dressed regally. Their capes had been smoked a beautiful golden hue, then covered with elk ivories, circlets of mammoth tusk, and painted with their clan symbols. She recognized each Elder by those symbols: *Elder Nashat from the Night Clan, Elder Satah from the Wolverine Clan, Elder Ta 'Hona of the Loon Clan, and Elder Khepa of the Ash Clan.*

The hem of Nashat's cape was decorated with white fox tails that almost dragged the floor. He seemed to be the youngest of them. Though he had a long white braid, his face bore few deep lines. The other Elders resembled shriveled winter-killed carcasses.

Just the sight of Nashat's face brought back that terrible night in the pen. She swallowed hard, willing her hands not to tremble. And from somewhere, perhaps the very blackness she had feared, courage came.

Skimmer's gaze was drawn upward to the high ceiling, which arched five body lengths over her head. Firelight fluttered over the dome. Truly, the Nightland Caves were staggeringly beautiful.

"Forgive us for being late," Ti-Bish said, and bowed to the elders. "A servant caught me just before I started down and—"

Nashat asked, "Was it that ugly little girl, Pipe? I haven't seen her for a while. I thought maybe you'd murdered her and I was finally rid of her."

Ti-Bish stood as if frozen. He didn't even blink.

Nashat turned to Skimmer and scowled as though he'd scraped her off his moccasins just that morning. "Please, step forward so that the Elders may see this 'Skimmer from the Nine Pipes band.'"

"It's all right," Ti-Bish whispered nervously, and gestured for Skimmer to walk forward. "They wish to speak with you."

Skimmer managed to keep from quaking as she stepped closer to the seated Elders. They whispered darkly to each other as she stopped before them.

Clenching her fists, she asked, "What do you want?"

Nashat strolled toward her, the fox tails on his exquisite cape swaying, the fur glinting wildly in the filtered daylight. His white hair had been freshly washed and braided. It shone.

"Did you organize your people to kill our Blessed Guide?" Nashat circled her like an eagle ready to dive for an unsuspecting rabbit.

She glanced at Ti-Bish, who stood near the entry with his shoulders hunched and his head down. He reminded her of a puppy beaten so often it always expected to be struck at any moment.

"I did," she answered.

The Elders hissed to each other and looked at her through narrowed hateful eyes.

Elder Ta'Hona turned his scarred face to look up at her, and the spotted loon painted on the front of his cape folded in the middle. He cradled a withered right arm in his left. "You wanted to kill our Guide. Why?"

"Because you're trying to steal our lands and have ordered the destruction of my people. Your warriors are murdering women, children, and elders. People who never wished the Nightland or their Guide ill until you butchered their relatives." She glared at them, feeling her hatred. "Can you think of a better reason for murder?"

Nashat grinned, and she fought the urge to spit on him.

Ti-Bish spread his feet, and his shoulders hunched more, as though he were trying to hide in plain sight.

Elder Khepa waved a trembling hand. "If you don't want to die, move. Then we won't have to kill you."

"Yes." Elder Satah turned white eyes on her. "We have far more people to feed than you do. We need your nut forests and hunting grounds. You can go somewhere else. Move farther south."

"I thought you were following the Guide to the Long Dark. Or are you just using him for an excuse?"

"Oh," Nashat responded, "we take the Guide very seriously."

A potent brew of anger and desperation pumped through her veins. "Why can't you go around us? You should move farther south, not us. The Sunpath People have lived in the nut forests since Wolf Dreamer first led us up through the hole in the ice. Our Ancestors lived and died on that land."

Nashat chuckled from her left. She turned to look at him. He tilted his head in an oddly seductive way and pinned her with cold black eyes. "It doesn't matter now anyway. In the past moon, War Chief Kakala and Deputy Karigi have destroyed most of your insignificant little bands. The few pitiful survivors have dispersed across the land. The Sunpath People are no more."

Skimmer's heart raced. Could it be true? Or a clever lie?

Ta'Hona ran a hand over his bald head and said, "Soon, we will head south and move into your old lands, perhaps even into your old lodges, those that are left standing. There's nothing you can do to stop—"

"No," Ti-Bish softly said, and his eyes went wide. "We won't."

Nashat scowled at him. "How dare you contradict an Elder? What do you mean?"

Ti-Bish stepped forward. His voice was like buffalo wool, soft and warm. "I've found it."

All of the Elders turned to face him. "Found what?" Khepa asked.

"The way."

Nashat turned to the other Elders and exchanged glances. No one seemed to know what the Guide meant.

Nashat said, "The way...to do what?"

"The way." Ti-Bish swallowed hard and lifted his chin. "The hole in the ice. I can lead our people to the paradise of the Long Dark!"

Chapter Twenty-Seven

Skimmer stared at Ti-Bish in disbelief. *The Paradise of the Long Dark? It was real?*

The Council chamber was silent for a moment, the expressions of the Elders that of shock. Even Nashat was speechless.

Khepa and Ta'Hona were on their feet in a heartbeat.

Satah walked up to Ti-Bish, and in a reverent voice said, "You've found the way to the Long Dark?"

"Raven Hunter showed it to me. He said I'd been good."

Gasps were followed by cheers; then laughter rose. Tears streaked their elderly faces. Nashat, however, sat to the side, fingering his chin, eyes narrowed to slits.

Ta'Hona asked, "When can we leave?"

"Soon. Raven Hunter told me that our people must start packing. But they can only take their most precious things. The trip is long and difficult."

Satah spun around, and the other Elders smiled

toothlessly at him. "We must tell our people immediately. We're going back. Back through the hole in the ice to the Land of the Long Dark, where we will never be hungry again."

Laughter again, joyous. The Elders rose to their feet, and as they filed out, each gently touched Ti-Bish's shoulder.

Skimmer watched, amazed.

They are old fools! Men who no longer think, no longer walk in the world like the rest of us! The image of puppets, the sort that adults used to entertain children, flickered in her soul. *And the one who guides them...?*

Only Nashat remained. He waited until the voices of the other Elders had vanished before he said, "Now that the foolishness is over, let's discuss Headswift Village."

Skimmer blinked. His entire demeanor had changed. His cold eyes fixed on Ti-Bish, and he said, "Guide, come and sit down. It makes me nervous when you stand by the door as though you're going to bolt at any instant." He pointed to the buffalo hides.

Ti-Bish came forward with a frightened look on his face and sat down as he'd been ordered.

Skimmer frowned, the memory of stone hammers whistling in the night, sounding in her head. Where once it would have brought horror, it now stirred a terrible anger.

Nashat...someday, I will repay you for all of this.

Nashat said, "First, what's this idiocy about the hole in the ice?"

Ti-Bish bowed his head. "I found it."

"You're going to have all of our people racing around

stuffing their packs full preparing for a journey they will never take."

Trembling, Ti-Bish had the courage to lift his gaze and look at Nashat. "We need to go soon. Very soon. Raven Hunter says—"

"Oh, Blessed Spirits, you're talking to *me* now, not the fools who believe you're going to lead them to the promised Long Dark. We have more important issues to discuss." He thrust an arm out at Skimmer. "It's a good deal more critical that we push the Sunpath People out of the nut forests, than it is—"

"We're going," Ti-Bish whispered. "I'm going to lead our people through the hole in the ice and back to the Long Dark, where tens of tens of mammoths, giant buffalo, and bears live. We don't need the nut forests. We'll never be hungry again. Raven Hunter will watch over—"

"Ti-Bish." Nashat propped his hands on his hips and shook his head as though terribly disappointed. "Try to listen for a time."

Ti-Bish kept quiet.

Nashat turned to Skimmer and malevolently said, "What's the last thing you saw at Headswift Village?"

Skimmer wet her lips. She could sense his hidden joy, as though he was about to reveal some terrible bit of knowledge that he knew would hurt her. "Windwolf was preparing to fight Kakala."

Nashat walked to the tea bag and dipped himself a cupful. He took his time swirling it before he said, "After that, Kakala overran the place. He tortured Windwolf to death, then hunted down and killed every man, woman, and child who had sheltered Windwolf. Including your daughter," he said pointedly.

Skimmer had to lock her knees to keep standing.

No, he's lying. He's lying!

Ti-Bish shakily got to his feet and stared at Nashat with his mouth open. "You...you ordered Kakala to kill the Lame Bull People?"

"Of course. They deserved it. But I also did as you instructed and told Kakala not to harm any Sunpath People. Though that was certainly a mistake."

"A mistake?" Ti-Bish asked in a tortured voice.

Nashat heaved a breath. "Ti-Bish, did Skimmer tell you that her friends, the Lame Bull People, sent her here to kill you? Did she mention that Windwolf was planning on attacking these caves, and hoped to kill us all?"

"What?" Ti-Bish whirled to stare at her. Every line in his face tensed with hurt.

She gave Ti-Bish a narrow-eyed appraisal, saying, "Don't worry, Guide. You're still alive. I think we both know the source of the problem." Her voice hardened. "And so does Raven Hunter."

Nashat ignored her, continuing to say, "Oh, yes, they sent her here specifically to keep you distracted while they organized their forces; then, at the last instant before they attacked, she was supposed to assassinate you."

Ti-Bish gaped at her. "Is that true?"

"I came to kill you in revenge for the murder of Nine Pipes women in the pen just south of the Nightland Caves. You ordered Kakala to destroy the Nine Pipes and have me brought here. Nashat took a woman called Blue Wing from the pen. The rest were clubbed in the head by Karigi's warriors. Murdered. When Nashat ordered it, he said it was *your* wish."

Nashat was giving her a slit-eyed stare. "Then how did you survive?"

"By hiding under the corpses of the dead, you piece of filth. If so many hadn't died of thirst, hunger, and cold, you would have got us all."

At the still, ravaged expression on Ti-Bish's face, she walked toward him and knelt at his feet. "I am telling you the truth, Ti-Bish. I came to kill the person responsible. And you are not he."

Nashat squeezed the bridge of his nose. "Don't be a fool, Ti-Bish. She's using your emotions against you. Can't you see that?"

Ti-Bish stuttered, "If S-Skimmer says she's telling the truth, I trust her." He looked up, stunned, tears beginning to leak down his cheeks. "But these other things? All of these horrible things? You have *murdered* in my name?"

Nashat laughed, throwing up his hands. "It was necessary. We needed the supplies. What do you think you've been eating for the last two winters? It's food taken from the Sunpath camps. And as to your friend, Kakala, a rumor has come that the fool managed to get himself trapped at Headswift Village. I have sent runners for Karigi and Blackta. We'll deal with the Lame Bull threat once and for all."

"No." Ti-Bish stiffened. "Send runners to bring our warriors home so that they can prepare for the journey to the Long Dark."

Nashat rolled his eyes and grinned, inspecting Skimmer. "With a bath and a clean dress she'd be a real—"

"No!" Ti-Bish cried. "You send those runners! If you

don't I—I'll tell the other Elders that you're trying to leave members of their clans behind!"

Nashat stopped and gave Ti-Bish an evil look. "Do you wish to challenge me?"

Skimmer stepped between Ti-Bish and Nashat. "He does. Come on, Nashat, you and me. Right here. Let us see who serves the Guide. I call on Raven Hunter's Power to aid me. What do you call on, you foul wretch?"

She saw his eyes widen, the first tremble of fear glittering behind his eyes.

"I need only call the guard," he said softly. "And you will be servicing the warriors one after another until you come to wish you'd died in that pen."

"I *did* die in that pen. I came here for justice, you pus-licking scum. And now I'm going to *have* it." She stepped forward, all of the anger washing up through her soul.

Nashat scrambled back, hands up, eyes wide with disbelief.

Ti-Bish grabbed Skimmer's collar, pulling her back. "No, no, let him go, Skimmer. This isn't the time." She heard him swallow, desperation in his voice. "*Please, Skimmer!*"

She hesitated, trembling with the desire to choke the very life out of Nashat.

"Skimmer?" Ti-Bish asked weakly. "Please? It's not the time."

"But it will be," she promised. "And soon."

Nashat fled to the doorway, calling, "Time, Guide, is a very fluid thing." Then he was gone, running for all he was worth.

Tears welled in Ti-Bish's eyes. Softly, he said, "Skimmer, come. We've got to go."

He pulled her after him, taking a side passage out of the chamber.

When they'd followed the tunnel around the first curve, he broke into a run.

"Why are you running?"

"Because as soon as he finds the right warriors, they'll be coming to kill you."

Chapter Twenty-Eight

N ashat hurried down the tunnel and out the front entrance, heading straight for the Night Clan's camp. He hadn't been so frightened in years. He'd looked into Skimmer's eyes and seen death there.

She would have killed me!

The knowledge sent a shiver down his spine and turned his guts runny.

The round lodges made of bent saplings tied together at the top and covered with hides looked tawdry in the bright sunlight. The paintings had faded to dull, indistinguishable images. And the soot of many campfires had furred the lodge tops, turning them black.

Get a hold of yourself!

He forced himself to slow, to breathe normally. Gods, he was Councilor Nashat! Not some simpering slave. For a moment, he stood, letting his heart resume its normal beat. Here, out of the caves, his old self returned.

The tall man standing with his friends before the fire stopped suddenly when he saw Nashat.

"Elder," he said, and bowed deeply. "You honor us with your—"

"What's the last thing you saw at Headswift Village, Homaldo?"

The muscular warrior straightened, fear behind his eyes. "War Chief Kakala was preparing to attack Headswift Village." He waved his hand uncertainly. "After that, Kakala ordered us to leave immediately, to bring Skimmer to the Guide."

A stiff wind gusted off the lake, flapping Nashat's cape around his long legs. "Would it surprise you to hear that Kakala walked into a trap? Perhaps it would shock you even more to learn he's holed up in some rocks, surrounded?"

Homaldo looked at the other warriors in the circle. They shrugged or shook their heads. Homaldo said, "Alive? He's alive?"

"That seems to surprise you?"

"Well, I mean...if what you say is true."

"I'll know soon enough. I've sent a runner to have Karigi's deputy, Ewiri, take a war party to Headswift Village on his way back here." He enjoyed the expression of terror on Homaldo's face. "But I have another task for you and your friends."

Homaldo swallowed hard. "Y-Yes?"

"You can go to the cages—you Kishkat, Tapa, and the other one. Or you can do me a slight service. Which would you choose?" When Homaldo just stood there looking at him, Nashat barked, "*Which!*"

"Yes, Elder, of course. We are honored to do you

any service. Let me get my weapons and my pack. Kishkat, Tapa, and Tibo will be most anxious to help."

While Homaldo ducked into his lodge, Nashat gazed around the camp. Curse the other Elders. The news must have already reached the people. Everywhere he looked, men and women ran from lodge to lodge, and happy voices rang out. Several people Danced and Sang. Before he knew it, they would be taking down their lodges and packing up for the journey through the hole in the ice to the Long Dark.

The fools.

Homaldo ducked out of his lodge carrying his weapons. His small warrior's pack rode his back beneath his cape, making him resemble a hunchback. His wife ducked out behind him and gave Nashat a scathing look. A little boy came out behind her with tears in his eyes. He gazed up at Homaldo and started to sob.

Homaldo knelt and hugged the boy one last time, then said, "Elder, what do you wish us to do?"

Nashat flipped up his hood against the ferocious wind. "You will take your friends and search the tunnels under the ice until you find the woman Skimmer. I think you remember what she looks like? Then, you will bring me her head."

"Where are we going, Ti-Bish?" Skimmer called up to him. The trail that twisted through his "secret" crevasse was steep and slick. Rivulets of meltwater ran down the trail. Her moccasins kept slipping on the wet ice.

"We're almost there." Ti-Bish gripped her hand and pulled her out into the bright gleam of Father Sun.

Skimmer climbed to the crest of the dirty, gravel-encrusted ice, and gazed westward. A rocky ridge thrust up in the distance, rising perhaps ten tens of hands above the tundra. Sunlight sheathed the boulders, turning them into a glimmering wall. To the south, lodges covered the tundra. Already, runners were sprinting from lodge to lodge, probably relaying the news about the sacred hole in the ice.

Ti-Bish sank down onto a boulder and lowered his face to his hands.

Skimmer asked, "Are you all right?"

"No." He looked up at her, soul sick.

"I'm sorry you had to hear those things," she said, laying a gentle hand on his head. "But you needed to know. Nashat has done terrible things in your name. Half the world hates you. I hated you."

In a tight voice, he replied, "I just need to pray for a time."

"I don't think praying is the answer, Ti-Bish. Nashat obviously disdains you and your Dream."

He paused as though judging his words before he murmured, "Prayer is always the answer. The problem is that humans no longer know how to pray."

She studied his tormented face. "Probably because so few people try these days."

"I know." His voice was small. He lifted his face and gazed out across the tundra at a herd of caribou grazing its way along the distant shore of Thunder Sea. Their shiny coats glinted in the sun. "Humans don't pray. But the world prays all the time."

"It does?"

He gestured to the lake. "Prayers are Sung every moment on the lips of breaking waves, and windblown branches, the whispering of leaves in the moonlight."

A strange tingling sensation began in her hip. She looked down at the old Spirit bundle tied to her belt. A mixture of fear and curiosity tormented her. Very faintly she heard a voice. A man's voice, deep and rich.

"Ti-Bish, I—I..." Her gaze was glued to the bundle as though attached with boiled pine pitch. "I hear..."

"Yes, I hear him, too." Ti-Bish swallowed hard. "No wonder he wished you to have it. He wants to speak with you."

"Who does?"

As though trying to decide if he should tell her or not, he twisted his hands in his lap. "Skimmer, I didn't tell you the whole truth when I gave you that bundle. I'm sorry. I was afraid of what you might do."

The tingling sensation had grown fiery. "Tell me now."

"Raven Hunter gave me that bundle. He told me to give it to you. He wanted you to have it."

Blood began to pound in her ears. "Why?"

"He didn't tell me that. I think he worried that I was too stupid to understand."

"You're not stupid, Ti-Bish. Just innocent."

"No, but there are times when I—I lose the"—he waved a hand uncertainly—"the boundary between myself and the world; it melts away, and I'm no longer sure if I'm seeing with my own eyes, or hearing with my own ears. I get confused."

Skimmer looked down at the bundle. The tingling had stopped. The voice was gone. Had she merely imagined it?

"Ti-Bish, whose eyes would you be seeing with if not your own?"

He grimaced down at his hands. "That's the problem. I don't know. There are times when I feel as though every rock and river, bird and buffalo, everything that has ever lived, has always been there in my soul. I could be seeing through any of their eyes. And they through mine."

"That doesn't mean you're stupid."

"*Stupid* may have been the wrong word. What I meant is that Raven Hunter can't rely on the fact that I am actually there when he explains things to me. So"— he sighed—"often he doesn't."

Skimmer flinched at the pain in his voice. "Why do you think he wishes to speak with me?"

"He speaks to a person when they need to hear him. Perhaps today you needed him. You did call on him."

In the villages below, voices had risen and there was a flurry of activity. People raced around shouting and weeping in what sounded like joy.

"The word is traveling," she said.

Ti-Bish nodded, then tenderly asked, "Skimmer, why didn't you kill me?"

As though all of her strength had vanished in a heartbeat, she hunched forward and braced her elbows on her knees. "I..." The words came hard. "I came to get justice. To pay you back for the horror in the pen. For the dead babies and husbands, and ruined lives." She paused. "Instead I found an innocent, a holy man. One doesn't kill the innocent and holy, Ti-Bish. No matter how many lives your death would save."

"My death would save lives?"

She made a sweeping gesture to the villages. "The

warriors would no longer have a reason to kill. You were the symbol, the heart, the Spiritual reason that drove them to do terrible things." She sighed. "And all along, it was Nashat."

"He is the leader of the Council of Elders. I am just the Guide. I have no right to give orders, though sometimes I make requests, and hope that Nashat will approve them. As he did when I asked for War Chief Kakala to bring you here."

"I have hated you for summers for things that were never your fault," she said. "Forgive me. If I had known the truth moons ago, my people would have assassinated Nashat, or the other Elders, but not you, Ti-Bish. I've never wished for the innocent to suffer evil."

"Suffering is not evil, Skimmer." His mouth smiled, but his eyes remained sad abysses. "All suffering forces us, in utter humility, to return to our own hearts. And that is where truth resides."

"You think suffering leads to truth?" She stared into his wide, appealing eyes. He seemed to beam at her with an inner peace that touched her soul.

"Oh, yes. Truth can never be found out there." He waved a hand to the world. "It's here, and here alone." He tapped his chest.

Her heart began to swell. "I don't know why your own people haven't killed you. What you say sounds like a rejection of Nightland beliefs. They should consider you a false Prophet, not a sacred Guide."

"Some do. But not as many these days. It's taken so long to find the hole in the ice. And so many warriors have died. People lose faith when fathers, sons, and brothers are taken from them."

"As did I." She sighed. "Perhaps, since I'm not going

to kill you, I should go home. My daughter needs me." She looked back at the soaring spires of the Ice Giants. "And something tells me Nashat isn't going to let me get my hands around his throat, or sneak close enough to run a dart through his pus-dripping heart."

Ti-Bish stood up. "You will go home. Soon. Raven Hunter told me you can't go with us to the Long Dark. But there's something magical I wish to show you before you go"

He extended a hand. She took it and got to her feet. At his touch, a sensation of peace and longing filled her. When had Ti-Bish wound himself so deeply into her heart?

"Where is this thing?"

"Deep in the belly of the Ice Giants." He fixed his warm eyes on hers. "It is the last, and greatest, wonder. I have longed for it, and now, I will be able to share it with you. For that, my soul is filled with joy."

Chapter Twenty-Nine

Windwolf sat on the hides before his fire, occasionally throwing branches onto the dwindling flames to fight the early-morning chill. The gray stone walls and high ceiling seemed to suck all his warmth away, leaving him bone-cold and weary.

He couldn't explain it, but he sensed something growing in the dark silence—some malignancy without form.

He cursed under his breath. One night with Keresa, and suddenly, for the first time since Bramble's death, he realized he had something to lose.

He stared at the fire, and then back to his bedding, imagining her there, seeing her smile up at him.

Windwolf lowered his head to his hands and massaged his forehead. He longed to send for Keresa, to start west for the Tills and a new life; but he couldn't just walk away from the people here. Without him, there was no telling what the Nightland warriors might be able to do. One tiny error and Kakala would be out of his cage and killing Lame Bull and Sunpath children in a frantic bid to save himself from the cages.

Voices came from the trail outside, and he heard someone running.

He was on his feet headed for the door before he'd even realized it.

Fish Hawk called, "Windwolf?"

He threw the door curtain back. It was still mostly dark. The last of the Star People twinkled overhead. "What's wrong?"

Fish Hawk caught his breath—he'd obviously run flat-out to get here. "Our scouts just reported in. There's a runner coming." While he sucked in a breath, a momentary flash of relief went through Windwolf. Silt, sending word that he'd reached the Tills. Then Fish Hawk finished, "He's definitely a *Nightland* warrior."

Windwolf's jaw clenched. He said, "Relax. Follow the plan. Notify the refugees. They know what they must do. Tell your men to get dressed. I'll take care of the rest."

"Yes, War Chief." Fish Hawk took off at a fast run, careening down the hill toward the Sunpath camps.

Windwolf let the curtain fall closed...and leaned heavily against the stone wall.

Kakala, tell me you value your hide as much as I suddenly do.

Goodeagle lounged on the floor, head propped on his hand, watching Kakala and Keresa. They knelt on the opposite side of the chamber. The thin veil of dawn penetrated the rocks over their heads and cast a pale

blue tracery across the floor. They were drawing in the dirt at their feet, whispering to each other. Plotting their escape.

A chuckle shook him.

The fools thought they could escape.

All around him warriors talked about their families, wondering if their wives and children were safe. The plans they made remained blissfully free of references to the cages when they finally returned home.

Goodeagle wiped his mouth with the back of his filthy hand. Since the deaths of his parents when he'd seen ten-and-four summers, he'd never had any family...except Windwolf and the friends who'd fought and hunted beside him those many summers. An ache built in his belly and climbed into his chest.

He glanced back at the tunnel they'd opened between the chambers. He ought to crawl back through to his own chamber, but two rocks covered the entrance. It was Kakala's order. They *always* rolled rocks over the entrance, coming or going. Kakala didn't want the guards above to know how many warriors he had in here. Since it was too much effort to roll them aside by himself, he stayed put.

Kakala said to Keresa, "If you're right that he only has a handful of real warriors and a gaggle of children playing at being warriors, we might have a chance if we..."

His voice went too low for Goodeagle to hear, but Keresa nodded and said, "We'll have to wait until he lowers the ladder again and hope he only has a few guards posted."

Goodeagle laughed; it was such a desperate sound that everyone turned in his direction. He said, "That moment will never come, Deputy. He will always have more warriors than necessary posted around this chamber. The greatest threat to his plans lies in here."

"But the last time I was out I saw only—"

As though speaking to a child, he leaned toward her and continued in a condescending voice, "He will never let you count his warriors. That would give you an advantage he doesn't wish you to have. If he's let you see ten warriors, he has three tens, maybe four. The instant you think you know what he's doing. Deputy, you are dead."

Keresa started to comment, but the rocks overhead grated shrilly. She hissed, "Goodeagle, get back to your own..."

He and two other warriors leaped to shove away the boulder that covered the entry to the next chamber. They moved it just enough for one warrior to slide through...then dawn light poured into the chamber as the rocks above them were rolled aside. Goodeagle and Mong froze, using their bodies to block the entrance.

Keresa shot Goodeagle a knowing glance, but kept her face blank.

Windwolf stood silhouetted against the dark blue sky— and looked Goodeagle right in the eye.

Goodeagle's heart stopped dead in his breast; he dared not even to breathe. He saw the instant recognition. Windwolf's expression hardened—painful remnants of old friendship mixed with hatred and silent questions of "why?"

Then Windwolf's gaze turned emotionless and passed to Kakala.

Goodeagle sank back against the wall, forcing

himself to take deep breaths while he pretended to stare at the floor.

If Windwolf knew, why hadn't he...?

Blessed gods, he—he's counting on me. He needs me.

"Kakala, Keresa," Windwolf ordered, "we have a problem."

Chapter Thirty

Kakala dragged himself to his feet and held up a hand, shielding his eyes against the gleam that poured in. He counted four warriors with war clubs in their fists.

Standing above, looking down, Windwolf carried a dart.

"What do you want, Windwolf?"

"Both of you."

The tall man's jaw was clamped so hard, his entire face seemed skewed. Whatever this was, it wasn't good. Kakala straightened. "What for?"

"My scouts just reported that there's a runner coming."

"And you need my help to talk to a runner?"

Windwolf used the point of his dart to motion to every warrior in the chamber. "It's a Nightland runner. I need all of you on your feet. Hurry. We haven't much time."

Kakala nodded to his warriors and said, "We're hurrying. Don't get nervous."

His warriors glanced at each other, obviously thinking the same thing he was—that this might be their chance. Keresa subtly held out five fingers, meaning "There are five of them." He nodded. Granted, Windwolf's people had weapons, but if the right opportunity arose...

Kakala gestured for his warriors to climb the ladder first. All the while, Windwolf stood rigidly, eyes glued to Kakala's every movement. Only when Keresa passed by him did his gaze shift. He glanced at her with a softness in his eyes.

Kakala climbed out last...and walked straight into three tens of warriors with clubs and nocked atlatls. Keresa bowed her head and smiled wearily.

Kakala grimaced. "What are we doing?" He took another look at the warriors, seeing no more than ten adults among them. Some looked as if they were hiding wounds. The rest were women and children, but each seemed to know how to hold a weapon.

Windwolf gave him a piercing look, almost pleading. "First, order your warriors to follow my directions."

"Why?"

If I ordered a sudden rush, we could probably break that pitiful bunch of warriors, seize enough weapons to make a real fight of it.

More to Kakala's warriors than him, Windwolf said, "Working with me does two things: First, it saves your lives, and perhaps the runner's as well. Second, it gives us a chance to keep you out of the cages." In a louder voice, he said, "Do you understand?"

Kakala looked back at his warriors, who shot questioning gazes in his direction. He turned to Windwolf. "You could just kill the runner."

231

A faint smile crossed the man's lips. "Then Nashat will *know* the rumors are true." He gave Kakala a challenging look. "You help me; I help you."

"Outside of keeping out of the cages, is there a reason I should?" He shot another measuring look at the pitiful band of warriors, women, and children.

"No games, Kakala. We don't have time for it. You choose: back in the hole, and I kill the runner, or we work together to find a solution that leaves everyone breathing, and with a future."

"We await your orders, War Chief Kakala," Keresa said formally. She managed to keep her expression wooden, but he could see the anguish behind her eyes.

She's leaving the choice to me.

In that instant, his soul swelled with heartfelt appreciation. If she would do this for him, he could do no less for her.

"We do as War Chief Windwolf instructs! No tricks, no foolishness. That is my order," Kakala shouted loudly enough for the rest. To Windwolf he said, "Tell me what you want me to do."

"You'll meet the messenger in the ceremonial cave, where everything will look perfectly normal."

"All right." Kakala started walking. His warriors followed. The Lame Bull warriors surrounded them with their darts nocked.

Windwolf matched his pace to Kakala's. "Let's discuss your conduct."

"I think I know how to act with another Nightland warrior."

"One wrong word, one suspicious move—if you blink too quickly, Kakala, I'll do what I have to do. But

I'll keep you alive to the last. Do we understand each other?"

Rage flared, but he controlled it. "We do." Then he asked softly, "Keresa, too?"

His shot went home. He saw the scream behind Windwolf's eyes.

"I die with my warriors," Keresa said stiffly. "No favors."

Kakala and Windwolf locked gazes, each taking the other's measure. A silent tug-of-war ensued.

Keresa noticed, averted her head, and made a *phiisst!* sound with her lips.

Then Windwolf broke the gaze, almost laughing. Softly, he said, "I want you to ask the runner one question for me."

Kakala squinted suspiciously. "What is it?"

"Ask him if anyone has reported the location of my warriors."

The question seemed to have a special importance to Windwolf.

By Raven Hunter, he doesn't know.

Kakala laughed. "And to think I've been worried—"

Windwolf's muscular arm slammed Kakala painfully against a boulder. His warriors started forward.

Keresa shouted, "Keep your places!" Then in a lower voice, "Windwolf, that isn't necessary."

To Kakala's surprise, Windwolf backed off, saying, "Just ask him."

"Of course," Kakala responded mildly. A seed of hope lodged in his breast, quickening his breathing. If Windwolf didn't know, they could be days away. Or dead.

He shot a quizzical look at Keresa, who lifted her eyebrows in a shrug.

Windwolf took a deep breath, remarking, "Keresa's right. You bring out the worst in me."

In a voice too low for Keresa to hear, Kakala said, "We don't have to like each other, but if this goes bad, you will make sure Keresa is safe?"

"Kakala," he said with a sigh, "I am a flawed man. For reasons I do not fully understand, I even want you safe."

They walked around the base of the rockshelters and passed through totally empty Sunpath camps. Every person was gone. Their belongings lay strewn in front of the lodges as though dropped by fleeing people. A few dogs skulked unhappily through the garbage, sniffing and growling at anything that moved.

"Where are all the—?"

"Keep walking," Windwolf said.

Kakala looked at him with new appreciation. "You've known someone would be coming."

Windwolf shot him a sidelong look. "And you didn't? Holding an entire Nightland war party is big news."

Kakala sighed.

I've been so busy keeping my people together and worrying about the cages, I haven't thought about those parties of Sunpath People headed west. Not all of them would have made it past Karigi.

"You irritate me," Kakala muttered. Then he laughed, more at himself than anything else.

"Good," Windwolf replied. Then he gave Kakala a serious look. "When I capture Karigi, you can have what's left of him when I'm through."

Kakala narrowed an eye. "When I take you back to the Council, I might let your bindings slip when we see him."

"Keresa told you about the Dreamer's vision?"

"The flood coming? Yes. She seems to believe it."

"So do I." Windwolf rocked his jaw. "But for the death, suffering, and misery, it makes our war appear even more insane."

"Assuming your Dreamer is correct." Kakala shrugged. "The Guide has been promising to lead us back to the Long Dark for a long time, now. It doesn't seem to ever happen."

"Maybe he serves the wrong Spirit."

"Or yours does." Kakala arched an eyebrow.

From behind, Keresa said, "Have either of you thought that perhaps they are both right? Raven Hunter wants to take his people into the ice, just as Wolf Dreamer wishes his people to flee to the Tills in the west?"

"Perhaps," Windwolf agreed.

They strode up the trail toward the ceremonial cave near the crest of the hill.

Kakala's eyes widened when he saw that every high point around the village had a red-shirted warrior standing on it. He grimaced. "So that's what you did with the shirts you took from my dead warriors. It might work. If the runner doesn't look too closely."

"After you speak with him, I want you to order him to run straight back home."

"What reason shall I give?"

"You have a message for the Nightland Elders."

Kakala exhaled unhappily. "What is it?"

"You're still hunting down some of the survivors, but

235

upon your return you will personally be bringing me back alive as a present to the Elders."

Kakala studied his hard expression. "I will?"

"Just tell him."

"Windwolf?" Keresa asked in surprise. "By Raven Hunter, do you know what they'll do to you?"

Kakala stared in open shock. "Nashat will order you tortured to death."

"No," Keresa hissed. "Windwolf, you do not have to do this thing for me! Have you lost your mind?"

"Probably," Windwolf said gruffly.

When they reached the ceremonial chamber, Windwolf gripped him by the arm. "Order your warriors to sit down in a circle around the fire and start having a delightful conversation."

Kakala roughly shook Windwolf's arm loose, walking out into the room. "You heard him. I want you to look tired. Think of this as the first rest we've had in a long time." He met their eyes, letting his stare bore into Goodeagle's. "Are you with me?"

"Yes, War Chief," they shouted in unison.

Kakala nodded.

He ignores Goodeagle, acts as if he doesn't exist. Is there something I can use here?

His warriors sat, delighted to find a skewered elk haunch slowly roasting. They dipped themselves cups of warm tea from the bag on the tripod and started whispering to each other.

Windwolf jerked his chin at his own warriors, and they slipped into the shadows of the cavern's walls.

Windwolf eased back to Kakala's right, hiding behind the lip of the cave, but his dart point stabbed uncomfortably into Kakala's kidney. He said, "Don't forget: Your warriors' lives are at stake."

Kakala shot a glare over his shoulder. "Do you think I'm an idiot?"

"That is a fascinating discussion we'll save for another time."

Kakala pulled himself straight. Forgetting where he was, his head struck the stone. At the impact he almost passed out. Trembling, he fought the urge to cry out. His warriors noticed. They looked at him breathlessly, some obviously worried that he was too ill to handle things. It made his gut ache as badly as his head.

Keresa's hard eyes assessed the Lame Bull warriors, then shifted to Kakala. "Are you all right?"

Kakala nodded, and in the calmest tone he could muster, said, "We'll proceed just as though this were a casual conversation with a runner from the Elders. No heroics, or our friend Windwolf will order his warriors to kill us all."

Windwolf said to Keresa, "Deputy, when the runner arrives, I would appreciate it if you would walk out and greet him."

She gave him a wary look. "I'll make him feel right at home."

I would appreciate?

Kakala looked back and forth between them, seeing the worry and concern in their eyes.

Oh, Keresa, what have you gotten yourself into?

On the hilltop across from the ceremonial chamber, the guard waved a hand.

"He's coming, Kakala. Are you ready?" Windwolf asked in a strained voice.

"As ready as I ever am when I have to answer ridiculous questions from the Elders."

A small round of nervous laughter went through his warriors, just as he'd intended. They all knew how much he hated clan politics.

"All right, Keresa," Windwolf said with a sigh. "He's running up the trail."

She stepped over to stand beside Kakala, looking down at the runner.

"Homaldo?" she called and lifted a hand. "What are you doing here? Where are the others? What happened to you?"

"We thought the fight was lost, got cut off from the rest of you," he called back, and pounded up the trail grinning.

When he got close, Keresa stepped out and smiled. "You should be home playing hoop-and-stick with your son."

Homaldo stopped in front of Keresa and took her hand in a strong grip. "We thought you were all dead! It's good to see you alive."

"Of course we're alive," Kakala said indignantly. "Do our Elders judge me so poorly?"

Homaldo's smile faded. "No, War Chief, not at all. I'm not supposed to be here. And if Nashat learns that I have come, the cages will be a merciful alternative to what he will do to me. Kishkat, Tapa, and Tibo are searching the caves for the woman Skimmer. We found her on the trail, and..." He glanced away. "We thought you were all dead, War Chief. But we took her to the Guide."

Kakala narrowed an eye. "With an eye to saving your necks, no doubt."

He gestured to the bandage on Kakala's head. "It must have been a tough fight."

"Windwolf jumped me at the last instant, but we got him. Even without your help." He pointed to his head. "I have been unable to travel."

Keresa added, "We're still hunting down a few survivors. We should be headed home tomorrow or the next day."

"With Windwolf," Kakala said, and lifted his chin proudly. "I will personally be bringing him back alive as a gift to our Elders."

Homaldo smiled broadly. "They will be glad to hear it. It's another piece of good news."

"Another?" Keresa asked.

Excitedly, Homaldo said, "Just before I left, the Elders came out and told us that the Guide has found the hole in the ice! We're all packing to return to the Long Dark."

The warriors sitting around the fire behind Kakala gasped and turned to listen.

Windwolf's dart pressed into Kakala's kidney." He winced and said, "Have you heard from Karigi? Where are Windwolf's warriors? We've been expecting them to show up at any time."

Homaldo spread his arms. "The news is mixed. Silt's warriors destroyed Hawhak's war party. He, his deputy, and the rest are in the cages. Nashat says that because of their disgrace, they cannot accompany the Guide to the Long Dark."

"And Windwolf's warriors?"

"Karigi sent word that they all fled west. Karigi attacked three more camps and is herding tens of captives to the Nightland Caves, where he's been ordered to set up a pen for them. And Deputy Ewin's war party is on its way here. He should arrive tomorrow."

From the corner of his eye, Kakala saw Windwolf's expression slacken, as though he'd just heard his own Death Song being sung.

"Why is Ewin coming here?" Kakala demanded. "Do the Elders think I am so incompetent that I require *his* assistance?"

Behind him, his warriors responded to his outrage by shifting disgustedly. Moans and curses laced the air. He wanted to kiss them.

Homaldo wet his lips nervously. "War Chief, I don't know. But there is a rumor that you had been captured. I, well, I'd die for you. We cast gaming pieces to see which one of us would come to see if it was true. I won the honor."

Anxiety tingled in Kakala's chest. If Ewin was headed here, Nashat knew of his failure.

Hawhak and his warriors are in the cages! They cannot accompany our people?

Kakala sagged against the cave wall, which forced Windwolf to pull his dart back. Unfortunately, he resettled it on Kakala's spine. "Homaldo, I want you to run home immediately and tell the Elders we will be right behind you with our 'gift.'"

Keresa pointed a finger like a bone stiletto at Homaldo. "And tell my clan not to return to the Long Dark without me."

Homaldo frowned. "I'll have to figure something out. I'm supposed to be searching the caves for Skimmer."

"Why?" Kakala asked. "This part, I do not understand."

Homaldo lowered his voice. "The guard at the Council is my cousin. As we were entering the caves, he told me that Skimmer was accused of plotting to kill the Guide. But in the Council, she accused Nashat of misdeeds. And then, after the Elders left, Nashat threatened the Guide. Skimmer protected Ti-Bish! Dared Nashat to try and harm him!" He blinked. "Can you believe that?"

Kakala and Keresa traded glances, and Kakala felt the dart point fall away, as if Windwolf had lost interest in holding it against him.

Kakala took the opportunity to step forward, out of visible range of the dart. "When it comes to Nashat, I can believe anything. Kishkat was there the night the Guide freed me. Ask him."

Keresa said, "War Chief? Perhaps it would be a good idea if Homaldo met Ewin? He could save him the trip here, urge him to hurry home and prepare to follow the Guide?"

Kakala gave her the expected look of irritation and said, "Homaldo, can you find Ewin?"

"I think so, War Chief." He frowned. "But who will carry your message to the Elders?"

"One of these lazy warriors back here." Kakala barked, "Washani! Bring Homaldo some of that meat to stuff in his pack. We have plenty."

"Yes, War Chief."

Kakala took a gamble, and walked over to clap his hand on Homaldo's shoulder. "Thank you, my friend. We all appreciate the risks you have taken on our behalf. I would ask you as a favor, find Ewin. Tell him the rumor of our capture is a lie formulated by the Sunpath. We are fine, and he shouldn't waste precious time coming here. By the time he arrives, we'll almost be home. Can you do that?"

"Yes, War Chief!" Homaldo cried with a grin. "Especially if it keeps me out of Nashat's way!"

A chorus of shouts rose behind him.

Washani emerged with a pack stuffed full of meat. He cast an inquisitive glance at Kakala, as if expecting some instruction, like, *Run off with Homaldo and tell him the whole story.*

"Thank you, Washani," Kakala said. "That will be all. Go back and fill your lazy belly."

"Yes, War Chief."

Kakala watched Homaldo turn and trot back down the trail. He called, "Find Ewin!"

"I will!" Homaldo waved over his back.

The Lame Bull warriors eased from the shadows with their nocked atlatls up.

Windwolf stepped forward and peered over Kakala's shoulder, watching Homaldo until he vanished down the trail. His voice came out unsettlingly soft. "That was good thinking."

Kakala blurted, "Well, someone had to save all of our skins. You'd just better hope Homaldo finds Ewin."

"The Guide has found the hole!" warriors called back and forth, excitement in their eyes.

"Yes!" Kakala snapped. "And Hawhak and his warriors aren't going! The Council has heard that we've been captured. If they believe it, we're not going either!"

They stared at him soberly.

Kakala turned. "All right, Windwolf. The other

night, you said that when we could talk like men, we should talk. Perhaps that time is now."

"What are you thinking?" Windwolf asked.

"I'm thinking it's not a coincidence that the Guide finds the hole in the ice just after your Dreamer warns of a great flood." He looked down at his fingers. "My people live on the Thunder Sea. Have you ever seen what happens when a mountain of ice falls into the water? A huge wave washes everything before it. My family died in one of those." He smiled wryly. "Perhaps, as you said, our war is insignificant."

At that moment, a low rumble rolled over the land; the ground shook. Kakala could see the warriors glancing nervously at the rock over their heads. Bits of gravel pelted them.

And then it was gone.

Chapter Thirty-One

W indwolf watched Fish Hawk climb up the trail. "Did it all go well?"

"They did exactly as Kakala ordered, War Chief. They walked right up to the hole and climbed down. I have already sent warriors to bring them robes and firewood." Fish Hawk fixed him with curious eyes. "War Chief, are you sure this is a smart thing to do?"

Windwolf turned and fixed him with knowing eyes. "I just met with Lookingbill. He understands that Homaldo may not be able to find Ewin. At Silvertip's urging, he reluctantly agreed that it was time to leave. I want every person packed and ready to move by first light."

"You mean, before Ewin's war party arrives?"

Windwolf nodded. "We can't fight them, Fish Hawk. We have only a few adult warriors; it's not enough. And our young warriors will fall like dry grass before a powerful hailstorm. You know it as well as I."

Fish Hawk swallowed hard, gaze inexorably drawn

to the children playing at the base of the rock shelters. He could hear their laughter rising on the gusts of wind. "This has been my home for all of my life. The idea of leaving...it just doesn't seem possible."

Windwolf asked, "Can you do it, War Chief?"

Fish Hawk nodded. "I can, but...where will we go? The Tills? I know nothing about them. My clan has been here forever."

A powerful gust of wind swept up the slope, and Windwolf's short black hair blew around his face. "I need to talk with Kakala and Keresa."

Fish Hawk jerked a nod. "My people will be packed by first light."

"And, in case I forget, you make sure you have a screen of scouts out. It wouldn't do to stumble into Ewin's war party on the way."

"Of course, War Chief." He hesitated. "Do you need guards for your talk with the Nightland?"

"No." He smiled at the irony. "Not anymore."

As Fish Hawk trotted away, Windwolf eased down on a flat rock and closed his eyes. So much had to happen so quickly.

Skimmer followed Ti-Bish along the sandy shore of the fiery lake, her way lit only by the luminous streamers that snaked through the water. The Ice Giants who stretched high overhead groaned, and the very air trembled with their pain. New cracks, like black lightning bolts, had split the ceiling since the last time she'd been down here. Some were over two tens of body lengths wide.

"Ti-Bish," she called, frightened. "Where are we going?"

"It's not much farther. Are you tired?"

They'd been walking for a long time, though she could not say just how long. The lack of sunlight and darkness left her completely bewildered. "No, I'm not tired; I'm just concerned. Won't your Elders wonder where you are?"

He shook his head. "They're busy packing for the journey. They know I'll return."

In the damp air, his two black braids had turned frizzy, but his dark eyes glowed as though a blaze had flared to life in his soul.

He pointed. "Do you see the bones ahead?"

Skimmer looked to where he pointed.

"That's the Monster Bone Trail," he explained in a whisper, as though the long-dead beasts might hear him. "I want you to see the path."

Skimmer's mouth dropped open when they walked through the rib cage of a huge animal; the bones arched over her head. From snout to tail, the beast must have stretched at least five or six body lengths. "What is this creature?"

He shrugged and stepped around a human skull. "One of the monsters that lived just after the creation, I think."

As Skimmer passed another human skull, she stared into the dark eye sockets, wondering who the man might have been. Another Dreamer? Someone else seeking the hole in the ice?

Then she saw the ax. It had been laid on an ice shelf. She stepped over, and picked it up, looking back at the skull.

Was this yours? A tool no longer needed?

She hefted it, staring at the handle. The wood had been carved with long grooves and drilled with dots. The binding, made of sinew, was crusted with frost. The stone head had been set in a Y in the wood and daubed with pitch. It had been chipped from a translucent brown chert she'd never seen before. She pressed her thumb to the sharp edge.

How long had it been since this had rested in human hands? Tightening her grip on the handle, she followed after Ti-Bish.

They walked in silence until Ti-Bish said, "There. Do you see it?"

"What?"

He gestured to the dark cavern ahead. A river spilled out through it and ran into the fiery lake.

She said, "It's a river."

Ti-Bish frowned at her. "Yes, but...that's the hole."

"The hole?" she said in confusion.

"The hole in the ice. We must go through it to get to the Land of the Long Dark."

Terror crept up around her heart. She stared at him. "That's it?"

He smiled tenderly. "Yes. That's it. It's a difficult journey. It will take many, many days, but—"

"How do you know how long it will take? Have you made the trip before?"

"Oh, yes," he murmured. "In a Spirit Dream. Raven Hunter took me."

"It's cold water, Ti-Bish. Walk in that for more than a couple of hands' time, and people's legs will go numb. If someone trips and falls, they'll be wet clear through.

You can't stop and make a fire to dry out. The children will die first"

"Raven Hunter will find a way. Perhaps, at the last moment, he'll divert the water." He searched the ice roof over their heads, as though expecting to see Raven Hunter swooping down to speak with him.

Skimmer pulled her cape more tightly around her shoulders and shivered. "Have you seen him lately?"

"Yes, often."

'Ti-Bish, doesn't it frighten your people when you tell them that?"

"Does it frighten you?"

"I...I don't know."

He bowed his head and smiled. "Skimmer, every man walks away from the herd sometime. When he chooses to stand alone in the meadow, he knows the predators will see him. He also knows they will be waiting. There was a time"—he hesitated—"a time when I moved too far from the herd. I'll never do that again. I only tell my people what they need to know. It keeps them at bay."

How strange that he thought of his own people as predators. But why wouldn't he? It had been only ten summers ago that he'd been a homeless outcast, loathed by almost everyone, chased from village to village.

They walked closer to the black cavern, and Skimmer said, "You once told me that you'd brought me here to pray with you. But we haven't prayed together. Not yet."

He stopped and looked at her with luminous eyes. "Prayer is...not what you think. Not what most people think. It isn't begging the gods for something. It isn't undertaken to enlighten or bring tranquility. It is an act of service done for the sake of the world. If people truly work to maintain harmony, the world will stay in balance. If they don't, the Spiral of life will tilt, and everything will wither and die."

Sorrow tinged the last few words, and tears welled in his eyes.

"Is that why there's been so much war and sadness? The Spiral has tilted?"

"Yes, Raven Hunter has been trying to bring it back into balance, but his evil brother won't allow it, and that's why we must go back."

"Back to the Long Dark?"

"Yes, back to a time before the brothers fought. Back to a time before they were even born."

As though in response, a deep agonizing groan shook the Ice Giants, and massive slabs of ice cracked loose from the ceiling and crashed down. When they splashed into the lake, brilliant sprays of light burst into the air. Waves washed high onto the shore, wetting her to the knees. She felt the sand slide under her.

Skimmer lurched back against the wall, panting like a hunted animal.

Ti-Bish just smiled. "It's all right," he said softly. "The pain is almost over."

Chapter Thirty-Two

Nashat caught his balance as the quake hit. Impulsively, he cast a quick glance up at the ice overhead. Only a couple of gravel pellets clattered down around him. He could hear the ice moan, screech, and crack.

"Blessed Raven Hunter, I can't *wait* to get out of this death trap!" Then he glanced around to make sure no one was close.

A sensation of doom was closing in around him, making breathing difficult. He hurried along, passed the opening to the Council Chamber, and stopped short. A huge block of ice had smashed down on his robes. Translucent tourquoise and crusted with bands of gravel, it had shattered to send angular chunks of ice around half the room.

If I had been sitting there...

No, don't even think it.

In half panic, he trotted down the tunnel, feet crunching the gravel underfoot.

At the great opening, he stopped, staring. People

had been corning from all over. Literal mountains of packs stood beside small camps. But for the moment, the people were congregated down at the shore. It took a moment for the meaning of the darkened sand to sink in. A large wave had washed up and then receded.

He glanced out at the Thunder Sea. He could see debris bobbing in the choppy water. Among the packs, boats, and floating hides, people splashed around. Some clung to wreckage, calling desperately.

Those on shore were dragging bull boats down to the water, intent on rescuing the survivors before the cold water claimed them.

He took a deep breath. When strong quakes shook the ice, it often broke off, splashing down into the Thunder Sea. His people knew better than to camp too close to the beach.

"Fools! Serves them right."

Then he returned his attention to the piled packs. The people were ready to move. He shifted his glance to the south, as if seeing beyond the tundra and spruce barrens to the oak and maple forest beyond. A land abandoned, ready for a new people to move in and enjoy the bounty, far from this miserable ice and cold.

"I am sorry, Ti-Bish. But I think it's time that Skimmer finally served her purpose." He actually felt a sense of delightful relief. His long ordeal was over. At last, he need no longer endure the wide-eyed innocence of the Idiot.

Keresa tossed a stick into Windwolf's fire. As the flames licked around it, she studied Kakala. He walked around, staring at the stone, fingering the bedding, and idly ran a finger down one of the long war darts leaned against the wall.

Kakala glanced at her as he studied the darts. "Do you think he remembered these were in here?"

"He's getting tired. Making mistakes." She flipped the bone stiletto from the top of her tall moccasin. "He never asked for this back, either."

Kakala picked up one of the darts, glancing down its polished length with a practiced eye. "You two must have spent an interesting night."

Keresa glanced at the fire. "I just hope it wasn't the *only* night we ever have together." Coolly she asked, "Why didn't you order us to rush Windwolf's pitiful little band of warriors when we climbed out of the hole?"

"Maybe it was curiosity. Maybe I wanted to see what Windwolf would do." Kakala was balancing the dart experimentally. "What does *pssst* mean?"

"*Phiisst!* It's the sound that one buffalo bull makes when another dominant bull walks up. You've heard it."

Kakala nodded. "And watched them tear up half the scenery. Is that what you think Windwolf and I are? Buffalo bulls?"

"You act like it when you get together."

"Well, at least he didn't kill me when I stepped out to clap Homaldo on the shoulder." He paused, bouncing the dart up and down in his hand. "Do you think the Guide has really found the way to the paradise of the Long Dark?"

Keresa shrugged. "I don't know."

Kakala searched her eyes. "Are you going?"

She shook her head slowly. "As much as it will

break my heart not to be close to you, no. I've been different all of my life, Kakala. The only place I felt at home was with warriors. If the Guide is right, and the Long Dark is paradise, where will the warriors be?"

"Hunting." He grinned. "And I will never have to look at another dead child and say, 'I did that.'"

"I wish you all the happiness in paradise, Kakala. You, of all people, deserve a little." She shot him a side-long look. "Give my regards to Karigi."

His expression fell. "Somehow, I forgot. I hope paradise is large enough that I can live on one side, and he on the other."

Keresa frowned. "What is this nonsense about Windwolf going with us as our captive?"

"I have no idea, but I will enjoy the reversal of roles."

Keresa gestured impotence. "It's madness. He doesn't have to do this! Our warriors can just leave. We can promise never to raid another Sunpath band. They're going west; our people are going into the ice."

She looked up as Windwolf—looking weary and concerned—stepped in. He stopped short, seeing the dart in Kakala's hand. "I hope you're not having creative thoughts about that."

Kakala balanced the shaft, feet braced. "Actually, I was. I was thinking how happy I am that it isn't sticking in one of my warriors' guts."

"Or your own," Windwolf said warily, ready to duck.

Kakala neatly bounced the shaft off his hard palm, caught it, and laid it back against the wall. "After all we've been through, War Chief, it appears that I am as flawed as you are. For some reason that defeats me, I don't wish you dead either." He smiled. "I'm tired, Windwolf. Sick of it. And after the last couple of summers wondering what it was all for."

"Don't we all?" Windwolf asked, and finally seated himself beside Keresa. He reached out and took her hand. "How are you?"

She smiled, tightening her grip in his. "Still confused." The smile fell. "Why do you think you have to go with Kakala to the Nightland villages? I don't understand. My warriors can take their chances, and by returning, no one will believe that they were captives. Homaldo can tell them otherwise."

Windwolf's probing look sent a shiver through her. "They have my people. Tell me, Keresa: Why would Karigi be herding still more captives north? Why do they need more women and children?"

Kakala exhaled bitterly. "The captives are to carry the Nightland possessions into the Long Dark."

Windwolf narrowed his eyes. "But I thought the reason you killed so many of us, destroyed our happiness, was to ensure that no Sunpath People followed you through the ice."

Keresa saw Kakala nod slowly. Then he walked over and seated himself across the fire from them. "It is Nashat's order. Probably without the Guide's knowledge."

Windwolf's look was grim. "The same Nashat who ordered the Nine Pipes women clubbed to death in the pen they were being held in?"

Kakala rubbed his face. "How did you hear about that?"

"Skimmer and her daughter, Ashes, escaped. They hid under the dead. Nashat ordered the attack in the middle of the night. Just before dawn, Skimmer and her daughter slipped away."

Keresa felt her heart sink. She glanced at Kakala. "And you wonder why I am not going with our people? They have lied to us from the beginning. We are sick, Kakala. Sick in our souls."

"They are our people, Keresa."

"The same ones who put you into the cage! And for what? Following Nashat's orders to attack Headswift Village with a force we both knew was too small for the task?"

"We have *had* this discussion before."

"And we're going to have it again," she insisted. "We have obeyed, followed their orders, and they put you in the cage for it But for the Guide and me, you'd still be there!"

Kakala's expression had grayed. "Don't *remind* me!"

Keresa glanced apologetically at Windwolf. "Forgive us."

"You sound like a married couple."

Kakala shot him a warning look. "You're the one who wants to marry her. I'd never have let myself in for that kind of irritation."

Keresa shot him a smile. "Marry? Windwolf might be as disgusted with me in next moon as you've been for summers."

Windwolf's amused smile died. "I still have to save as many of my people as I can." He looked at Kakala. "Unless you have some objection to that?"

'If my warriors can go free, and you can find a way of doing this without killing my people, I have no objection." Kakala frowned. "If the Long Dark is such a paradise, why do we need to take so many things with us?"

"The journey is supposed to be long," Keresa answered. "The captives carry the extra food."

"And what do they eat?" Windwolf asked. "Each other?"

Keresa met Kakala's suddenly dull eyes. "Nashat wouldn't care about feeding slaves. That's why he had the Nine Pipes women murdered."

Kakala propped his chin on his knee. He glanced curiously at Windwolf. "You sent your warriors to the Tills?"

"It kept them alive. And, with party after party of refugees, they're so busy hunting and getting people settled that they don't have time to come back and get themselves killed over misguided heroics."

"So, it's just us?" Keresa asked.

"Just me," he amended.

"I'm with you," she insisted. "I helped put a lot of those women in there."

Kakala gave a harsh laugh. "Windwolf, you've been so lucky you've come to believe you can't die. Well, you can. I could have killed you when you walked through that opening. You're tired, making mistakes. And one man isn't going to free tens of tens of captives. Not from under Karigi's very nose."

Windwolf's eyes hardened. "Karigi? It's even more tempting. I have an old score to settle with him."

"We both do," Kakala insisted. Then he threw his arms up. "*What* am I doing?" He gave Keresa a pleading look. "He's a madman!" Then, "Windwolf, you can't help them by dying!"

She watched Windwolf and Kakala lock gazes.

Then Windwolf said in a soft voice, "They're my people, Kakala. If they were yours, what would you do?"

Kakala's mouth opened, then slowly closed. He shrugged in weary defeat.

Keresa said, "Kakala, after all the planning we've done, and the raids we've pulled off, this shouldn't be that difficult."

He climbed stiffly to his feet. "I don't know. My head has been aching since I banged it on that rock." He looked at Windwolf. "I'm going back to my warriors. Do I need a guard?"

"It would be a good idea. First, it would stop you from entertaining any foolish ideas. Second, it would keep some angry Sunpath or Lame Bull widow from taking out her wrath on you."

Keresa sighed, pulled her hand from Windwolf's, and stopped when Kakala smiled. "Stay, Keresa. Maybe you can talk some sense into him."

Windwolf smiled at her. "I'll escort him myself."

"No guard at the door?" Kakala asked.

"Why would I need one?" Windwolf replied. "I assume Keresa still has that stiletto tucked in her moccasin."

Chapter Thirty-Three

The pain is almost over. Skimmer ran the words through her soul as she stared at the forbidding blackness of Ti-Bish's chamber. She could feel his warm body pressed against hers where they lay together under the hides.

Upon their return from the long trek to the hole in the ice, the fire had been burned out. Ti-Bish had been concerned that no wood had been carried in, and he refused to discuss what had happened to his slave girl, Pipe.

Skimmer, still wet from the wave that had washed up her legs after the quake, had been shivering, exhausted, and heedless of anything but getting warm. Ti-Bish, too, had been nearly blue from cold. She had removed her moccasins and damp dress to climb under the hides.

Unable to bear his shivering, she had looked across the room where he'd sat back against the wall. In the flickering light of the little lamp, he'd looked pathetic as he huddled and shivered.

On impulse, she'd invited him to share the hides.

The pain is almost over.

But what had it been for? She stared out at the darkness, sensing a presence in the very air. The little lamp had long ago burned out. Did something hover in the room?

She almost turned over to wake Ti-Bish, then felt a movement in the air, as if a great wing had spread over her. The sensation was oddly reassuring, as if a covering against her thoughts.

I am alive when so many are dead.

She closed her eyes, remembering with clarity the attack on Nine Pipes Village, the shock of her captivity and the long journey north. She relived each instant of the horror of the pen, right down to the snapping of skulls as Karigi's warriors waded into the captives. Again, she smelled the cloying odor of death.

So I came here to kill, and found a humble and honest man who Dreams of peace.

The Song of the Ice Giants changed harmonics, little creaks and groans of the ice adding to the effect. Why did she feel so at peace?

"Ti-Bish loves you with all of his lonely heart."

Did she hear, or just imagine the soft voice in the darkness?

"Loves me?" she asked under her breath.

She thought back to Hookmaker, and what they'd shared.

"You live," the faint whisper from the darkness assured. *"Take the moment."*

She closed her eyes, trading one darkness for another. She was aware of the beating of her heart, the blood in her veins. She reveled in the air filling her lungs. She could sense Ti-Bish, feel his warmth and life, where it pressed against her.

Alive.

At that moment, Ti-Bish rolled over to mold his body against hers. A delighted sigh escaped his throat as he slid his arm over the curve of her waist.

She should have stiffened, repulsed by his body against hers. Instead, the disarming memory of his worshiping eyes lingered within her. She could recall each of his gentle movements, the joy that filled his face when he looked out at the marvels of his world.

She had never known a soul as pure as his. That left her oddly disturbed, but with a curious warmth down in her core.

How odd that she'd instinctively placed herself between Ti-Bish and Nashat, understanding the role that Power had cast for her.

Her eyes opened as she felt his penis harden against her buttocks, and from the purling of his warm breath on her neck, knew that he still slept.

How long did she lie there, aware of his hard shaft? Considering its implications?

She had come expecting this, believing it was part of the ruse to gain his trust.

And now?

Without thought she rolled onto her back and wrapped her hand around his stiff manhood.

He started, coming awake.

"What...?" The words froze in his throat.

"Don't speak," she told him softly, and tightened her hold.

She heard him swallow. With her other hand, she took his, laying it on the swell of her breast. He moved awkwardly as he explored her, the touch reverent and gentle. Then, hesitantly, he settled onto her body. As he slid into her ready sheath he took a deep breath, whispering, "I love you."

"I know."

Keresa blinked awake, aware of the dull gray light that filtered in around the door hanging. She lay for the moment, deeply content with the warmth from Windwolf's body. She could hear his deep breathing, feel his back pressed against hers.

If only we could stay like this forever.

What a joyous miracle that would be.

She replayed their coupling during the night, relishing the memory of their bodies moving in unison. She had tried to pull the whole of him inside, as if to press his body right through bone and muscle. If only she could keep him there, inside her, somewhere close to her heart.

Turning over, she pressed herself against his back, slipping her knees behind his and hugging him tightly.

"Morning?" he asked gently.

"It is."

He groaned. "Got to get up."

"Can't we take time?"

"The Lame Bull are packing."

"They don't need you to put blankets in packs. I'm sure they can do that on their own." She hesitated. "This might be our last chance."

Her inquisitive fingers snaked down past his navel

to find him. She had greater powers of persuasion than logic.

When they finally lay spent, the glow fading from their loins, he propped himself up to stare down at her. "If anything should happen, if we are separated, I'll wait for you at the Tills." He arched an eyebrow, "But I wouldn't travel there dressed in a Nightland war shirt."

She laughed. "Come, let's get on with the day."

"War Chief ?" a voice called from outside.

"Silvertip?" Windwolf asked. "A moment please, and then I will be out."

"I need to see you both," the boy said. "Call me when you are ready."

"How long has he been out there?" Keresa whispered. "He would have heard everything."

"I don't think he heard anything he didn't already know," Windwolf muttered, reaching for his war shirt.

Keresa pulled on her dress, running fingers through her hair. What she'd give for a proper washing. The miracle was that Windwolf didn't hold his nose when he was coupling with her.

"Enter, Dreamer," Windwolf called.

Ashes ducked beneath the hanging, her careful eyes taking in the room's contents. The war club filled her hands.

Silvertip followed, his face expressionless, but when Keresa looked into his eyes, it was like staring into deep pools, knowing that the bottom might be an illusion.

"Dreamer," Windwolf greeted. "Can I help you?"

Silvertip walked over and settled by the cold fire. "I am leading my people west, War Chief. Some insist on staying, though I have told them the price they will pay."

"People must make their own choices, Dreamer."

He smiled. "That they must." His young face lined. "Wind, Water, and Fire. It is a Powerful combination. Opposites crossed." He stared right at Keresa, and her soul shivered. "When you are in the north, you will find the Earth."

"The Earth?" Windwolf and Keresa asked in unison.

Silvertip smiled. "Power comes in fours: the directions, the great forces, the seasons, it is all part of the unity."

"Some say six, Dreamer," Keresa replied. "The four directions, and up and down."

"Or light and dark," Silvertip agreed. "Darkness and light. I am one; the Guide is the other. Do you begin to understand?"

Keresa frowned. "He is Raven Hunter's. You serve Wolf Dreamer."

"I walk in the light," Silvertip told her, a question in the set of his lips.

"...And he walks in darkness."

"Opposites crossed. We all serve Power."

Windwolf nodded, as if some great revelation had been born in his soul. "What is my role, Dreamer?"

"To serve Power, War Chief." Silvertip leaned his head back. "In the end, our peoples will have paid the cost of disharmony, as Wolf Dreamer and Raven Hunter are paying."

"I don't understand." Keresa frowned. "How do Spirits pay?"

"By finally understanding that neither can win." He smiled. "Opposites cannot exist without the other. Can men exist without women? The very existence of light can never be pure by itself. Look beneath the rock,

263

Deputy, and you will find shadow. Revel in the blackness of midnight, but it will yield to morning."

"And Wolf Dreamer and Raven Hunter are bound by this?" She gave him an uneasy look.

"Oh, yes. Though it has taken time for them to realize that while they must, by their very nature, oppose one another, they are brothers, born of the same womb. Is it possible, Deputy, to receive without something being given?"

Windwolf took her hand, giving it a press. "We understand, Dreamer."

"Good. The lesson is surprisingly simple, but infinitely difficult at the same time." Silvertip pressed his palms together.

"Isn't that always the way of it?"

"The final pieces are in place," Silvertip told him. "Opposites crossed. When you find the Earth, you must head south. The west will be impassable. I would urge you to make all haste. You will not have time to tarry. Once across the river, you will have to follow the southern margins of the lakes to the Tills."

"I see," Windwolf replied.

"What of my people, Dreamer?" Keresa asked. "We have heard that the Guide has found the way to the Long Dark."

He smiled at her, eyes seeing somewhere in the distance of his Dream. "The Sunpath People ignored Raven Hunter and cast his teachings from their souls. They have paid dearly for that."

"But my people have turned their backs on Wolf Dreamer!"

"And now, the balance must be restored," Silvertip said sadly. "Deputy, remember, there is no life without death. Sometimes, terrible steps must be taken to restore the harmony."

Keresa's fumbling thoughts tried to make sense of it The Sunpath and Lame Bull were beaten, leaving. Who could possibly challenge the Nightland now? She was about to ask, but Silvertip had stood, nodding politely at them.

"Dreamer?" Windwolf asked, rising. "Will we see you again?"

He looked back, one hand on the door hanging. "That depends on Wind and Water, Fire and Earth." And then he was gone, Ashes silently following behind.

Chapter Thirty-Four

What have I become? Who have I become?

Skimmer sat in the darkness, her back to the contoured wall of Ti-Bish's chamber. She had placed a folded hide to both cushion and insulate her back from the ice.

She felt Ti-Bish shift, his head cradled on her lap. Her fingers carefully smoothed his hair, running strands of it between them the way she had once done with Ashes.

"Are you still alive, Daughter?" she asked the darkness.

"She is."

Skimmer heard the voice from the Raven Bundle, could feel its pulsing warmth.

"Where is she?"

"Headed west, toward the Tills."

"Why should I believe you?"

"Because I have no reason to lie."

"Oh? You have Ti-Bish believing he can lead the Nightland People up an icy river to find paradise."

"And Wolf Dreamer led your people to believe that through peace, and the search for the One, they, too, could find paradise."

"We were fools."

"That is the lesson you needed to learn."

She heard the shift in his voice, and looking through the darkness, thought a darker shadow moved in the room. She could feel the change in the air on her cheek. "So, what are you going to do? Let all those people climb into that hole, splash around, and wash out as corpses?"

"No. The Dream, my Dream, is about to die. The bargain is struck. Opposites crossed. I have taken from Wolf Dreamer; he has taken from me. I have given him his Dreamer; he has given me mine."

"And what comes next?"

"The struggle begins again. It is the nature of creation."

"Why struggle?"

"Why not just live in the One?"

"Because it becomes stagnation. It leads to weakness and death."

"You begin to understand."

"So all that is left is war and struggle?"

"Until you met Ti-Bish, what did you have?"

"Hatred and rage." She smiled at the darkness. "And I still have it."

"Good." A pause. *"But you now have something to go with it."*

She frowned, and then nodded, aware of the spark deep in her breast "Hope."

"My mistake...I failed to anticipate the Power of it."

"You should have listened to your Prophet. Ti-Bish is full of it"

"Ti-Bish is not my Prophet."

"Spirits take me, if it's Nashat, I'm going to bum your bundle."

"Oh, no." The soft voice sounded amused. *"Nashat cares nothing for Spirit Power. He lives only to serve Nashat."* A pause. *"I sought a Dreamer who believes but has a strength of soul and dedication. Someone who would offer his life and happiness to a cause he believed in. My Dreamer had to understand down to the soul's core why the One, tranquility, and order were flawed, like tool stone riddled with cracks."*

"Have you looked closely at Karigi?"

"Karigi is too much like Nashat."

She saw the darkness shift felt movement in the still air.

"Come. Let me show you something."

"I'll wake Ti-Bish if I get up."

"He sleeps more soundly than he has since he was a child. He loves you with all of his heart."

She carefully lifted his head, slipped to the side, and eased it to the hides. Standing, she followed, oddly aware of his black presence. To her surprise, she could sense the corridor, as though her soul reached out and touched the ice walls, could feel the twists and turns in the passages.

"It's as if I can see in the dark."

"It is my gift"

"Do you give such gifts often?"

"As often as you do" A pause. *" You have given the greatest gift to Ti-Bish. He has loved you for a long time."*

"He once said that lying with me would have dire consequences."

"It was your final decision."

"And that means...what?"

"Pleasure, creation, fertility, love, and sharing. The balance of harmony, peace, and order. To seek the One is to deny the needs of the flesh."

She wound around a sharp twist, the tunnel leading upward. It took all of her concentration to scramble over a fallen boulder.

"I should have felt guilty. My husband isn't that long dead."

"You have survived a lifetime's worth since Hookmaker's death. You have learned a valuable lesson."

"All I have learned is that moments can be precious."

"Come. Climb up here."

She frowned. "That looks steep. What if I fall?"

"You won't. The water has washed just so, leaving stones exposed that will hold your weight."

She watched the dark shadow rise, felt puffs of air, heard the flapping of wings. Then, following her instinct, grasped a protruding stone and levered herself up. How long she climbed was hard to assess, but finally she struggled out, amazed to find herself in a narrow valley between masses of jumbled ice. A trail of gravel, stone, and silt showed where meltwater had run before a crack drained the runoff away.

"That takes you to tundra. Trust me, you need only follow it."

"My way out?" She turned back, seeing a human form, a great black-feathered cape falling down from his shoulders. His face, achingly handsome, seemed to glow with the same radiance as the waters in Ti-Bish's hidden lake. He watched her with knowing dark eyes.

"Raven Hunter?" She placed one hand to her heart,

the other dropping to the bundle tied to her belt. She could hear it Singing, as if with tens of tens of voices.

He extended a dark wing, pointing off to the east. "The crack is opening there. When it goes, it will wash most of the Thunder Sea south. Imagine slapping your hand into a puddle, but on a much grander scale."

She stared off to the east, aware only of jagged spires of the ice rising toward the night sky.

Raven Hunter's other long wing unfolded and extended to the west. "There, a moon's travel to the west, the ice dam has given way. That was the quake you felt in Ti-Bish's chamber. The huge lake it held back is already washing everything before it. When you find the others, you will need to hurry south. Once past Lake River, find high ground. You will be safe."

"But what about the people?" She stared out to the south, seeing the distant high point that marked Headswift Village.

"*Ask Wolf Dreamer. He's the one who is supposed to be merciful.*"

She heard the change in his voice, but when she looked back, it was to see a dark form flapping up into the night sky.

Kakala's entire party of warriors heard the unearthly Singing of the Ice Giants—like tens of voices Singing slightly different notes—long before the trail ran down the rugged tundra to the Thunder Sea. But there was a new sound today, like bones cracking deep inside the Giants. Occasionally, the earth trembled.

Kakala glanced behind him, watching his warriors follow in a winding line.

At least they're alive.

He noticed Goodeagle at the rear and glanced speculatively at Windwolf. The man pointedly ignored his old friend, acted as if he didn't exist And that, Kakala realized, tortured Goodeagle even more than outright looks of disgust would have.

Keresa led them through the maze of boulders that littered the shoreline. To his left, the massive peaks of the Ice Giants rose like gleaming white shark's teeth. Icebergs floated in the deep blue water. He lifted a hand to shield his eyes and, in the far distance, thought he saw bull boats out on the sea, people fishing, or hunting seals.

Keresa had been keeping up a steady pace, just fast enough, but not too fast to drain Kakala's strength—though his head had been pounding nauseatingly all day.

Kakala tried not to glare at Windwolf. The red shirt the man wore irked. He kept wondering which of his dead friends it had belonged to. Somehow, the war club, stiletto, and darts the man carried didn't seem as menacing anymore. Even the warriors accepted the presence of an armed enemy, and one by one, they had been sidling up to Windwolf, making introductions, almost anxious to talk to the legend they had hunted, fought, and hated for so long.

The grudging respect they showed each other came as a revelation.

But for the Elders, and their insistence on war, we would have been friends.

"It's not much farther," Kakala said. "One hand of time, maybe."

"I know." No emotion lay behind Windwolf's replie.

The closer they got to the Nightland Caves, the harder Windwolf's expression became. This afternoon, his square-jawed face might have been carved from wood, and his body a statue set with glittering stone eyes.

The path curved around to the bizarre side of the Thunder Sea, where drifting icebergs had grounded offshore and melted into strange shapes. They resembled a forest of dirty half-human monsters. As Father Sun descended in the west, sunlight reflected from the ice sculptures with a fringe of opalescent fire.

"Let me stop, just for a moment," Kakala said. "I need to drink."

Keresa nodded, panting. "How's your head?"

"Feels like a Sunpath warrior split it in two."

The faintest of smiles flickered and died on Windwolf's lips.

The rest of the warriors dropped into squats, conserving their energy, taking the time to sort through their packs. The pickings in Headswift Village had been lean after the grand exodus.

Kakala dropped to his knees by a large pool of fresh water spawned by the melting icebergs that had come ashore. He dipped up water with his hand. As he drank, he watched Windwolf and Keresa trade desperate glances. Their longing brought a pang to his heart. He remembered sharing the same with Hako, two cages down.

And the way that ended ruined my life.

Kakala wiped his wet hand on his pant leg. "Gather around. We have planning to do."

The old familiarity of his warriors gathering, the looks of anticipation in their eyes, brought a surge to his heart. "All right, my warriors, here's the situation: We must assume that Homaldo found Ewin, since we didn't see his ugly, fat warriors drifting into Headswift Village. That being the case, he is probably off to the west somewhere, running straight home with Homaldo. He may even beat us there, which means the Council will hear directly from him that all went well at Headswift Village."

They grunted assent.

Kakala narrowed an eye at Windwolf. "We owe a debt to Windwolf. He could have killed us. The Lame Bull and the refugees were most anxious to pay us back for our attacks."

Another grunting of assent.

"My warriors do not leave debts unpaid." He walked around, looking them in the eyes, one by one. "Many of you know that I have often disliked the orders we have received. You know that I often warned Sunpath villages to expect people seeking refuge after our attacks."

The grunting was muted this time.

"This is the situation: Nashat is going to try and use Sunpath slaves to carry our possessions through the ice to the Long Dark. He is doing so in violation of the Guide's direction that no Sunpath should follow us, bringing their beliefs about Wolf Dreamer to soil the Long Dark."

He got worried looks in return and nodded. "Yes, you see the problem. We all know that Nashat, for reasons I can only guess at, changes the Guide's orders to suit himself."

Sour chuckles erupted.

"I would cast one stone to knock several birds from the sky at once." He ground his fist into his palm. "So, my warriors, here is what we are going to do. Just at dusk, we will approach the slave compound. As high war chief, I will order the guards to leave, to return to their villages for the purpose of packing their belongings, or, if they've done so, to ensure that their belongings are carried to the Nightland caves in preparation for leaving."

He looked from face to face, emphasizing his words. "When they are safely out of sight, you will simply go home."

They gave him a puzzled look.

"That's right," Kakala said. "Go home." He made a gesture. "It's over. We're finished. Go to your families, pack your things, and join the rest of the people. Say nothing about what we have been through. Say nothing about me, or the deputy. You have done all...no, *more* than your duty to your people. You have earned the right to live the Guide's promise."

"And what of you, War Chief?" Corre asked.

"When I have ensured that Windwolf has his people headed south, I will be along." He smiled. "I, too, will have fulfilled my obligations." He glanced at Windwolf. "All of them."

They nodded. Only Goodeagle looked perplexed. But since traveling with Windwolf, the man had remained unusually quiet. Contemplating his faults, no doubt.

"Any questions?"

Keresa asked, "What if one or more guards refuse to leave?"

Kakala shrugged. "He might be surprised to wake up after taking a short but very unexpected nap. You know, caught by surprise from behind when the Sunpath made their break."

"If that happens, War Chief," Bishka pointed out, "the Elders might put you in a cage with Hawhak."

Kakala shrugged. "I'll take my chances. I owe a debt to Windwolf. I have given him my word that he can take his people home." He searched their eyes. "We all know the fate of those women and girls if they enter the Long Dark. The war is over. We have won. Having fought this from the beginning to the end, I say it is not too much to let them go."

He could see the agreement.

"Very well, warriors, you have your last orders from me. I ask only that Raven Hunter bless you all, and especially those who are not with us today. They will live in our memories forever."

More grunts followed. Kakala gave Windwolf a slight nod, then gestured to Keresa. "Lead the way, Deputy."

Windwolf trotted along behind Kakala, asking, "That's it? Just walk in, tell the guards to leave, and open the gates?"

Kakala said, "What do you expect? I lay awake that last night at Headswift Village, asking, 'What would Windwolf do?'"

Chapter Thirty-Five

S kimmer glanced up at the rounded ceiling of ice over her head. The fact that she could see so well in pitch blackness still amazed her.

Raven Hunter's gift!

She prowled up the winding tunnel, awed by the way it rose and fell, only to twist to the left or right. The place reminded her of the wormholes she had observed in a clod of freshly turned earth.

"And now I am a human worm." Was this how the little beasts felt? Oddly safe and protected? She had never thought of the earth as a thing to live *in*, but something to walk on.

She closed her eyes, letting her soul drift, feeling the cold eternity of the ice, but this, too, was passing. Year by year, it melted, the waters draining away. One needed only walk north from the distant oak and pine forests to see the moraines, kettles, and boulders left behind.

"Where will it end?" she mused. "With all of the world's ice melted?"

She remembered the ever-present winds blowing up from the distant south, warm and balmy, even in winter. The world was changing, warming. The old ways were about to die, and how were people to adapt? Could they become one with the new land, the new plants? And what of the animals, creatures like the mammoth, sloth, and short-faced bear who clung to the spruce barrens?

"We live with death," she murmured. "Everything in its time." But now time was running out.

So, she stood, savoring the darkness, feeling the ice. It moaned and creaked, the wind keening through the tunnels, forever drawing warm air into the depths, only to have it cool, and suck more warm air down into the slowly melting ice.

For that moment, she felt eternal.

A voice broke the peace.

She turned, hearing someone say, "This way, Kishkat...I think."

The faint flicker of a light shone around the tunnel's curve.

Skimmer reached down and slipped the ax from where it rode on her belt beside the Raven Bundle.

"Kishkat?" she called. "Is that you?"

Silence. Then a tentative voice called, "Skimmer?"

"I'm just around the corner."

She squinted at the faint light the warrior held before him. His eyes widened in surprise as he stared at her.

"You have no lamp!" he stated.

She looked past him. "Greetings, Tapa. But what are the two of you doing here?"

Kishka lowered his eyes. "Looking for you."

277

She smiled grimly. "Missed my company?"

Kishkat sighed, and to her surprise, slumped to the floor. "We're supposed to kill you."

"I see."

"Where's your lamp, Skimmer?" Tapa asked.

"I don't need one."

"You don't?" Kishkat wondered; then he stared down at his flickering flame. "This is the last of our fat. When it burns out..." He closed his eyes. "What seems like an eternity ago, when the big quake struck, it blocked the tunnel we were in." A pause. "Tibo was on the other side."

"I just want out," Tapa said fervently. "Nashat can lock me in a cage. Break my back, but I'll be able to see the stars."

"Nashat," Skimmer said softly. "He ordered you to murder me?"

Kishkat nodded. "We found out why. It's because you protected the Guide." He looked up. "But I guess you're as lost as we are."

"Nashat ordered you to kill me..." She stiffened. "Ti-Bish!"

"What?" Kishkat asked.

"Come. We have to hurry."

"Is it on the way out?" Tapa asked anxiously.

"It is. Follow me. As soon as we know the Guide is safe, I'll show you the way out."

She left at a run, chafing at the slow progress they made trying to follow her. They didn't dare let their precious flame blow out in the draft rushing through the tunnel.

With his light flickering before him, Nashat stalked down the tunnel; gleamings of yellow reflected on the ice around him.

He took the familiar turn, watching his footing as he descended a steep slope, then rounded a bend. He paused, listening.

No voices could be heard.

He swallowed hard, hating the fact that he couldn't bring a warrior with him. He'd thought about Karigi, but wasn't sure he could trust the man in the long run. Karigi had an utterly practical streak, one that might be used as leverage against Nashat in the future.

Nashat crept closer, holding his lamp behind him to shield the light, and peeked past the hanging. Ti-Bish sat, back straight, eyes closed. He had a slight smile on his lips and wore a ragged-looking hide shirt.

Nashat could see no one else as he slipped his head back and forth. Relieved, he let the flap fall, calling, "Guide? Are you there?"

"Y-Yes?"

Nashat pulled the hanging back and stepped into the room, satisfied that his first impression was correct. No woman waited to ambush him.

"I'm surprised to find you still alive. I would have thought Skimmer would have murdered you by now."

Ti-Bish stood, then gave a small shrug. "She's off with Raven Hunter."

"Oh, is she?" He fought the urge to smile.

"Are the people ready?"

Nashat paced idly around the room, staring in

disdain at the shabby hides, the piles of clothing. "They have most of their things packed. In fact, that's what I've come to discuss with you."

"We can leave in the morning. Raven Hunter told me the water is coming."

"Water?" Nashat frowned. He had no interest in water.

"We don't have much time to get everyone into the tunnels."

"Yes, well, Ti-Bish, that's the problem."

"H-How?" He swallowed hard. "The Councilors told them, didn't they?"

"Oh, yes. Everyone is excited. Ready to go. Even the Lame Bull People are gone. The Sunpath have fled west to the Tills. All of the south is open. Ewin sent a runner with that information, and Karigi arrived last night with a large contingent of slaves."

Ti-Bish frowned. "Then what is the problem?"

Nashat reached down to his belt, fingering the handle of a stiletto crafted from an elk's brow tine. "The caves. Guide. We don't want to go starve ourselves to death in some hole in the ice that leads to who knows what kind of disaster."

Ti-Bish gave him a look of absolute incomprehension. "But that was Raven Hunter's Vision."

"I'm sure it was." Nashat smiled. "But it is certainly not mine."

Ti-Bish's confusion grew. "But, you heard—"

"I did, and it worked splendidly! We have opened the entire south, driven the Sunpath People out. All of those nice forests are ours for the taking. The people are packed. just ready for their Guide to walk out and give them a new vision."

"I don't...What new vision?"

"The one where you raise your arms and tell them that Raven Hunter has changed his mind. That instead of into the ice, we're headed south, to spread the word of Raven Hunter throughout the great forests of the south."

"That wasn't the Dream."

"Ti-Bish, it doesn't matter. They will believe anything you tell them."

Ti-Bish closed his eyes, shoulders slumping. In a voice little more than a whimper he said, "You have never believed."

"Oh, I believed. I believed in you. Now, come, like a good Guide, and tell the people we are headed south."

Ti-Bish shook his head. "It's too late, Nashat. The water is coming. A fast warrior might make it, but women and children carrying loads, and the elderly and frail, they'll be washed away."

"We can take the high trails," Nashat mused. "It might even make the tale easier to accept."

Ti-Bish opened his mouth, but words seemed trapped behind his tongue.

"It's not so bad," Nashat told him, his finger tapping on the stiletto top. "You will have everything you need. Just do as I say, and you can even keep Skimmer. What do I care who you fill your bed with? As long as she keeps a decent tongue in her mouth and stays out of my way, I won't even insist on taking a turn or two with her myself. You'll have more—"

"No!"

"What did you say?"

"I said no, Nashat. I am going up and telling the

people to pick up their packs and start into the tunnels." Ti-Bish crossed his skinny arms.

"That is your final word?"

"It is. You've worked your poison long enough. You've broken the Dream, muddied the Vision, and I have let you."

"I'd reconsider," Nashat said as Ti-Bish walked past him.

"No. Raven Hunter protects me." Ti-Bish reached for the door hanging as Nashat spun on his heel and drove the sharpened tip into Ti-Bish's back.

Nashat watched Ti-Bish stiffen as he twisted the antler cruelly, pulled it out, and drove it in again. Then he grasped Ti-Bish's collar, thrust the stiletto in a third time, and jerked the man back into the room.

Ti-Bish sprawled on the hides, staring up in pain and disbelief. His mouth hung open in a surprised circle. With one hand, he reached around and felt the crimson rush that poured from the punctures in his back.

"Raven Hunter protects you?" Nashat laughed. "It seems he doesn't do a very good job."

Ti-Bish made a gurgling sound, eyes blinking.

"That punctured your liver, and most likely the bottom of your lung. It won't take long."

"Why?" Ti-Bish croaked.

"Because, with you dead, we have no choice but to head south. No Guide...no way to find the way to the Long Dark." He made a face. "Long Dark? Who'd want to live there?"

"Those who believe," a sober voice said from behind.

Nashat whirled to find Skimmer, breathing hard, standing behind him. He backed up, raising the stiletto.

"This time I'm armed. And, well, your timing is perfect. A Sunpath assassin has taken our Guide from us. All the more reason for the people to joyously head south. It makes reaping the benefit of your old lands even more precious to them."

Skimmer smiled coldly, stepping forward.

Nashat caught the cold glow of her large dark eyes, as if they no longer had pupils, but watched him like some great raven's. "Better that you ran, Skimmer. You'd at least have a chance before we hunt you down."

"There's no running, Nashat."

Even as she spoke, Kishkat and Tapa stumbled in behind her, staring first at him, then at the bloody stiletto he held, and finally at the Guide, flat on his back, blood pooling blackly on the hides.

"Take her," Nashat said. "Drag her out to the people. Let them tear her apart. She's killed the Guide."

Skimmer's smile grew. "It's too late, Nashat. You've uttered your last lie." She cocked her head as a low wailing rose from the ice tunnels. The sound was eerie, keening, one he'd never heard before.

Skimmer fixed him with her liquid-dark eyes. "Hear them? Those are the voices of the Sunpath dead. The Nine Pipes women are screaming for your soul." The smile widened. "And I'm going to give you to them."

He watched her pull an old ax from her belt, raising it. Then, she jerked her head toward the door. "Go on, run. But leave the lamp behind. They're waiting for you. Just out there in the darkness."

Nashat swallowed hard, hearing the eerie wail rise like a thousand screaming voices.

"Kishkat, Tapa, seize her. I'll give you anything you

want. Women? I have them. Would you like to be war chiefs? Elders? I can make it happen."

"Go," Skimmer ordered, her voice little more than a whisper. "Run! They're reaching out, their fingers as cold as the very ice."

"Skimmer?" Kishkat asked, staring in honor at the Guide.

"Let him go." She continued to glare at Nashat. "Death at the hands of the ghosts will be more horrible than anything we could imagine."

Nashat turned, threw down the stiletto, and bolted for the doorway. He shoved past the two warriors, scrambling down the tunnel, slipping, falling, grunting as he ran headlong into the walls.

Then something cold plucked at him from the solid blackness...

Will he make it back to the main caves?" Kishkat asked. He glanced at Tapa, finding his friend wide-eyed, speechless.

"No," she said softly, crouching down beside Ti-Bish. "He only thinks he knows the way." She turned, looking up at Kishkat, her large eyes as black as the caverns themselves. He stepped back. It was as if he'd looked into some night creature's face, something not quite human.

He felt Tapa's reassuring grip on his arm. Then, mustering his courage, he bent down, lifting the Guide, seeing the blood draining from the back of his shirt.

Ti-Bish coughed, frothy red bubbling on his lips. "Too late," the Guide whispered.

"I know," Skimmer told him. "The world is dying. You understand, don't you?"

Ti-Bish jerked a slight nod, crimson leaking past his lips. "Skimmer? Do...do you love me?"

"With all my heart, Ti-Bish."

He smiled slightly; then his voice changed. "Raven Hunter, is that you?" His eyes had widened, sightless. "Thank you, the light was getting to be too much." He coughed, spewing red. Then he whispered, "...Let's fly now..."

Skimmer reached out, running her fingers along his blood-smeared cheek. Then she closed her eyes.

Kishkat watched for a long moment, and then saw her nod. She said, "He's going to the Long Dark. Raven Hunter kept his promise."

Somewhere from down the tunnel, they heard Nashat's terrified scream.

Skimmer turned her strange black eyes on Kishkat, and his blood ran cold. "Nashat has found the dead," she said simply.

Scream after hideous scream echoed from the darkness.

Chapter Thirty-Six

Ashes sat with her war club across her lap. Throughout the long day's walk, she had kept it in hand, swinging it, practicing a leap, skip, strike, and then whirling, preparing to block a blow.

Silvertip had watched her, as if he'd seen it all before. Once she'd raised an eyebrow, asking, "Problem?"

"Nothing that will not fix itself over time."

She had swung the club up onto her shoulder, shooting him a sidelong look. "It's been four days now. Why did you turn us to the south?"

"You will know soon enough."

"I suppose." She matched her pace with his. "I thought I heard Mother's voice last night."

"I'm sure you did," he had said simply.

She had pondered that, wondering what it would be like to know everything, including another person's Dreams. The idea of it was unsettling.

Now, as they sat by the evening fire, Lookingbill snored softly, his mouth open. Dipper placed the last of the wooden bowls in her pack and shot a curious smile at her father, saying, "He's not as young as he used to be. A full day's walk used to be nothing for him."

Silvertip watched the fire crackle and spit, and then looked out toward the north again. He had insisted that they camp on the highest point. Across the moonlit night, the distant waters of Loon Lake could be seen, its surface silver against the black land.

"He will make it, Mother. Most of the danger is past now." Silvertip rubbed his nose, as if it itched.

Dipper glanced at Ashes. "Are you ever going to lay that club down?"

"No," she replied. "They put me in a pen once. They will never do it again."

Silvertip turned his large eyes on hers. "The pens will be gone soon. No others will be built in our lifetimes."

"Idiocy," Dipper murmured, "putting people in pens. We don't even do that to animals."

Ashes felt the sudden tension in Silvertip, watched him rise to his feet, staring out at the darkness. Then he started to walk out past the fire.

"Where are you going?" Dipper called.

"I have to speak with someone."

"You don't go past the line of guards," she insisted.

Ashes walked a step behind, casting suspicious glances around. The Lame Bull camps had been laid out in a large circle, and Silvertip walked past one after another until he reached the outer edge.

People watched them pass, pointing, some whispering, others smiling and waving. Ashes carefully nodded, her gaze roving, searching for danger.

Passing the last camp, she said, "Going beyond the fires could be dangerous."

"No," he answered. "Not tonight." He glanced at her. "If you weren't Raven Hunter's perhaps you could hear him as clearly as I can."

"Hear who?" She shifted her war club, trying to widen her eyes to the dark forest beyond the camp. The way led downhill now, winding around spruce and patches of sumac. Moonlight limned the prickly spruce needles and silvered the sumac, budded now with the first hints of spring.

Ashes gasped, tightening her grip on the club.

A large black wolf stood in a clearing where a great spruce had toppled and now lay rotting into the duff. Even in the moonlight, the animal's eyes seemed to glow an odd yellow, as if lit from within.

"Greetings, Grandfather," Silvertip said respectfully. For a long time, he and the wolf stared at each other, Silvertip whispering under his breath, then pausing, as if receiving an answer.

Finally, Silvertip nodded, saying, "I understand."

Ashes felt rather than heard the rasping of feathers on the cool night air. She looked up, seeing her breath cloud in the moon's white light.

The raven sailed around the clearing, gliding on midnight wings to perch on an old branch that stuck up from the long-fallen tree. The raven—a bird comfortable in the daylight—now peered intently at the wolf, as if distrustful.

Silvertip nodded respectfully to the bird, turned to Ashes, and said, "The Guide is dead."

For a moment, Ashes wanted to leap and scream

out a whoop of victory, but something held her back. "Did Mother kill him?"

Silvertip shook his head. "She would have saved him."

"Why? She hates him. I hate him."

He reached down, fingers tracing the old worn sides of the Wolf Bundle. "She has accepted her destiny. Another part of the balance is restored."

"How?"

"Keresa came to Wolf Dreamer; your mother has gone to Raven Hunter. A trade—opposites crossed. Keresa has turned to peace and light, your mother to chaos and darkness."

"What does that mean?"

"It means that she now carries the Raven Bundle."

Ashes pointed at the raven. "Is that why he is here?"

He nodded. "You are Raven Hunter's. He has sent a Spirit Helper to ensure the balance is kept."

She walked out toward the bird, fully aware of the wolf watching her intently. She lifted the club. "I can take care of myself. But thank you."

Silvertip grinned in the moonlight. "In many ways, yes. But we have a long way to go. Listen to him, Ashes. He was sent for you."

To the north, a low rumble could be heard.

"It comes," Silvertip said. "I would see this."

"What?" she asked.

"The end of the world."

He led the way down a little farther. From a rocky knoll, they could see Loon Lake, glowing silver in the light. It came from the west. The surface seemed to roil, changing slightly in color.

"Can you see the beach down there?"

She followed his finger to the pale strip of sand in the distance.

"Watch it," Silvertip said, seating himself. He seemed oblivious to the wolf and raven, as they perched beside them, and watched as the sandy strand slowly disappeared.

Evening gloom lay on the land as Windwolf followed Keresa toward the compound that held the Sunpath captives. He could just make out dark forms through the gaps in the fence. The enclosure had been constructed of rocks, sections of mammoth rib, and long bones all laced together with roots and strips of old hide. It was the sort of thing the Nightland people cobbled up for caribou drives.

And, like caribou drives, he suspected that the warriors gleefully darted anything that tried to wiggle through the flimsy barrier.

As Kakala trotted toward the fence, he glanced up at the scattered puffs of cloud that blew steadily northward to blot the early-evening stars.

Windwolf could just see Kakala's ironic smile. "Thinking of something, War Chief?"

"Only that you must have your guts tied in knots, Windwolf. One wrong word from me, and you'll be in there with the rest. I'll be a hero. You'll be the captive."

Windwolf's thin smile reeked of danger. "Perhaps you shouldn't have allowed me to keep my weapons."

"A couple of darts won't do you much good."

"Good enough," Windwolf said softly. "You'll be dying at the same time I am."

Kakala chuckled under his breath. "Well then, perhaps we should just do it my way. Unlike Karigi, I keep my word."

When they got to within atlatl range, shouts went up from the compound, and two warriors trotted out toward them.

Kakala said, "It's time to Dance. I hope you brought your sacred mask."

"I'm wearing it," Windwolf muttered.

A skinny bald warrior called, "War Chief Kakala! What are you doing here?" Then he smiled. "It is good to see you here. You wouldn't believe the rumors that have been flying about you."

"Rumors are like songbirds; they sound filling but make a poor feast." Kakala stepped out to meet the men and said, "What is your name, warrior?"

"Jaron." The man bowed, nodded to Keresa, and looked at Windwolf.

Kakala quickly said, "This is...Water."

Jaron bowed slightly. "The Elders said they would send someone to inspect the slaves, but we didn't know it would be you."

He thinks the Elders sent us...

"Thank you, Jaron," Kakala said. "But I come with orders of my own. Have your warriors seen to the packing of their things?"

"Yes, War Chief."

"Then you are to take your warriors, have them return to their camps, and carry all of their belongings to the caves."

Jaron hesitated. "But Karigi said—"

Coldly, Kakala said, "I was unaware that Karigi had been appointed high war chief by the Council."

"He has not, H-High War Chief." Jaron swallowed. "As you order, High War Chief." He glanced past Kakala. "I assume you will take responsibility for the captives?"

Kakala looked back. "Fan out; take the others' places so they can get about their business."

Windwolf watched Kakala's warriors trot out to either side, gesturing the others to head home. He could hear calls of greeting in the night. But then, Kakala's men had always been well trained.

Only after Jaron trotted off after the others did Keresa say, "Well, that went easily."

Windwolf muttered, "I'm not used to things being easy." He glanced around worriedly. "Let's see what we've got."

They walked up to the narrow gate, little more than a couple of worn poles that marked the entrance. Inside he could see people squatting, huddling together for warmth. In the gloom, he couldn't make out faces.

"Are Jaron's warriors far enough away?" Kakala asked.

"I think so." Keresa stared off into the distance. "Bishka, keep a watch for us."

"Yes, Deputy." He trotted off around the curve of the enclosure.

Windwolf laid his darts to the side and began sliding the poles off the rocks on which they'd been braced. To those closest to the opening, he said, "These are your orders. You will walk out with your belongings. You are to head straight south. No one is to speak; no one is to laugh or shout. You must be across Lake River by no later than four days."

"Who are you?" a man asked.

"I am called Water. The Council has decided that they have no need for captives." Then he added, "But that could change at any moment. If you're going, go. Anyone who lingers might be called back."

People rose, filing past him. He watched as they hurried along, slipping out into the night, heading back south.

Windwolf stepped back and turned to Kakala. "Thank you for this, War Chief."

Kakala nodded, an anxious set to his shoulders. "You're not finished yet, Win...Water. They only have a night's head start. Karigi will be after them as soon as he discovers the escape."

"Hopefully, he'll be too anxious to follow the Guide."

"We can hope."

A woman paused. "There are some who cannot walk."

She gestured. "Back there."

"I'll see to them." Windwolf nodded, and watched the trickle of people passing by.

"I'll come, too." Kakala turned. "Keep watch, Keresa."

"Of course. I think our people are fidgeting to get home."

"Dismiss them. Tell them I will speak with them later."

"Yes, War Chief." She turned, trotting away.

Chapter Thirty-Seven

A s he entered the compound Windwolf caught the stench of feces, urine, and human fear. "How did we come to this?"

"Arrogance," Kakala muttered, "and Nashat's poison."

They walked into the enclosure, peering around. A hide-covered hut sat in the back, a low fire burning before it.

Kakala prodded a human form on the ground. "Come on, get up." Then he bent down, fingering the body. "Dead," he said. "A young woman. Club wound to the head."

"Nightland honor?" Windwolf asked.

"Karigi's sort," Kakala replied, failing to take the bait.

Several more dead lay here and there; two of them, Windwolf noted, were children. Kakala said nothing as they passed.

The hide-covered hut was a low-domed thing made of willow stems bent over and tied together.

Windwolf stepped up to the fire. In the feeble light

it cast, he could see three naked women and a little girl. They sat, backs to the wall, hunched over for warmth.

A warrior lay sleeping opposite them, his body covered with a bearhide robe.

The little girl stared up with horrified eyes, and said, "Not again. Please?"

Kakala asked, "Again?"

Not realizing it was a question, the little girl crawled out onto a filthy hide, settled on her back, and spread her thin legs. Windwolf's heart sank as he watched the child, no more than eight summers of age, opening herself to the next man who demanded her.

"By Raven Hunter's filth," Kakala growled. "Put some clothes on, child."

The warrior blinked, sat up, and yawned. As he stretched lazily, the women lowered their heads, doing anything to avoid the man's attention.

"Come for your turn?" the warrior asked muzzily. "I recommend the woman on the right to start with. She's—"

"My turn?" Kakala asked, stepping forward. "How does this work?"

Windwolf cast a sidelong glance at Kakala, surprised by the deadly calm in his voice.

"We each get a couple of hands' time." The warrior rolled his shoulders as he stood up. "Compensation for having to do this stinking duty. Most of us have taken a turn or two already. Sorry for the leftovers."

"And the child?" Windwolf asked in a mild voice.

"She's tight. You'll have to spit on your shaft first." The man was ducking through the low doorway.

Windwolf sensed Kakala's bunching muscles, heard

the whistle and crack as Kakala's war club crushed the back of the man's head.

The warrior dropped with a hollow thud, his limbs twitching. Kakala stood over him, raising the club and bringing it down again and again on the back of the man's head. The body jerked with each sodden impact.

"Worried he might still get up, War Chief?" Windwolf asked dryly as Kakala raised himself for another blow.

"I just can't..." The war club hammered the pulped head again. "...abide..."

Windwolf watched the women flinch at the snapping impact of the club as it continued to hammer at the man's crushed skull. He reached out and laid a restraining hand on Kakala's bulging arm, feeling the rage.

"The captives have been freed," Windwolf told the women. "Find your clothing, or take what you need from here. The robes will be a comfort during the cold. But go now. Stay silent until you are far away. Head south. Follow the others."

The little girl still lay on her back, legs spread, her naked body pathetically vulnerable in the flickering light.

"See to her!" Windwolf ordered. "I am making you responsible! And, by the Spirits, if you fail me..."

"Yes, warrior," one of the women said, and they bundled the little girl up as they stripped the lodge and hurried out into the night.

Kakala sank down beside the fire, his face working. He looked up. "Are you made of wood?"

"It splinters too easily. What do you mean: Am I made of wood?"

"How can you be so calm after seeing this?"

Windwolf sighed. "It is nothing new, Kakala."

"It is among my warriors. A child. *A little child!*"

"Are you telling me you didn't hear the stories?"

Kakala spread his hands, looking at the palms. "Somehow, it was different this time."

"Then perhaps you have finally found your soul. You will have plenty of time to become acquainted with it in the Long Dark."

Kakala smiled bitterly. "The Long Dark? What right do I have to enter paradise?" Then he slapped his knees and rose. "Come. Let's see if there are any others, and then you and Keresa can be on your way."

Passing occasional corpses, Windwolf almost dismissed the huddled forms at the distant end of the enclosure. He walked over, kicking at a foot.

"What?" a man asked, sitting up in the darkness.

"You're leaving, quietly."

"Windwolf ?" the man asked incredulously.

"Quiet. Just get up and walk. Leave and head south. Make no noise. You have to get as far as you can by morning."

"Yes. *Yes!*" The man turned the next figure, trying to rouse the sleeping man. "Wake up! Grandfather, let's go!"

Windwolf pressed on, kicking each corpse, investigating each pile of clothing.

He met Kakala and Keresa at the gate. "I think that's the last of them. Did the women take the girl with them?"

"They did." Kakala was still looking downcast, staring at his hands.

"All of our warriors have gone," Keresa added. "I

don't want to remind you about Silvertip's flood. We don't have much time to get south."

"No," Windwolf agreed. He glanced around, noticing that more clouds had moved in, the darkness increasing. "Kakala, I thank you for this."

"My debt is repaid, Windwolf."

"What debt is that?" a voice asked from the darkness.

Kakala spun. "Blackta?"

Dark shapes formed in the night. Windwolf eased his war club from his belt. How many? Four? Five?

"So, you've captured Windwolf after all?" Blackta walked up, peering in the darkness. "Brought him to the slave compound? Not the Council chambers? Are you insane? He'll give the slaves hope after we've taken so much time to beat it out of them."

Windwolf gripped the handle of his war club, feeling the familiar smooth grain of the wood. He started forward, only to feel Keresa's restraining hand grip his forearm.

Kakala stepped breast to breast with Blackta. "You are dismissed, War Chief. Get away from me before I break your neck!"

Blackta seemed to consider it, then cocked his head. "Quiet in there." He bent, craning, trying to see into the compound.

"Like you said, you beat half the life out of them." Kakala seemed to swell in the night. "You make me sick."

"Oh, do I?" Blackta chuckled. "You've been in the cages how many times? Twice?" He turned, "Tanga, see to the slaves. Make sure they're not up to mischief."

Kakala barked, "Tanga! You, and the war chief will

return immediately to your camps. As high war chief, I order it."

"No," Blackta said crisply. "Check, Tanga. Now."

"You would disobey me?" Kakala demanded.

Tanga stepped to the side, lifting himself above the wall to say, "I think it's empty!"

Blackta's movement was a blur in the night. Kakala snapped back from the impact as Blackta drove a fist into his jaw. Then the man was on him, kicking, beating.

Windwolf whipped his war club up, pivoted, and caught the surprised Tanga on the side of the head, knocking the man back. From the feel of the blow, he could tell it hadn't connected well, but might be enough to stun.

Blackta's warriors waded in, each clawing for his war club. Keresa had rushed forward, trading blows with a barely seen assailant.

To fight in such a way was madness, slashing at dark forms, trying to dodge and weave flailing clubs.

Keresa! Spirits, where is Keresa?

Windwolf ducked a hissing war club that would have missed him by a hand's width anyway.

"Now, Kakala," Blackta grunted. "I've waited too long for this."

Windwolf ducked down, peering, seeing Blackta hunched atop Kakala's prostrate body.

He's only half-recovered from the blow at Headswift Village.

Blackta was choking the life out of him.

Windwolf leapt, slamming his body into Blackta's. A hot rage burst through him, remembering Bramble's naked body: the dart jutting from her chest; the bite marks on her skin; the stains between her thighs...and a little eight-summers-old girl lying spread-eagled with tears running down her face.

Windwolf bellowed, raising his war club, smashing it down on the scrambling man beneath him. Time slowed as Windwolf methodically worked his club, hammering away, feeling each satisfying impact as stone crushed flesh, bone, and skin.

He reveled in the droplets of gore spattering his hands and face, and battered away, revisiting each burned camp, each haunted expression. The smell of smoke from burning lodges stung his nose. The shrieks of the dying sounded over and over as he pounded his rage into Blackta's body.

"Windwolf?" a voice asked. *"Windwolf?"*

He turned, ready to lash out, as a hand landed on his shoulder, and pulled him back.

"Windwolf!"

"What?" he gasped.

Kakala, voice hoarse, rasped, "Worried that he might get up again, War Chief?"

Windwolf nodded, panting, staring around at the darkness. "Keresa?"

"Here." He heard her voice. "The rest have fled."

"Not all of us." Tanga's voice came from the dark gap of the gate. "The first man who moves, dies. I swear, I'll drive a dart right through him."

"Put your weapons down, Tanga," Kakala ordered. "It's over."

"Oh, no. The pen's empty. The slaves are gone. So help me, Kakala, you're going to rot your life out in the cages. But first, Windwolf, stand up. Stand where I can see you."

"Why?" he asked, wondering how much cover Blackta's body would give him.

"Because I'm killing you. Now. Tonight. Your head is my trophy to carry into the Long Dark."

Keresa's calm voice said from the side, "If you hurt him, Tanga, I'll hand you your balls."

"You?" he asked. "Side with Windwolf ?" He chuckled. "Oh, Nashat has waited for years to have you for his own. And you, you cold-blooded camp bitch, will be my gift to him...But then, sharing Nashat's bed is better than dying in the cages."

Windwolf caught the faintest movement in the darkness behind Tanga. Then the warrior stiffened and jerked, taking a half stumble. Tanga glanced down, atlatl and darts clattering to the ground. He weaved, coughed. His knees gone weak, Tanga pitched sideways to the ground, kicking, gasping as he fingered a dart point that protruded from his chest.

A dark form rose behind him, saying, "War Chief Windwolf ? I think that's the last one."

"Who are you?" Windwolf stood slowly.

"Sacred Feathers, War Chief." The man stepped over Tanga's body, staring down in the darkness. "I found one of your darts by the gate. Grandfather Drummer is dead " He straightened. "He was right all along." He took a deep breath. "My daughter, Elk Leaf...she was in the warriors' tent...They..." His voice broke.

"I know," Windwolf said. "The other women have already taken her. She's headed south."

"Which is where we need to go," Kakala said, rising stiffly.

W. Michael Gear & Kathleen O'Neal Gear

A man screamed in the darkness. Windwolf turned on his heel, lifting his war club.

"It's all right, War Chief," a low voice called. "It's Kishkat and Tapa. I hope we didn't get here too late. But there were two warriors out here that were going to stick you like fish as soon as they had a shot."

"A third one ran," a second voice called. Forms emerged from the darkness. Windwolf could make out three of them.

Keresa said, "Come on, Windwolf, let's get out of here before Nashat sends the whole Nightland world down on us."

A familiar woman's voice said, "Nashat is no longer a concern."

Windwolf cocked his head. "Skimmer? I thought you were dead."

"Oh yes, War Chief. Skimmer died long ago. But we have no time for talk. This world is about to be washed away."

"What about the Guide?" Windwolf asked anxiously.

"Dead," Skimmer told him, "by Nashat's hand."

"Blessed be the name of Wolf Dreamer," Windwolf said softly.

"May he be cursed," Skimmer spat. "But you and I can argue the Spirits later. That third warrior will make fast time back to the Nightland Caves."

"It's dark as pitch," Keresa murmured. "We're not going to make much distance getting away from here."

"I can see fine, Deputy," Skimmer told her. "Just follow my instructions." Then the woman turned, stepping off into the darkness.

"Skimmer?" Kakala asked.

"Call her the Earth," Keresa replied.

Chapter Thirty-Eight

awn grayed the skies as Keresa climbed through boulders atop a pile of glacial rubble and looked back. In the faint gray light she could see the Ice Giants rising against the glow. Their sharp peaks seemed to saw at the sky.

On the trail below her a line of women and children, all looking haggard, walked wearily toward the south.

Windwolf climbed up beside her, breathing deeply. He'd spent most of the night encouraging, cajoling, and keeping the freed captives moving. The rest of the time he had devoted to Kakala, who had had trouble of his own keeping up.

"Everyone keeps hitting me in the head," Kakala had muttered once when his balance had deserted him, and he'd had to lean on Windwolf's arm.

"It's because it's such a tempting target," Windwolf had replied.

"Why?" Kakala had been foolish enough to ask.

"Because anything that ugly just begs to be hit."

Kishkat had laughed, and then made himself scarce when Kakala turned his hard glare that way.

Keresa glanced at Windwolf, aware that the war chief was staring back the way they'd come, judging the progress they had been making. "What are you thinking?"

"That one of Blackta's warriors got away."

Keresa pinched her lower lip and nodded. "When Karigi hears, he'll be after us."

Windwolf reached down and helped Kakala up the rough boulders to the high spot. The war chief looked gray, his scarred face set against an inner pain that came from more than just a bump to the head.

"Karigi's not going to give up." Kakala looked down at the ragged band of refugees.

"No," Windwolf agreed, eyes on the north. "He's already collecting warriors."

"And how do you know that?" Kakala asked, staring down where Skimmer made her way toward them.

"I've got that same old feeling I used to have when you were chasing me."

Keresa turned thoughtful eyes on Skimmer. The woman was climbing up the trail below them. "Do you really think Nashat's dead, like she claims?"

Kakala shrugged. "That's what Kiskhat and Tapa say. I got the whole story from them last night. Nashat killed the Guide with an antler stiletto. They say they saw it."

"And Nashat?" Windwolf asked.

"That's the curious part. Kishkat and Tapa swear the ghosts of the dead got him. Both of them were shivering when they told the story. They said his screams were awful to hear."

Windwolf exhaled slowly. "Power's loose on the land."

Skimmer stopped on the rocks just below them. "Looking for Karigi?"

"No sign of him yet," Keresa told her.

"Soon, Deputy." Skimmer braced her feet. "Very soon. In the meantime, we must break up this party. Have them scatter."

"And why is that?" Windwolf asked.

She stared up with oddly large eyes that seemed to suck at Keresa's soul. Keresa felt a shiver go down her spine. Windwolf, too, took a sudden breath. Kakala, however, remained undisturbed.

In an eerie voice, Skimmer replied, "You know the answer to that, War Chief."

Keresa glanced at Windwolf, seeing his expression tighten.

Windwolf gave the slightest of nods. "I will send the order."

Kakala was already climbing down. Keresa took a final look down the backtrail, seeing only a couple of their stragglers limping along behind.

"What did she mean?" Keresa asked.

"There will be fewer to kill when Karigi finally catches up with us." Windwolf made a face as the wind buffeted their high rocky point.

Windwolf watched as his little band of people splintered into small groups, each winding its way through the torturous tundra with its piles of rock, holes, and boulders.

Satisfied, he trotted along the trail to where Keresa, Kakala, and his two warriors waited with Skimmer. They crouched in the lee of a boulder pile, out of the worst of the wind.

"That's it," Windwolf told them as he approached. "Karigi should find the trail confusing from here on out."

"Then we should go," Keresa added. "Silvertip was specific about crossing Lake River by the fourth day."

"Silvertip," Skimmer mused, a hardness in her expression, "Wolf Dreamer's tool." Then she sighed. "But he sees clearly. We're in a race with the end of the world."

Kakala ordered, "Kishkat, Tapa, take scouting positions. Ewin might still be out here someplace. We don't want to run right down his throat and have to make uncomfortable conversation with the man."

Windwolf gestured for the others to take the trail ahead of him and then matched his pace to Skimmer's. They hadn't made two tens of paces before she asked, "Questions, War Chief?" and turned her eerie eyes on him. The effect was like cold water dribbling on his soul.

"You haven't asked about Ashes," he said.

She smiled slightly, not even breaking her confident stride. "She is fine."

"You know this for a fact?"

"Raven Hunter told me. Though I am a little disappointed about her attachment to this Silvertip."

"I thought you no longer believed."

An ironic smile bent her lips, and the too-large eyes narrowed. "Let us just say that I serve a different Power now."

The hair at the back of Windwolf's neck prickled.

He glanced down at the leather-covered bundle at her waist. The premonition of danger worsened. "I didn't think you had it in you to kill the Prophet."

"He was innocent," she said simply.

"What about the lives you could have saved?"

"Do you question the thunder, War Chief?"

"Of course not."

"Then do not question the ways of Power."

He gave her a thin stare. "But I do question, especially when it involves the lives of my people."

"Then you have your answer, War Chief." She laughed, the sound like something echoing from a deep cavern. "Perhaps, in a way, I did kill Ti-Bish. But it's a complicated give-and-take— something in the very balance of the Spiral itself."

He shot a sidelong glance at her, aware of her finely formed face, the skin smooth, her lips full and sensual. Rich black hair hung in long and glossy luster. She walked with a light grace that swung her hips, and the cloak she wore couldn't hide the swell of her high breasts.

Was she this beautiful last time I saw her?

He remembered her as an attractive woman, but this magnetic allure puzzled him.

"Yes, War Chief ?" she asked, shooting him a knowing glance. Her dark eyes seemed to swell, as if drawing on his very soul.

"Nothing."

"Good. You would hate yourself if your thoughts strayed too far from Keresa."

He frowned. "I don't know you anymore."

"You *never* knew me, War Chief." Then she relented. "I shouldn't be so harsh. You don't know

Raven Hunter's Dream; none of us did. Not even poor Ti-Bish."

"And just what is Raven Hunter's Dream? Death and war?"

She smiled slightly, as if in the presence of a naive boy. "It's life, War Chief. All of it right down to the last spurt of blood in your veins. It's seizing life and savoring it, milking it of every last drop of bliss." She lifted her hand, watching her slim fingers curl into a fist. "The goal is to struggle and win, and enjoy the fight with every step you take. In the process, we are to love and hate with all of our hearts. Don't you understand? Life is creation, fertility, change, and curiosity. I didn't begin to understand until I was locked away in the bowels of the Ice Giants." She shook her head. "Only then did the terror I'd survived make sense."

"That's what the Nightland Prophet taught you?" He asked skeptically.

"Ti-Bish wasn't a Prophet, Windwolf. He was a Dreamer with only half the Dream. No, he taught me just how deeply rooted love was in the soul. My days with Hookmaker were passionate, and I did love him. But not with the complete dedication of being that Ti-Bish loved. It was elemental to him, as much a part of who he was as the beating of his heart. He gave all of himself in the attempt to save our world, right down to his last dying breath."

"But he couldn't?" Windwolf guessed.

A wistful smile died on her lips. "Ti-Bish lacked the courage. He was only the final step along the trail to save Raven Hunter's Dream."

"And what is that final step?" he asked, unsure if he

wanted to hear the answer. "This terrible flood that's supposed to roar down on us?"

"I am," she replied simply, and lightly stroked the leather bundle at her hip. "All of the death, suffering, and anguish—everything hinged on getting me to the ice caves. The terrible things we lived were the means to prepare our world for the end." She gave him a half-lidded look that pierced his soul like a sliver of ice. "Did you really think it was happenstance that brought you to Kakala's camp that night you discovered me in the rocks?"

Windwolf chuckled. "You're saying *you* are Raven Hunter's Dreamer?"

"Power is swelling on the wind, War Chief." She raised her right hand high, clutching it into a fist. "Those with Power can call it at will."

Windwolf heard the rasping of wings on air and ducked instinctively as a great black raven hissed through the space where his head had been. The big bird backed air, and settled on her raised fist to stare at him with a gleaming black eye.

"Blessed Spirits!" Windwolf cried, recovering. He glanced up at the bird that rode so easily on her hand.

"Welcome to the end of our world," Skimmer told him, her eyes on the glistening black raven that clung to her hand. The bird threw its head back; the hoarse cawing seemed to shake the world.

Chapter Thirty-Nine

Karigi trotted at the head of his warriors. Looking behind, he could see four tens of his trusted men. At the distance-eating dog trot at which they traveled, they could go all day. Each man carried a handful of long darts in his left hand, his atlatl, war club, and a pack tied to his back.

They had passed several women already. Wounded or dying, they had fallen back, finally succumbing to fatigue. From them, Karigi knew that the others weren't all that far ahead.

"Look, War Chief," Terengi called from behind.

Karigi glanced back and followed his deputy's pointing finger to where a great dire wolf watched them from on high.

"He won't bother us." Karigi chuckled. "If anything, he ought to be grateful. That last woman we killed will fill his gut for a week."

Karigi ignored the animal, concentrating on the rough trail. Here and there, where the silt had blown in, he could see tracks. A lot of moccasined feet had passed this way.

Kakala! You always had a ridiculous soft spot in your soul. I should have known you'd turn against us.

Blackta's warrior's report had been succinct: High War Chief Kakala had helped to release the captives.

My captives!

Karigi reached up to run his hand along his jaw, as if he could still feel the blow Kakala had landed there that day in Walking Seal Village.

I'm coming, Kakala. And this time, you'll wish you were only going to be locked in a cage.

The mountains of packs amazed Goodeagle. Some were piled as high as a man's head. Around them, the Nightland people sat, squatted, or lingered around little fires. Children were everywhere, running, playing, calling happily. Among them he could see Sunpath children, many serving as slaves.

So this is the wreckage of my world? This is what I did?

The cramp of grief rose in his belly, swelling the sickness that lurked like a black fog around his heart.

The trail here from Headswift Village had tortured his very soul. For four long days, he'd trotted along at the back of the line, having a full view of Windwolf as he ran side by side with Keresa. At their nightly camps, Windwolf hadn't once looked in Goodeagle's direction.

I am dead to him. He laughed, half-hysterically. *I am dead to myself.*

Every now and then he'd nod to a warrior he knew.

Most nodded back, old enmities forgotten in the excitement of the migration into the Long Dark.

He recognized Washani where he stood talking to Klah and Degan. He hesitated, unsure of his welcome, and walked over.

Washani gave him a slight nod, expression tightening.

"Have you heard the rumors?" Goodeagle asked.

"That Karigi is after Kakala and the escaped Sunpath captives?" Degan asked in a low voice.

"The same." Goodeagle glanced around. "People are wondering about it."

"Do you think one of us has talked?" Klah asked.

Off to the side, by a huge pile of hides, an old man cried, "How long are we going to have to wait? It's been days!"

Grumblings of discontent followed as the closest camps picked it up.

"People are getting angry," Degan noted.

"There's been no word from the Council," Washani remarked. "It's unlike Nashat to be missing for so long."

"Word is that Councilor Khepa sent a group of warriors into the caves, searching for the Guide." Klah glanced around uneasily. "Something's wrong."

Washani nodded. "I know." He rubbed his jaw, eyes on the piles of loot and the uneasy people who stood by them. "Tensions are rising."

Degan crossed his arms. "My family wanted to bring a mountain of things. I told them no. It didn't make my wife happy."

Klah shuffled his feet uneasily. "Since I have been home, it is as if I were a stranger to my family. They have changed, grown fat and lazy."

Goodeagle looked around. "Who's going to carry all this?"

Washani smiled uneasily. "With the Sunpath captives gone, I'd say most of it is going to be left behind."

Klah's expression soured. "Think of how many good friends died to obtain this. And now it's going to be wasted?" He shook his head. "On the war trail I longed to be home. Now, home, I long for the war trail." He lifted a skeptical brow. "Even seeing stinking Goodeagle is a relief."

Goodeagle gave him a weak smile. "Well, I won't bother you with my stink."

He turned, walking toward the great cave. The way threaded through packed people. The odor of their sweat, the smell of urine, and piles of feces almost gagged him. He could see the stewing resentment on the Nightland faces.

"When is the Guide going to *call* us!" kept echoing in his ears.

He wound through the mass, doing his best to ignore the swell of humanity. He raised his eyes, looking up at the thin arch of ice overhead. He could see boulders up there, frozen in place, but ready to fall.

What kinds of lunatics live in a place like this?

It made his skin crawl, and he had a sudden longing to be outside, in the air, where the world was still fresh.

Instead he forced himself through the crowd to where Bishka stood beside Rana, a war club in his hand. The warriors were glaring out at the crowd, who glared back at them.

"Good day," Goodeagle greeted.

"Is it?" Bishka asked. "I've been on my feet keeping

the people back since before dawn." He shot Goodeagle a hard look. "Is it true that Karigi's chasing down Kakala?"

"It is."

Bishka glanced at Rana. "We should be out there, protecting our war chief."

Rana muttered, nodding in agreement.

"What of your duty to the people?"

Bishka gave him a dark shrug. "The people? These same ones who are cursing us because we won't let them go search out the Guide?"

Rana growled. "We've been out dying for them for moons. Now they would as soon split our heads as look at us."

Goodeagle looked back at the crowd. The gazes were hostile, but none of the fishermen, hunters, and women had quite mustered the courage to press the warriors.

"Where's Nashat?"

"No one knows," Bishka whispered. "No one has seen him for three days."

Goodeagle considered leaving but hated to face the mass of humanity again. "I heard warriors are searching the tunnels. I'll go see if I can learn anything, and I'll let you know."

Either the ruse worked, or Bishka could care less anymore. He allowed Goodeagle to pass.

Winding his way along the gravel-packed floor, Goodeagle marveled at the grandeur of the great ice caves. In his warrior's shirt, no one bothered to ask his business.

He saw the woman first, recognizing her as she hurried down the gavel path. His first instinct was to ignore her; then, screwing up his courage, he turned to intercept her.

Blue Wing carried a pack slung over her back, a desperate expression on her face. She kept peering back over her shoulder, as if expecting a shout at any moment.

"Blue Wing," he greeted as he stepped into her way. She glanced up, startled, and he watched her fear turn to loathing.

"Goodeagle." A resignation filled her voice. "My life is truly cursed."

"What's happening back there?" He indicated the deeper caverns.

"Why should I tell you?"

He gave her a ruthless smile, remembering how soft her body had been against his when he'd taken her during the long march north from Nine Pipes territory. "Because I'm ordering you to."

She narrowed her eyes. "I'm Nashat's now."

"And where is he?"

She gave a terse jerk of her head toward the rear. But he saw through her bravado, could sense the panic in her.

"Taking the opportunity to run?" he guessed.

The widening of her eyes betrayed her.

"Come, into this side cavern. Let's you and I talk."

She slumped in defeat, gave a nod, and walked slowly into the side tunnel.

Goodeagle lifted a hide flap, finding a storeroom in the ice, and motioned her in. She entered, staring about in the gloom. The place had been emptied in advance of the great journey to the Long Dark.

"What do you want?" she asked wearily.

"Where is Nashat?"

"I don't know."

"And the Guide?"

"I don't know that, either. But Nashat thinks he's a fool. All of this, it's a great trick. There is no hole in the ice. No paradise in the Long Dark. Nashat told me that much." She lifted her eyes. "If you ask me, Nashat's fled."

He reached up, fingering her long black hair. "Then it was all for nothing?"

She looked up at him with wide dark eyes. "What do I have to do? If I lie with you again, will you let me go?"

A slow smile crossed his lips. That might be just what he needed to restore his wounded soul. "I would like that."

She lowered the pack from her shoulders, unrolled a hide, and spread it on the floor. With a flourish, she pulled her dress over her head, and flipped her long black hair back. She stood before him, letting him admire her perfect body.

Whatever Nashat did to her, this new lack of modesty serves her well.

He undid his weapons belt, letting it clatter to the floor. She sighed, stepped back, and lowered herself to the hide, saying, "Your war shirt, too. Take it off. I'm tired of being chafed."

Goodeagle grinned, pulling his war shirt over his head, feeling the cold air prickle on his skin. He turned, selected a stone, and laid the garment there. When he turned back, Blue Wing was lying, ready for him, an odd gleam in her eyes.

Goodeagle stepped over and lowered himself, the tingle of anticipation already rising in his loins.

It annoyed him that she was dry when he forced himself into her. How long had it been since he'd coupled with a woman who wanted him? What did it say about the quality of the life he'd come to lead?

With that knowledge, the wound in his soul opened. *You are not the only one with a cursed life, Blue Wing.*

She had locked her legs around his hips, her arms clasped at his back. He could feel her fingers, pressing, as if following his ribs.

The moment began to build, the anticipation of release stirring deep in his hips.

She sensed it, tightening herself around him, her arms shifting.

He was lost in the pulsing waves of pleasure. The faint pressure against his skin barely registered...Then a terrible pain lanced deeply into his chest.

In that instant, he stared down into her eyes, feeling the white-hot agony drive into the center of his being.

"I have had the pleasure of your shaft," she hissed, "now you have felt mine!"

He rolled off her, reaching around to finger the handle of a bone stiletto where it protruded from between his ribs just below the shoulder blade.

Numb with pain and shock, he barely registered as she grabbed up her dress and fled past the door hanging.

"By Raven Hunter," he whispered. "No."

He got his fingers around the handle, and with one desperate jerk, pulled it free. His scream echoed in the ice. He stared stupidly at the bloody stiletto, the ground and polished bone so familiar. *Mine!*

His gaze went to the weapons belt; the stiletto's sheath gaped empty.

When did she...?

His war shirt lay folded on the stone. He clamped his eyes shut, remembering how he'd turned his back on her.

He blinked at the pain burning in his center, heart hammering with fear. His chest seemed to scream with searing agony, and an odd tingle began deep in his throat. He stared in disbelief at the bright red blood frothing down his side.

A lung. She punctured a lung.

Goodeagle could hear shouts from beyond his shelter. Had they caught her?

He forced himself to his feet, wincing, hating the fear more than the pain. He staggered past the hanging, wandered down the tunnel, and stopped short, propping himself against the cold ice, heedless of his bare skin.

"Dead!" a warrior called, running toward the front. "The Guide is dead! Murdered!"

More shouts broke out from near the entrance. Goodeagle coughed, feeling warm fluid on his lips.

He forced himself to stagger forward, blinking, feeling as if his soul were already loose in his body.

He slumped to the floor, oddly weak, and watched the milling confusion as Bishka and Rana were overrun by the pressing crowd. In an endless stream, people hurried past, filing into the caverns.

Goodeagle watched them go, coughing blood, gasping for breath. He leaned back against the ice, thankful for the cold on his skin.

No one noticed him, but the Nightland People

continued to pass, shouting in fear and confusion. It all grew faint as Goodeagle began to shiver.

The pool of blood around his buttocks spread, frothy and red, as his life drained away.

"Bramble, Windwolf, I'm so sorry..."

He toppled on his side as the world turned gray.

Chapter Forty

The spruce gave way to willows as Kakala led the way down the sloping bank that led to Lake River. He pushed through the greening stems of willows, aware of the first mosquitoes that hummed up from the damp earth.

Summer would be coming, and with it, a plague of insects. Time was close when he'd need to brew a concoction of spruce, sticky geranium, and nightshade leaves to mix with grease. The concoction worked to keep the worst of the mosquitoes, bots, and black flies at bay.

But that was for another day, assuming they all lived that long. By pushing, they had reached the river, and just in time. He had seen the worry on Windwolf's face as the weaker of the captives that dogged their path dropped behind. Now only three women remained with them. All Windwolf had managed to save.

Kakala stepped out onto the gravel shore. Was it his imagination, or was the river running higher? The normally wide channel should have been covered by interlaced snakes of current. When he had crossed no less than a moon past, there had been six distinct channels. Now there were four.

"I don't know," he muttered as the rest of them stepped out onto the rocky beach beside him. "Water's up. Most of the stones in the ford are covered. Think we ought to make camp and try it in the morning?"

Skimmer fixed him with her oddly luminous eyes. "No. Karigi is right behind us."

Kakala looked back at the willows, able to see the tips of the spruce rising above them. "You're sure?"

"Trust her," Windwolf said, as he wearily stretched his tired muscles. "Only a fool argues with a Dreamer. She may serve Raven Hunter, but he also serves his Dreamer."

"We go," Keresa decided, her attention on the river. "But if Karigi's that close, we should take measures."

"Wade up the current? Hide our trail?" Skimmer asked in a hollow voice. "No time."

Kakala took matters into his own hands, picking his way through the rounded stones to the first channel. He splashed into the water, trying to remember where the shallow places were.

Cold leached through his moccasins, biting his tired feet. He stared at the water, reading the ripples of current, winding his way across the slippery bottom. The amount of silt in the water surprised him; it obscured the bottom, hiding the rocks he hoped to use for purchase.

Behind him, Skimmer, Kakala, Windwolf, and the rest followed behind.

"You know what you're doing?" Windwolf called over the purling water.

"Of course," he lied. "This was my main trail south. I had to cross this every time I made a raid."

But the river hadn't been running this high. He looked nervously upstream. Had a storm passed? But when? And why hadn't he seen the distant clouds?

"The end of the world, War Chief," Skimmer chided, her knowing eyes flashing. "We don't have much time. You had best hurry."

Kakala wadded onward, sloshing through the cold water, wincing as the current tried to pull his feet off the rounded rocks.

He was up to his thighs, fighting for purchase, as he studied the rushing water. What gave the current such added strength?

Slogging into shallows, he reached back, giving Skimmer a hand. Her skin was cool against his; her knowing smile as she met his eyes sent a curious calm through him.

What was it about her? He shook his head, making sure the rest climbed, dripping, onto one of the rocky islands.

Even as he watched, the water seemed to be rising, creeping in around dry stones.

"Come on," he ordered, almost trotting across the dry rock and wading into the next current.

Then he stopped, staring at the rocks. Yes, that black one. A gravel bank lay just to the west of it. He changed his course, splashing along upriver as he hurried.

"Look!" Windwolf shouted, pointing.

A tree came floating down the next channel, branches broken, roots rotating as the great pine rolled along with the river.

"One of those catches us, we're gone," Keresa reminded.

Kakala led them safely to the next narrow strip of dry riverbed. He thought he heard a faint shout over the sound of the river and looked back. The willows they had just left remained empty, almost forlorn in appearance.

Kakala watched as one of the Sunpath women stumbled, went down, and scrambled for shore. She emerged wet to the bone, looking cowed and worried.

The great tree had been beached, water breaking around the roots where it had come to rest against a submerged rock.

"No time to waste," Skimmer cried, wading into the next of the braided channels.

"No!" Kakala barked, pointing. "Over here. It's shallower."

He hurried forward, feeling the cold in his feet. Gods, they were already going numb! That's when he noticed the first piece of ice. He took a second glance, seeing a thin band of gravel in it as it floated past. Glacial ice? Here? This river drained Loon Lake, and he could think of no glacial ice anywhere around the perimeter of Loon Lake.

So where did it come from?

With rising unease, he frowned at the silt-choked water, trying to remember the path he'd used to cross last time. The great rock with the white quartz scar was the key. He lurched to the downstream side, where the current split, following a long flat rock that lay just under a U-shaped ripple.

Then he took a step, lost his footing, and sank. Cold washed around him, numbing, shocking his skin. He floundered around, losing his grip on his darts, letting the current take them. He got his feet under him and pushed off the bottom. Orienting himself, he fought the current and climbed up on a submerged gravel bank.

"I don't know another way!" he cried. "We'll just have to cross it."

He watched Skimmer bravely leap, splash, and barely keep her feet as she fought her way across. Then, one by one, they each made the crossing to the shallows.

"Trouble!" Keresa called as she rose dripping from the water. She pointed back to the bank.

Warriors were emerging from the willows they had just left. Kakala squinted across the distance, recognizing Karigi out in front. The river drowned the man's orders as he gestured his men forward.

"Does he know the ford?" Windwolf asked.

"As well as I do." Kakala turned, trotting into the next channel. He knew this one: Take the route that winds between the two gray boulders. Each had a long gravel bar behind it.

He sloshed through the water, stepped in a hole, and went down again. Fighting for purchase, he struggled as the current whirled him around. Frantic, he braced on a stone, and floundered ahead. Behind him, the others were coming, but one of the women was in trouble. The current was carrying her downstream.

"Leave her!" Skimmer ordered. "There's no time."

Windwolf cried, "But, someone—"

"No!" Skimmer pinned him with hard eyes. "We make it now, or die!"

Kakala forced his way ahead, taking a quick glance over his shoulder. Karigi's men were splashing through the first channel, war darts in their hands.

"Up there!" Skimmer pointed as she hurried beside him. "That high rocky point!"

Kakala nodded, seeing where shale bedrock rose above the bank. A narrow trail led up the side, a place more fitted to deer than humans.

He splashed into the final channel, wading through water up to his chest. Mercifully, the current was slow here, but it kept dragging him downstream, his progress more swimming than anything else. Then, with each sodden step, he rose higher, finally climbing out on the rocks.

Karigi's warriors were crossing the second channel, just out of dart range.

"Hurry!" He pulled Skimmer up, indicating the trail. "Climb! Help the others up."

He pulled Keresa and then Windwolf up the steep bank. Kishkat stopped to help, adding his strength as the floundering women, fear bright in their faces, were pulled from the water and started up the nearly vertical trail.

Windwolf's attention was fixed on the pursuing warriors. "I don't suppose you have any ideas? I lost the last of my darts splashing around in the river."

"We all did," Kakala replied. "Let us hope they lose theirs, too."

Windwolf chuckled grimly, then attacked the steep trail. He made it partway up, moccasins slipping on the mud left by others. Kakala watched him grab a root and muscle himself up.

He barely heard the hissing dart over the growing roar of the river. It missed his shoulder by a finger's width and splintered against the shale.

Kakala scrambled for the now-greasy trail. He leapt,

caught Windwolf's root, and prayed it would take his weight. Spruce root was fibrous stuff, good enough for constructing baskets. This one ripped loose, dropping him a couple of hands' length, then held.

Handhold by handhold, Kakala pulled himself up until Windwolf reached down to jerk him the rest of the way.

Gasping, Kakala flopped onto the moss-covered soil and asked, "Now what?"

He looked back at the river. Four lines of Karigi's warriors were tracing their way across the channels.

Keresa took long enough to ensure that Kakala was safe, then looked around. "We need weapons."

Windwolf nodded. "Did we lose all of our darts?"

"Oh, yes," Kakala told him darkly. "Running isn't going to do us much good, either. Not with that many behind us."

"Sticks, rocks, anything. Find them!" Keresa ordered, staring desperately around the shale formation on which they stood.

"It is time." Skimmer's voice had an eerie certainty that stopped Keresa short.

"'Time?" she asked.

Skimmer unlaced the leather bundle from her belt and walked to the high lip of the shale formation. She raised the bundle high, a soft Song rising from her lips.

Windwolf started forward to pull her back out of sight, but Kakala laid a hand on him, saying, "No, this is Power."

Keresa searched her soul, trying to hear the words

that Skimmer Sang. They seemed oddly familiar, but alien, as if from another language. Then an odd prickling sensation began along Keresa's limbs, as though a warm wind was blowing.

A dart hissed through the air above them and vanished among the spruce branches. Keresa ducked, dropped to her belly, and crawled up to the edge. The river below them was washing over the small beach where they'd just passed.

"I wish she'd get down," Windwolf muttered as he slipped up next to Keresa."

"Can't you feel it?" she asked.

"Feel what?"

"The Power."

"No."

Keresa shook her head. "You belong to Wolf Dreamer."

In the river, Karigi's men were having troubles of their own. As she watched, two of the lead warriors waded into one of the channels, fighting the current, searching for footing. Both went under at the same time, bobbing up to be carried away thrashing and splashing. One managed to pull himself out in waist-deep water; the other continued to flounder about as he was carried farther downstream.

The great pine, Keresa noted, was no longer beached, but had been washed away. Two of the small islands they had crossed were no longer visible. A large chunk of ice came bobbing and spinning down the closest channel.

Skimmer's rich voice called, "Come, Raven Hunter! The time is now!"

Keresa watched in horror as the waters rose,

sweeping more of Karigi's warriors away, whirling them about, whisking them downstream. Others turned back, desperate to return to the far bank. Some even made it.

"Karigi!" Kakala pointed as he came to kneel beside them.

She could see the war chief where he had climbed up onto a great boulder, wet and bedraggled. He kept looking about him in bewilderment as more and more of his warriors lost their footing and were swept away.

Terengi started to crawl up on the rock, only to have Karigi kick him viciously in the face. The man fell back, splashing into the current, and was carried headlong in the rush of the murky waters.

"Wolf Dreamer's flood," Windwolf said in awe. "These bits of floating ice are from the broken ice dam far to the west."

"Here? It's come this far?" Keresa shook her head.

Skimmer bent her head back, shouting to the sky, "Call the thunder, Raven Hunter!"

The quake was unlike anything Keresa had ever felt. A great jolt shook the earth, pitching her body up from the ground.

Her reeling senses recorded a confusion of sights and sounds: the water in the river leaping, vibrating, and rising in spikes of spray; Karigi toppling from his boulder as it rose and fell; trees swaying; and odd spurts of dirt, duff, and twigs rising from the very earth.

Somehow she managed to grasp Windwolf s hand as they bounced like cones on the pitching shale.

Somewhere through the roar, she swore she heard a great mammoth trumpeting in fear.

Chapter Forty-One

Blue Wing gasped for breath as she climbed to the high point and looked back. She could barely see the Nightland camps where they tucked up under the jagged wall of the Ice Giants. From this distance, the great cavern was little more than a dark spot in the grimy ice.

I am free.

She walked up to one of the erratic boulders that littered the high ridge and leaned against it, looking back, wondering at what she had lost: her husband, a son and daughter, the sanctity of her body.

"And part of my soul," she whispered. She looked down at her hand, remembering the feel of the bone stiletto she'd driven between Goodeagle's ribs.

Did I really do that?

The great quake caught her by surprise. The land leapt, and a rolling thunder filled the air. She barely had time to claw her way to her feet when she pitched sideways. The great stone she had been leaning against rolled on its base and toppled, just missing her.

For too many heartbeats the ground shook, pebbles and gravel leaping as she staggered for balance. Silt rose in a low cloud, only to be carried away by the wind.

And then it was gone. She lay panting, trembling with terror, the thunder fading off to the south.

For a moment, the world was silent, as if holding its breath.

An earsplitting squeal erupted from the Ice Giants, followed by a deep-throated groan.

"Wolf Dreamer, help me." She started, rising to stare back at the Ice Giants.

Blue Wing watched as the first massive slab of ice cracked loose. It seemed to hang, moving slowly, as if lowering tentatively into the Thunder Sea. Where it sank, white water foamed and a stunning wave of water rolled away from it, traveling at unbelievable speed. The floating bergs rose and fell like a ripple of dots.

Blue Wing stared in disbelief as the great wave spread like a huge ring. It raced across the narrow band of water, rushing up the southern shore, covering the tundra. As it engulfed the land, it dislodged the grounded bergs, tossing them high up on the pock-marked land. Then the water seemed to settle for a moment, filling the hollows, swirling around the hillocks and drumlins.

Behind it, the beach remained bare, reefs of rounded rock sticking up like pimples on the naked seafloor. Then the remnants of the wave began to flow back across the denuded shores, and the roar of it came thundering across the land. She felt the power of it by the trembling of the earth beneath her, and the rumble that deafened her ears.

As she watched, a series of cracks shot through the

bellies of the Ice Giants, racing away in every direction, and another slab sloughed off. It crashed into the lake. Then another peeled off and fell with what seemed an agonizing slowness. The massive waves that rolled away smashed into the backwash of the first. Giant geysers of white shot high into the air; the mist rainbowed in the sunlight.

Terrified birds fluttered this way and that like disoriented bats. An arctic hare ran past her in panic.

In one gigantic grinding wail, a piece of ice bigger than all of Nightland country broke free.

The inlet exploded. A wall of water raced through the pitching waves for the shore.

It came like thunder, the sound growing louder by the instant. The great wave overwhelmed the draining waters of the first, thrusting them back into the rocks and old ice that lined the tundra.

Blue Wing watched in stunned amazement as the edge of it rushed across the land below her, churning, dashing, shooting high as it engulfed the country she had just crossed. The rumble of it shook her, shivering her very bones.

In panicked immobility, she watched wide-eyed as it rolled up almost to her feet and slowed.

To the south, the Thunder Sea rushed through the hilly moraines, spilling out across the uneven ground in a wild torrent.

The earthquake trembled to a stop, but a new roar filled the air.

As more and more water poured through, the gap widened and sent the icy water crashing down what had been the narrow channel of Windigo River. The wave pushed a flood of enormous rocks and chunks of frozen earth before it, scouring the channel.

The water had overflowed the banks of the river and was flooding out like a black sea, washing toward the distant ridge where Headswift Village stood.

Blue Wing climbed uneasily to her feet as the water below her began to drain away. Every hollow was filled; rivulets were being cut into the slopes before her eyes.

Every vestige of the Nightland Caves and villages had been wiped clean. The beach below the camps stretched empty, the water far down the gentle slope. Damp mud glistened in the sunlight with an eerie sheen. Here and there, great rivers of backwash roared back toward the dancing waters of the Thunder Sea.

She had no idea how long she stared, but a distant wall of white caught her eye. It lay along the eastern horizon of the narrow Thunder Sea, a hazy thin band.

She looked at the exposed mud flats where water had once rested, thought about the waves that had washed out of the basin, and looked back at the distant band of white.

Was it bigger now?

"Water always finds its own level," she whispered. And the Thunder Sea ran right into the ocean.

She turned and ran.

Chapter Forty-Two

For two days following the great quake, Silvertip led his people eastward along the ridges. Behind them, the water continued to rise, slipping up valleys, spilling into hollows.

At last he topped a final ridge, following a path between large pines. He stopped, staring, stunned to see with his eyes what his Spirit had known only in Dreams.

Ashes came to stand beside him, her war club resting on her shoulder. He heard her sudden gasp of disbelief. Lookingbill and Dipper walked up on either side, standing in silent awe.

Below them, what had been Lake River Valley had become what at first appeared to be a flat plane that extended almost without relief to the distant peaks of the Ice Giants. To the eye it seemed like flat land at first, until a decided movement became apparent, as if the great expanse of plain moved inexorably to the east.

Looking closer, the observer realized that what passed for matted earth was floating debris consisting of rafts of uprooted trees, icebergs, tangles of wood, sticks, and branches. Most, however, was duff and leaves floated from the forest floor. Occasional clear patches of water, like cracks, gleamed a gray granitic sheen.

Close to the shore Silvertip could see the bloated carcass of a mammoth, the long red hair of its hide clotted with debris. The great cow floated on her side, bobbing slightly, head turned down into the filthy brown water. He spotted other carcasses: a bison, two elk, and the dark hide of short-faced bear. All animals that had no chance to flee the great sprawling mass of water that had rolled out of the west.

In places, high ground stuck up, catching the great rafts of debris, holding it for a time, until the relentless eastern flow spun it one way or another and bore it relentlessly toward the distant ocean.

"So much water!" Lookingbill whispered under his breath. He swallowed hard. "Where...where is Headswift Village?"

Silvertip pointed. "There. That little knob in the distance." He turned his eyes on the pinprick amidst the debris-matted water.

"No one who stayed would have lived," Dipper said softly. "That water's up to the highest rocks."

"It's flowing through the passageways," Silvertip told them, "eating away at the base. Even the great rocks are collapsing, sinking down. When the water drains away, it will only be a low mound covered with silt."

"Is that a mammoth?" Dipper pointed to where a single calf stood perched on a shallow island to the east. It kept raising its trunk, as if scenting for its mother. Then it would whirl, splash down into the water where wood had collected. Raising its right foot, it would press anxiously at the floating wood, as if in search of solid footing. Finding none, the calf retreated to the limited sanctuary of the rounded hump of land. Even as they watched, the saturated ground seemed to be sliding under the calf's feet. Panicked, it whirled and dashed about in ever smaller circles, destroying its haven as it went.

Ashes swallowed hard. "When will the flood subside?"

"Our children may see it." Silvertip watched the mammoth calf with a leaden soul. "The trees will slowly wash out into the ocean, carrying the carcasses of dead animals, and those few that survived by clinging to the wood: squirrels, raccoons, some beaver."

"The size of it," Lookingbill cried. "It runs all the way to the Ice Giants. What of the Nightland?"

"Gone," Silvertip told him. "Washed away. Their corpses have already been carried off by the tides of the Thunder Sea."

"Raven Hunter's Dream?" Ashes asked.

"Alive," he said simply, and pointed to the south. "The Raven Bundle is there. I can feel it, like a darkness on the land." He glanced at Ashes. "Your mother lives."

"What now, Dreamer?" Lookingbill asked. "What do we do?"

Silvertip filled his lungs, smelling the odors of wet wood, earth, and water. "We go south. There we will meet up with the remains of the Sunpath People who are fleeing to the Tills. It will not be easy. The forest peoples down there won't be pleased to see us encroach upon them. We will need Silt's warriors."

"More war?" Dipper asked.

"Raven Hunter has rebalanced the Spiral," Silvertip

whispered. "Where there is order, there will be conflict."

He bent down, grasping a handful of soil. Then, slowly, he opened his fingers, letting it trickle away through his fingers.

In the distance, the mammoth calf trumpeted in fear as the fragile island crumbled beneath its feet.

Epilogue

Windwolf sat on a high outcrop of limestone and watched the northern horizon. The band of brown hung low in the sky, like a great distant smoke that ran from horizon to horizon. Wind whipped white strands of hair around his lined face.

He coughed, hating the nagging tickle in his lungs. It had become a constant thing over the summers after the end of the world.

He could never rest on a high place without thinking of the great flood. Memories of the time they'd spent watching Lake River swell into a huge torrent remained, as did their frantic flight to the south as the river washed over the shale bench and pursued them through the forest trails.

He wondered: Was any of that country left?

Below him, the great forest—oak and hickory, walnut and beech—stretched off to the distant north, still and green in the summer. The carpet of forest undulated over distant ridges until it merged with the far brown haze.

In the valley below him, a great river ground away at its limestone banks. So much water, but nothing like he'd seen in the north.

At the soft padding of Keresa's feet, he looked up, smiling as she came to sit beside him. The faint breeze tugged at her graying hair. He envied her for that; his own had gone white years ago.

"Any change?" she asked, pointing at the distant brown cloud. Her hands had hardened with time, the bones knobby under thin and wrinkled skin.

"No." He turned his eyes to it. "The winds are still carrying it east."

When the west or north winds blew across the great empty lake beds of the north, they picked up the loose silt and rock dust, carrying it far and wide to settle on the land in a fine dust. Most of the country up north had been abandoned, unfit for man or beast. In places the wind-blown silt could be seen in cut banks, taller than a man. It had suffocated the land. Where once mammoths had fed on lush grasses, dark silt now piled in rippled dunes that stretched for as far as the eye could see. According to the few hardy individuals that dared journey there, the north had become a dead zone.

Winters had grown colder as well.

When the silt blew south, people tended to stay in, their faces wrapped with cloth. Despite that, most people had developed the common cough after years of enduring the fine dust.

Windwolf grimaced. At those times, the sun was gone for days. People huddled in their lodges, waiting out the long dark days. He wondered if that was what Ti-Bish had meant. If so, it was certainly no paradise.

On the other hand, where the silt fell, and the rains came, the forest seemed to swell with life. Nut crops were plentiful; cattails and goosefoot grew. The deer, elk, and bison thrived.

Keresa said, "Silvertip and Ashes have sent a runner. They are holding a gathering again this summer." She shot him a curious glance. "As usual they have invited Skimmer."

"And again, she will have nothing to do with it." Windwolf reached down, toying with the grass before him. "Did Kakala show any interest in going?"

"No. He's happy to stay with her." Keresa looked out at the distant brown haze. "Now that Black Bird has taken the Raven Bundle, Kakala wishes to concentrate on raising his own sons."

Windwolf shot her a knowing look. "She had the boy less than six moons after Kakala began sharing her robes."

Keresa kept her level eyes fixed on the distant haze. "Black Bird is Ti-Bish's child. No doubt about it. He has that wide-eyed look."

Windwolf pulled the grass up, chewing thoughtfully on the stem. "Kakala doesn't care. He owes his happiness to Skimmer. Only a woman with her Power could have put his ghosts to rest."

"Then I must be full of Power, too." She gave his bony knee a squeeze. "Not only did I cure your ghosts, but I gave you four strong children in return."

He gave her his wary grin. "They tell the other young people that they had two fathers for parents. That you were tougher on them than I was."

She chuckled at that; then her voice turned serious. "Chief Silt sent a message to you. He wanted you to know that Blue Wing died last moon."

Windwolf nodded. She hadn't been doing well. "I owed her. Had she not survived and married Silt, I would never have known what happened to Goodeagle."

"Would it have mattered after all these years?"

"It would have."

She studied him. "Windwolf, so many summers have passed, Kishkat's and Tapa's children have grown and married into Silt's band. No one cares that some of us were once Nightland People. We could join their band, become one with them."

Windwolf shook his head sadly. "Skimmer wouldn't go. She and Silvertip...they just wouldn't see eye to eye. War Chief Ashes would side with her husband, even if she follows Raven Hunter's Dream."

"Separate and opposite?" she asked.

He nodded. "Silvertip told me the Spiral is just beginning to regain its balance. Let's give the earth some time before the Wolf and Raven Bundles clash again. Until we are gone, our little band will be the last of the Nightland and of Ti-Bish's Dream."

She wound her fingers into his. "I don't care. As long as I can Dream it with you."

In the forest behind them, a great black wolf watched with glowing yellow eyes. He often followed the man through the forest, watching, studying the man's ways.

The only warning came as the soft whisper of wings. The black wolf ducked nimbly to the side, then leapt and snapped as the big black raven dove low over his head.

The bird cawed, flipped over on its back, and disappeared behind the trees.

The wolf watched it go. There would always be another opportunity. This thing between him and Raven was only beginning.

Afterword

At the time of the cataclysm, PaleoIndians lived near the ice, and made their camps along the borders of the gigantic lakes. In fact, some of the oldest archaeological sites in North America are found close to what was—when the prehistoric peoples lived there—the edge of a melting glacier: the Udora site in Ontario; Debert site in Nova Scotia; Michaud site in Maine; Whipple site in New Hampshire; Meadowcroft Rockshelter, Shawnee-Minisink, and Shoop sites in Pennsylvania; Bull Brook in Massachusetts; the Hiscock and Dutchess Quarry Caves sites in New York; the Hebior-Schaefer in Wisconsin; and in Michigan, the Holcombe, Gainey, Rappuhn, and Barnes sites—all of which reliably date to between 11,000 and 14,000 years ago.

In the area where *People of the Nightland* is set, archaeologists have identified three distinct cultures of PaleoIndian hunters. We call them Gainey, Debert, and Parkhill, after the locations where their distinctive fluted spear points were found. For a general introduction to the archaeology, we recommend Peter L. Storck's excellent *Journey to the Ice Age*. Other resources are contained in the bibliography.

Why would human beings have been drawn to one of the most inhospitable environments on earth? First of all, the area immediately adjacent to the ice was certainly tundra and there is evidence of permafrost, but a short distance to the south, the Pleistocene taiga—which formed a belt along the southern margin of the ice—consisted of spruce, jack pine, and oak. The taiga also had many parklike meadows filled with shrubs. At Meadowcroft Rockshelter in Pennsylvania, the archaeologists discovered nutshells, wood, and charcoal from walnut and hickory trees. We call these places *refugia*, that is, sheltered locations that fostered a more temperate ecology. Probably many such refugia existed around the glacial margins.

This is important because the taiga meadows would have provided big game animals with better grazing and browsing opportunities, and *that's* why prehistoric peoples camped there. Kill a ground squirrel and one person can eat for a night. Kill a mammoth and a village can eat for a month.

Try to imagine a world where extinct animals like mastodons, mammoths, giant ground sloths, tapirs, and camels walked alongside deer, fox squirrels, raccoons, and elk. Each year, huge flocks of ducks, geese, herons, and other migratory birds winged north with the spring. The largest bird in the sky was the California condor; its range extended over all of North America.

The prehistoric peoples were outstanding hunters. Their spear points—fashioned from a variety of stones and propelled by an atlatl, or throwing stick—could penetrate the rib cage of an adult mastodon. In fact, bones from mastodons, and to a lesser extent, mammoths, are among the most common Pleistocene fossils in the Great Lakes region. Paleoindians were also master traders, exchanging goods across much of eastern North America. As well, we know from the Hiscock site in New York and Meadowcroft Rockshelter in Pennsylvania that they weaved nets and textiles.

So what happened 13,000 years ago?

Global warming peaked. The glaciers collapsed. Ice dams must have partially blocked the Mississippi River drainage and opened a new spillway along the eastern edge of Lake Agassiz, which resulted in catastrophic flooding. Eighty-five percent of the lake's volume rushed into the Nipigon Basin in western Ontario, and from there into the Superior and then the Huron Basins, and finally flooded out into the North Atlantic through what paleoclimatologists call the Champlain Sea. A small remnant of that sea is what we know today as the St. Lawrence River.

The final triggers for this cataclysmic event may have come from three sources. First, when sea levels rose enough to flood the Bering Strait 13,000 years ago, it established the Trans-Polar Current that sent warmer waters flowing into the Arctic Ocean, melted the sea ice there, and flooded the North Atlantic. Second, as the glaciers melted, the land that had been weighed down by the ice began to spring back. This is called isostatic rebound. (Incidentally, this is happening today in the Alps. Recent surveys have demonstrated that the Alps are losing 1.5 billion tons of ice per year to global warming, and as the massive glaciers melt the reduction in weight on the peaks is causing the entire region to gain altitude. Italian glaciologist Claudio Smiraglia and his colleagues reported this in their excellent article in the July 28, 2006, issue of *Geophysical Research Letters*.)

Also, 13,000 years ago, when the land began to spring back, there were strong earthquakes that probably helped to further destabilize the glaciers. Lastly, ice cores taken in Greenland verify that one of the most volcanically active periods in the past 100,000 years was the period from about 8,000 to 15,000 years ago. It's possible that this flurry of volcanic eruptions resulted from the stresses on the earth's crust that accompanied isostatic rebound. But whatever the reasons, these eruptions spewed enormous amounts of dust and sulfuric acid into the atmosphere and dramatically affected the global climate, resulting in decades of "volcanic winters."

Also, keep in mind that glaciers grind up rock and gravel, creating a fine dust. As the glaciers melted, this powdery sediment settled into the meltwater lakes. As the lakes in turn drained, wind scoured the thick layers of fine dust and silt, blowing great clouds of it to carpet eastern North America. Geologists call this wind-deposited dust loess, and in places deposits were sixty and seventy feet thick. We can only imagine the terrible impact those huge dust storms had on the local flora and fauna. Suffice to say that when the dust finally stopped blowing, mammoth, mastodon, dire wolf, short-faced bear, condor, giant beaver, and giant sloth were extinct in eastern North America.

Our goal in writing the *People* books is to allow our readers to see through the eyes of prehistoric cultures, in the hope that we can learn from them. In this regard, we are often helped by historical records. For example, eyewitness accounts of similar volcanic events proved extremely valuable in writing *People of the Nightland*, particularly accounts from the second century AD, when there were a series of explosive eruptions in Alaska. Chinese historians during this time period recorded that "several times the sun rose in the east red as blood and lacking light...only when it had risen to an elevation of more than two zhang (24 degrees) was there any brightness..." Perhaps one of the most chilling chronicles of these eruptions was written in AD 186 by the Romans: "The heavens were ablaze...stars were seen all the day long...hanging in the air which was a token of a cloud..."

We are also helped a great deal by the oral histories of the native peoples. There are many stories of terrible floods. After the Yavapai emerged into this world, they failed to close the hole to the underworld and it caused a great flood. Tears of mourning often cause floods, as in the Kathlamet story about Beaver crying for his lost wife, or among the Cherokee when Mother Sun's beloved daughter dies from a rattlesnake bite and her tears cause a flood. The Wiyot story of Above-Old-Man and the Arapaho story of Neshanu tell of how the creator grew unhappy with human beings and flooded the world to cleanse it. The Pawnee creator, Tirawahat, flooded the world to kill the evil giants who lived there. The Cree culture hero, Wesucechak, fought the powerful water lynxes after the great flood to avenge the death of his brother.

These stories may have been inspired by the great flood of 13,000 years ago that brought about a global climatic reversal, rolling the Earth back into an Ice Age we call the Younger Dryas.

Afterword

Academically oriented readers may question whether people inhabited the ice caves. While the violence of the collapsing glaciers probably erased any such evidence, we know that modern Inuit build houses out of ice and snow for protection from the elements, and the honeycomb of glacial caves would have provided similar shelter from the winter winds, as well as a handy deep-freeze for long-term food storage. Finding evidence for such is a daunting task, but a fertile field for investigation.

Lastly, for those who think the Pleistocene Ice Age ended ten thousand years ago, let us suggest that it may not have. This current warm episode, the Holocene, encompasses only about half a percent of the Quaternary Period. Which means today's climate could be just another in a long line of brief warming periods.

As you listen to the news tonight remember that Ice Ages are almost always heralded by sudden episodes of global warming.

In fact, with atmospheric carbon dioxide at the highest level it's been in the past 750,000 years...we're overdue.

A Look At: Buffalo Justice

deliver a gripping western filled with murder, corruption, and the battle over the American government's most famous and controversial buffalo herd.

When high-profile conservation lawyer Ryman Banks is gunned down on his own doorstep, Montana Department of Justice Agent Jillian Masterson is assigned to the case. What should be a routine investigation quickly spirals into a deadly web of greed, deception, and bloodshed, all tied to a legal war over the management of Yellowstone's bison. As Jillian digs deeper, she finds herself caught between ruthless power players—corrupt politicians, conservationists with deadly agendas, and a psychotic assassin who will stop at nothing to silence those who stand in the way.

Framed for the crime is Wyoming buffalo rancher John Cody, a man with everything to lose if Yellowstone's bison are declared endangered. As the evidence stacks against him, he races to clear his name while battling an undeniable attraction to the very woman determined to put him behind bars.

But the real killer is still at large...and as Jillian gets closer to the truth, she becomes the next target. With enemies lurking in the shadows and a final showdown looming in a remote Wyoming buffalo corral, Buffalo Justice is a heart-pounding story that will leave you breathless.

COMING SOON.

About W. Michael Gear

W. Michael Gear is a *New York Times, USA Today,* and international bestselling author of sixty novels. With close to eighteen million copies of his books in print worldwide, his work has been translated into twenty-nine languages.

Gear has been inducted into the Western Writers Hall of Fame and the Colorado Authors' Hall of Fame —as well as won the Owen Wister Award, the Golden Spur Award, and the International Book Award for both Science Fiction and Action Suspense Fiction. He is also the recipient of the Frank Waters Award for lifetime contributions to Western writing.

Gear's work, inspired by anthropology and archaeology, is multilayered and has been called compelling, insidiously realistic, and masterful. Currently, he lives in northwestern Wyoming with his award-winning wife and co-author, Kathleen O'Neal Gear, and a charming sheltie named, Jake.

About Kathleen O'Neal Gear

Kathleen O'Neal Gear is a *New York Times* bestselling author of fifty-seven books and a national award-winning archaeologist. The U.S. Department of the Interior has awarded her two Special Achievement awards for outstanding management of America's cultural resources.

In 2015 the United States Congress honored her with a Certificate of Special Congressional Recognition, and the California State Legislature passed Joint Member Resolution #117 saying, "The contributions of Kathleen O'Neal Gear to the fields of history, archaeology, and writing have been invaluable..."

In 2021 she received the Owen Wister Award for lifetime contributions to western literature, and in 2023 received the Frank Waters Award for "a body of work representing excellence in writing and storytelling that embodies the spirit of the American West."

Selected Bibliography

Agenbroad, Larry D., et al. *Megafauna and Man: Discovery of America's Heartland.* Northern Arizona University, Flagstaff, and the Mammoth Site of Hot Springs, South Dakota, 1990.

Bonnichsen, Robson, and Karen L. Turnmire. *Clovis: Origins and Adaptations.* Corvallis, Oregon: Center for the Study of First Americans, 1991.

Bradley, Raymond S. *Paleoclimatology: Reconstructing Climates of the Quaternary.* Amsterdam: Elsevier Academic Press, 1999.

Bryant, Vaughn M., and Richard G. Holloway. *Pollen Records of Late Quaternary North American Sediments.* Dallas: The American Association of Stratigraphic Palynologists Foundation, 1985.

Deller, Brian D., and Christopher J. Ellis. *Thedford II: A Paleo-Indian Site in the Ausable River Watershed of Southwestern Ontario.* Memoirs of the Museum of Anthropology. No. 24. University of Michigan, 1992.

Dixon, E. James. *Bones, Boats, and Bison: Archeology and the First Colonization of Western North America.* Albuquerque: University of New Mexico Press, 1999.

Ellis, Christopher, and Jonathan C. Lothrop. *Eastern Pale-oindian Lithic Resource Use.* San Francisco: West-view Press, 1989.

Fagan, Brian M. *Ancient North America: The Archaeology of a Continent.* London: Thames and Hudson, 2000.

Guthrie, R. Dale. *Frozen Fauna of the Mammoth Steppe: The Story of Blue Babe.* Chicago: University of Chicago Press, 1990.

Hansel, A. K., D. M. Mickelson, A. F. Schneider, and C. E. Larson. "Late Wisconsinian and Holocene History of the Lake Michigan Basin." *Quaternary Evolution of the Great Lakes.* Eds. P. F. Karrow and P. E. Calken. Geological Association of Canada Special Paper No. 30, 1985: 39-53.

Haynes, Gary. *Mammoths, Mastodons, and Elephants: Biology, Behavior and the Fossil Record.* Cambridge: Cambridge University Press, 1991.

Helm, June, ed. *Handbook of North American Indians.* Vol. 6. Washington, D.C.: Smithsonian Institution, 1981.

Jablonski, Nina, ed. *The First Americans: Pleistocene Colonization of*

Selected Bibliography

the New World. Memoirs of the California Academy of the Sciences. No. 27.

Jackson, Lawrence J. *The Sandy Ridge and Halstead Paleo-Indian Sites: Unifacial Tool Use and Gainey Phase Definition in South-Central Ontario*. Memoirs of the Museum of Anthropology. Ann Arbor: University of Michigan, 1998.

Martin, Paul S., and Richard G. Klein. *Quaternary Extinctions: A Prehistoric Revolution*. Tucson: University of Arizona Press, 1989.

Mead, Jim, and David J. Meltzer. *Environments and Extinctions: Man in Late Glacial North America*. Orono, Maine: Center for the Study of Early Man, 1985.

Pearson, James L. *Shamanism and the Ancient Mind: A Cognitive Approach to Archaeology*. New York: Al-tamira Press, 2002.

Peilou, E. C. *After the Ice Age: The Return of Life to Glaciated North America*. Chicago: University of Chicago Press, 1991.

Roosa, W. B. "Great Lakes Paleo-Indians: The Parkhill Site, Ontario." *Amerinds and Their Paleoenvironments in Northeastern North America*. Eds. Walter S. Newman and Bert Salwin. New York: Annals of the New York Academy of Sciences, 1977. No. 288: 349-354.

Saunders, Jeffery J. "A Model for Man-Mastodon Relationships in Late Pleistocene North America." *Canadian Journal of Anthropology* 1.1, 1981: 87-98.

Storck, Peter L. *The Fisher Site: Archaeological, Geological and Paleobotanical Studies at an Early Paleo-Indian Site in Southern Ontario, Canada*. Memoirs of the Museum of Anthropology. Ann Arbor: University of Michigan, 1997.

Storck, Peter L. *Journey to the Ice Age: Discovering an Ancient World*. Vancouver: UBC Press, 2004.

Straus, Lawrence Guy, et al. *Humans at the End of the Ice Age: The Archaeology of the Pleistocene-Holocene Transition*. New York: Plenum Press, 1996.